ONE DAY IN SUMMER

SHARI LOW

Boldwood

First published in Great Britain in 2020 by Boldwood Books Ltd.

A CIP catalogue record for this book is available from the British Library.

Paperback ISBN 978-1-83889-170-1

Large Print ISBN 978-1-83889-744-4

Ebook ISBN 978-1-83889-172-5

Kindle ISBN 978-1-83889-171-8

Audio CD ISBN 978-1-83889-239-5

MP3 CD ISBN 978-1-83889-741-3

Digital audio download ISBN 978-1-83889-169-5

Boldwood Books Ltd
23 Bowerdean Street
London SW6 3TN
www.boldwoodbooks.com

This book is set on the 30th May 2020, but it was written long before that, so it describes a world that is now barely recognisable. In these pages, there is no pandemic, no lockdown, no worries about new terms like 'social distancing.'

So while you read it, please suspend belief, and remember a time when we could all gather for family meals, meet friends at airports and squeeze the people we love.

Those days will come again.

And in the meantime, this book is dedicated to every single person who went out to work to keep our lives turning – the NHS staff, the teachers and staff in hub schools, the shop workers, the delivery drivers, the carers for our elderly and vulnerable, the forces, the post office, the bin collectors, the police and fire services, public transport workers, the volunteers and all the many other cogs in the wheel.

You're all bloody brilliant.

Thank you

x

ONCE UPON A TIME THERE WAS...

Agnetha (nee Sanders) McMaster, 45 – owner of The Ginger Sponge, a coffee shop in the Merchant City area of Glasgow, divorcee with twin daughters, Isla and Skye.

Skye McMaster, 20 – Focused and driven, studying law at the University of Glasgow.

Isla McMaster, 20 – Working with her mum in The Ginger Sponge until she decides what she wants to do with her life.

Mitchell McMaster, 46 – Agnetha's ex-husband, a lawyer whose negotiation skills come in handy when co-parenting their daughters.

Celeste Morrow-McMaster, 45 – Mitchell's second wife and stepmother to the twins, a successful event planner who was formerly Agnetha's best friend.

Yvie Danton, 31 – Agnetha's friend, confidante and a nurse on the geriatric ward of Glasgow Central Hospital, founder of bereavement group, The Wednesday Club.

Val Murray, 60-something (she refuses to confirm) – Another of Agnetha's pals. Also a member of The Wednesday Club, and a gregarious gem who takes all newcomers under her wing.

Will Hamilton, 48 – A bereaved dad who bonded with Agnetha over loss and sorrow, but who is now giving her a reason to smile again.

Hope McTeer, 22 – An adoptee who has decided to search for her biological parents, planning to be a doctor, in her fourth year of studying medicine, while moonlighting as a health care assistant at a Glasgow hospital.

Maisie McTeer, 24 – Hope's adoptive sister, drama queen and jobbing actress.

Dora McTeer – 56 – Adopted Hope and Maisie as babies, an English teacher who is always on hand with support and calm reason.

Aaron Ward, 48 – Divorced father of two who had a wild holiday romance with Agnetha in LA in 1997.

Zac Stone, 48 – Aaron's best friend and flatmate back in 1997; Celeste's lover on the same nineties holiday.

The rest of the Wednesday Club:

Marge and Myra (septuagenarian sisters), Jonathan and Colin – bereaved survivors who come together every week to support each other as they navigate the loss of their loved ones.

PROLOGUE

I remember her so clearly.

There's an image in my mind of her standing on the observation deck at the top of the Empire State Building in New York. She was about twenty-one and it was a cold day, but she didn't care that the wind made her long red hair fly and her eyes glisten as she threw her arms out wide. The sheer joy she was feeling radiated from every pore, her smile wide and irrepressible. Like it would never fade.

Another memory. Maybe a year later. Sitting on the end of a cold Scottish pier in the early hours of the morning with a man she was madly in love with. She said he was the third love of her life. Or was it fourth? It was a standing joke with her friends that her romantic history was like a constant repetition of death defying leaps. She'd fall from a great height into the abyss, but, as if on a bungee cord, she'd snap right back out again at warp speed a day, a week, a month later, leaving a few cases of whiplash along the way.

Another flashback, to the following summer. On a beach in Malibu, watching the surfers at dawn, making lines in the sand with her toes. I knew the whole holiday had been put on a brand new credit card and the expense sent it straight to its limit, but she gave that no thought at all. All that mattered was that moment. That experience. Life is for living. Her mantra. A cliché, but, yep, life is for living, she'd say.

Along the way, she'd met him. The one who made her forget everyone else. Dizzy with love and optimism, she said yes to the happy-ever-after dream, and prepared to waltz up the aisle with him. But they didn't make it. Life took her on another path and into the arms of someone else.

It was just a detour. A blip.

Still, she would dance, she would throw back shots and bounce the glass on the bar, she would start a party in an empty room and watch as people flocked to join the fun.

She would talk about how there were no limits to how great her life could be, and you couldn't listen to the enthusiasm and certainty in her voice and not believe her.

At twenty-three, she thought nothing could stop her, that she was indestructible, that there was absolutely nothing she couldn't do or achieve if she wanted to.

Perhaps it was the naivety of youth, but she didn't even see the perfect storm coming.

Marriage. Children. Ailing parents. A mind-blowing betrayal. A chain of events that would hijack her world, changing her until the person she was no longer existed.

Yep, life is for living, she would say.

Until she became nothing more than a battle-weary survivor, who set aside her own life just to get through the days.

I remember that young, carefree woman so clearly.

Because she was me.

8AM – 10 A.M

1

It was like the sound they played to warn of imminent tornadoes in disaster movies. Agnetha McMaster – 'Aggs' to her pals – banged the button on her phone, silencing the alarm that was wailing like a foghorn about twelve inches from her ear. Thankfully, there was no tornado. And, also thankfully, the mug that she knocked off the pale grey chest of drawers beside her bed was empty. This wasn't her first 'tea dregs flying across the room first thing in the morning' rodeo, so she'd been sure to drain the cup before switching off *Grey's Anatomy*, snuggling down alone and falling asleep.

Pushing herself up in bed, she stretched her arms to the top of the silver velvet headboard. Redecorating this room had been her twins, Skye and Isla's, idea and they'd all spent last weekend sanding, painting and then scouring the aisles of Dunelm for new furniture and accessories to replace ones that had been in residence here since Aggs was a teenager. They'd come home with a thick white duvet, a grey and pink tartan throw and scatter cushions that she wasn't entirely sure what to do with. She didn't mind. All that mattered was that she was glad she'd given in to the pressure from her daughters to treat herself, and now, on the morning of her forty-fifth birthday, and ten years after she'd sold up her house and moved back into her parents' flat above their family's cafe, it no longer felt like her childhood bedroom. It still felt like her home, though; the one she'd had for most of her life. She'd grown up in this very room, with her parents in the next bedroom, and her grandparents at the end of the hall. She'd moved out when she got married, then moved back in with her girls after her divorce, finding comfort in the aromas that drifted upstairs from the café that had passed from her grandparents, to her parents and then to Aggs.

She pulled on her specs, gathered her long red messy mane up into a ponytail and picked up her phone, grinning as she saw that Skye had already sent a 'Happy Birthday' gif to the WhatsApp group she shared with her daughters.

She checked the time: 8 a.m.. The doors of The Ginger Sponge would be opening downstairs, but Isla had insisted that she didn't come down until at least noon. It was her first lazy morning in years and she intended to milk it – at least until 8.30, when she'd inevitably succumb to the guilt that would no doubt get the better of her, and she'd make some excuse to go down and get to work. Café owners – especially this one – didn't have the luxury of sleeping late.

The bedroom door slammed open and her twenty year old daughter marched into the room, tray first.

'Don't even think about it,' Isla warned. She was already in her warm-day work uniform of a black vest top, jeans that were cut off just above the ankle and black Vans.

Aggs automatically adopted a face of innocence. 'Think about what? Brad Pitt on a sunlounger, wearing nothing but suncream and a smile?'

'No and eeeew, that's so inappropriate. Mothers your age are not allowed to have sexual fantasies. I'm sure there's a law about it somewhere,' Isla winced as she placed the tray down on the empty side of Aggs' new double bed. It was laden with a huge mug of coffee, two slices of pumpkin-seeded toast and a glistening apple Danish that Aggs knew would have come out of the oven five minutes ago.

'Fine. I won't tell you about what Matt Damon might get up to in my utility room then. Anyway, what have I not to think about?'

Isla made gagging sounds before dissolving into giggles. 'Don't even think about getting up and coming downstairs.'

'I wasn't even contemplating it.' Blatant lie number one of the day was met with a knowing grin, hands on hips and raised eyebrows of doubt. Aggs immediately buckled. 'God, I'd be a rubbish spy. One sign of a sceptical look and I fold like a deckchair. Okay, so I was planning to come down. But only because I don't want to leave you on your own in case it gets busy.'

'I'm not on my own. Val and Yvie are downstairs. They came to help because they knew you wouldn't be able to relax. Val says if you come down before noon she's shutting up shop and picketing the front door with placards saying we've got mice.'

Despite the undoubted authenticity of the threat, Aggs found herself laughing at the thought of her two friends pitching up and doling out orders. And she knew better than to call Val's bluff.

Isla squeezed onto the bed next to the tray, tucked a tendril of red hair the same shade as her mum's behind her ears, then leaned over and gave Aggs a hug. 'Happy birthday, Mum. Are you okay? Are you missing Gran?'

Aggs hesitated, giving her time to swallow the lump in her throat. This time last year her mum had still been with them, although she'd been in the final stages of her illness. Now, the pain of watching her suffer had been replaced by the pain of losing her, but her mum, more than anyone, would be telling her to 'just get on with it, love'.

'I am, but you know what she'd be saying...'

'Just get on with it, love,' Isla said softly, her impersonation of her grandmother's voice absolutely on point. Isla had been in the fifth year of high school when they'd discovered she'd been bunking off lessons for years, by calling the school and using her gran's voice to claim Isla was sick. Aggs had been furious, but her mum had thought it was hilarious. She never could get upset with her granddaughters. Isla shifted the mood back to happiness. 'So that's what we're going to do. We're planning to give you your presents later when Skye gets here, but in the meantime please stay here. Relax. You deserve it.'

Isla's last word was restricted by the tightness of the squeeze Aggs was delivering, her heart bursting with gratitude. 'I love all this. And you. Thanks so much, sweetheart. How did I get so lucky to get you?'

'Because God had to make up for Skye somehow,' Isla shot back with a grin.

'Hey! Don't talk about your sister like that.' Aggs feigned outrage, but Isla was already up and out the room, chuckling as she went.

'Tell you what – if she decides to grace us with her presence, I'll be nice to her all day.'

'Best birthday present I could have!' Aggs shouted in her wake.

Twins. Double trouble. Isla and Skye definitely had a love, irritate, love, relationship. It didn't help that while they looked undeniably alike, with their flaming hair (Isla's falling past her shoulders in waves, whereas Skye had a more reserved chin-length bob) and green eyes, their personalities were completely different. Isla was more of a free spirit who had taken a couple of years out after school to volunteer with a school-construction charity in South America. On her return, she'd come to work in The Ginger Sponge for a couple of weeks until she decided what to do next. A year later, she was still there, still undecided and that showed no sign of changing any time soon. The fourth generation of the Sanders family to work in the café. After running it for a decade on her own, Aggs harboured a hope that Isla would one day take over from her, but she'd leave that up to her daughter to decide.

Skye, on the other hand, was following in her father's footsteps and studying law at the University of Glasgow. She had already mapped out the next ten years of her life, set on being a top-flight international property lawyer by the time she was thirty. Moving in with her dad the year before had been a strategic decision and Skye made no secret of the fact that she'd done it so that she'd have his brilliant legal mind on hand to help with her studies. Aggs completely understood, and saw the sense in it, but the house was definitely too quiet without Skye around. Aggs even found herself longing for the familiar sound of her girls bickering about the most inane and trivial stuff. If it wasn't for the resemblance and the fact that Skye dropped into the birthing pool just two minutes before Isla, Aggs wouldn't be convinced that there was any genetic link between them at all.

The coffee scalded her lips as she took a sip, but she barely noticed, enjoying the heat of the mug on her hands as she stared at the tiny specs dancing in the rays of sun that were forcing their way through the slats of the shutters on the wall next to her. A sunny day. She'd hoped it would be. Although, this was Glasgow, so there could be torrential rain by lunchtime, a heatwave in the early afternoon, and a warning of frost by dinner time.

A sigh escaped her. So here it was. Her forty-fifth birthday. She was normally far too busy with the café, the accounts, the ordering, the invoices and the other hundred jobs she did every day, to allow herself the indulgence of introspection, but now the peace and silence was giving her way too much time for reflection. This was the first year without both Mum and Dad, the first one since the flat and café had officially passed to her, the first one since Skye had moved out, but definitely not the first one without someone lying beside her in bed.

It had been ten years now since the divorce. Ten years since that crushing betrayal that had spurred her to return here with the twins. Ten years with no time to herself to think about the simple things like getting her roots done, never mind the big stuff like personal relationships and life plans.

History had shown that neither were exactly her areas of expertise, but it wasn't too late, was it? Decorating her bedroom had been a first, tiny step towards doing something for herself. It was a notion that had grown since her mum's funeral.

She missed her every single day. Missed her laugh. Missed her company. Missed her love. Missed chatting over cups of tea in the morning and getting told off for not making the most of herself. 'The day I go out without my lippy is the day it's over for me,' her mum would tut.

Aggs doubted that there would ever be a day that she didn't think of her, but over the last few months she'd worked on picking up the pieces of her life. Now, for the first time in twenty years, she didn't have the responsibility of looking after other people. The girls were taking care of their own lives, her parents were gone and there was no one depending on her but herself.

Her eyes went to a photograph that the girls had found in an old suitcase when they'd been clearing out this room to decorate it. They'd slipped it into a new white satinwood frame and put it on her dressing table.

It was a picture of Aggs. Around twenty-three. In a white bikini on a Malibu beach. Head up. Hair blowing behind her in the wind.

Arms outstretched. Laughing at the sky. That's who she used to be. And that wild, free, young woman bore no resemblance to the exhausted, depleted, weighed-down person that she'd become, someone who went through the motions, did what was required of her, but put herself at the bottom of the priority list.

After laying her mum to rest, though, she'd gradually taken steps to heal the scars left by too much loss, and after a while something in her had shifted. Years of tension had begun to unfurl and something else had taken its place. Was it... hope?

An involuntary shiver made her toes curl as another glance at the picture threw up a memory that popped her bubble of bliss. This date had another significance, another association, one that now, over twenty years later, still made her stomach twist with regret and embarrassment. With a ferocity that almost made her glasses rattle, she shook her head, shutting down that thought.

That birthday, twenty-two years ago, had been the day that changed everything.

Nope, not going back there. Hadn't she learned that you could do nothing to change the past? Hadn't she been doing her best to have a new, bright, sunny outlook? From this day forward, the Agnetha 'Aggs' McMaster of the last two decades was behind her. The woman who'd lived for other people, who'd taken care of everyone else, was going into retirement, and the new independent, optimistic version of herself was in charge now.

A buzz from her phone made her jump and she picked it up to see a text with that familiar name on the screen. The flush that crept up from her neck was equal parts excitement and guilt.

Happy birthday, gorgeous. Have you told them yet?

She'd promised she would break the news before today, but of course she'd chickened out. It was too big. Too scary. Too radical.

With a sigh, she turned the phone over without replying.

She'd tell them at some point, when the moment was right.

Today was the first day of Aggs McMaster's plan to claim back a life on her own terms. She just had to take the first step. And then decide if she had the courage to see it through.

2

MITCHELL MCMASTER

The thud of the pavement under his feet provided a steady rhythm that Mitchell used to synchronise his breath. As he turned into the crescent that housed his three storey sandstone home, he barely even registered the early-morning dog walkers, the couple from No. 15 running on the other side of the road in matching Lycra, and the parents from No. 4 shepherding two boys in rugby kits into their Audi estate.

The west end of Glasgow, with its beautiful Victorian terraces and tree lined streets, was his favourite part of the city, yet living there, like everything else in his life, was just something he took for granted now.

He pressed his thumb on the biometric lock on the front door. He'd had it installed the year before when he'd upgraded the security and CCTV systems. It was probably an unnecessary expense – the company he'd founded ten years ago specialised in commercial law, not criminal law, so the personal risks were considerably lower – but it was tax deductible, while adding to the value of the house, so it made sense. And at least he didn't have to faff around with keys any more.

'Morning, Sweatman,' Skye greeted him with a grossed-out wince, before returning her gaze to the pile of textbooks in front of her. Half-past eight on a Saturday morning and she was already on the books, preparing for her exams next week. That apple didn't fall far from the tree.

Mitchell gave her a kiss on the top of her head as he passed her, earning a disgusted 'Eeeeew,' in return.

'Sweat*dad* to you,' he retorted, letting the teasing go over his head. Just about every morning in his life, he rose at 5.30 a.m. and did a workout in their basement gym, followed by a five kilometre run. It kept him lean, toned and in the same size suit trousers he'd worn since he was in his twenties. More than that, it gave him the clear head he needed every day of the week to get the best deals for his clients and maintain his reputation as one of the top corporate lawyers in the city.

He took pride in his appearance, in his home, and in his business and he was laser-focused on putting in the effort to maintain them all. Today there would be no work, but he'd definitely need to be on his A game because there was every chance the next twelve hours or so could be life-changing.

The coffee machine, integrated into a wall of cream gloss Poggenpohl units, began to gurgle as soon as he switched it on to make the first of his four daily espressos. He liked order and structure in his day. It was the only way he got through the demands of a busy practice while keeping himself in the best possible shape.

He leaned against the quartz worktop while he knocked back the bitter liquid.

'Need help with anything?' he asked Skye.

'Nope, I'm all good.'

Maybe it was the morning light streaming in through the window, but as she lifted her head he noticed the dark circles under her eyes. Was she getting enough sleep? Was she eating properly?

Had she lost weight? It was hard to tell under the standard uniform of gym leggings topped with massive oversized sweatshirts that she wore in the house. She'd been on study leave for the last month, so he'd barely seen her in anything else.

It had been almost a year since she'd come to live here, and they'd developed an easy relationship based on love and a shared passion for the law, but he didn't want to drop the ball. Aggs had been great about Skye moving here, accepting that it gave her more space, peace, and resources in her studies. After living separately from the girls for a decade after the divorce, Mitchell was loving the new closeness.

'You haven't forgotten it's your mum's birthday today, have you?'

'No, of course not. Isla says she's forcing Mum to relax this morning. I'm going round for lunch with them though. We've arranged for a few of Mum's friends to be there too, but she doesn't know that, so that'll be her first surprise of the day. The second surprise – because we're amazing daughters who are milking this to death – will be her party tonight. Are you and Celeste still coming so you can all pretend to be progressive adults working together to form the perfect blended family?'

Mitchell wasn't sure if it was the amused, teasing tone or the accuracy of her perception that made him roll his eyes.

Agnetha's surprise birthday party. Since the divorce, and his remarriage to Celeste, they'd celebrated every event together for the sake of the kids, no matter how hard it was. In the beginning, it was very bloody tough, but he only had himself to blame for that.

'Thanks for the sarcasm, madam. This is why I always preferred your sister,' he quipped, ducking immediately as a pencil came flying in his direction.

Of course, they both knew it wasn't true. He and Aggs loved both their daughters absolutely equally and if they'd done anything right at all it was to try to bring them up knowing that they were both loved beyond measure. Skye living here full time was such a joy, and Isla had a room here too, even if it was only used on the occasional weekend. In fact, since she'd come back from her travels and started work in the café, she'd barely stayed over at all. Still, he made a point of meeting her a couple of times a week for lunch or dinner and he was grateful that they both allowed him to be central in their lives. Even if it did come with some high grade cheek from both of them. Small price to pay.

He was still laughing and Skye was still feigning outrage when he picked her pencil out of the sink and tossed it back to her.

'To answer your question, yes, we are both coming and, yes, we'll be the perfect progressive parents,' he joked. 'How have you managed to keep it a surprise?'

'Lies, optimism and taking advantage of her aversion to modern communication,' Skye replied proudly. 'We've told her that we are taking her out for a quiet 'mum and daughters' dinner, just the three of us. And thanks to the fact that she refuses to use social media, we've plastered the party all over Facebook and Insta to try to make sure we reach everyone. Look...'

Skye clicked the trackpad on her MacBook, then spun it round so Mitchell could see the post.

The announcement was on the The Ginger Sponge's Facebook page.

To all friends, family and regular customers!

Tonight we're having a SURPRISE party to celebrate our lovely owner Agnetha's 45th birthday. If you love her, like her, or if she makes you a cup of tea more than once a week, you're very welcome! Cake supplied, but bring your own bottle!

7 p.m. The Ginger Sponge.

And, remember, it's a SURPRISE – anyone who spills the beans will be barred for life.

'That looks great. She deserves it,' Mitchell mused, almost to himself.

Skye nodded. 'She does. She's been through way too much and it's time for some happy stuff.'

There was a tiny hint of a reprimand in Skye's words, but he let it go, mainly because she was correct, but also because there was no point in opening up old wounds that time had already healed.

'You're right.' Something tugged at his gut as he said it and he tried to pinpoint it. Unease? Doubt? Dread? All of the above, he decided. 'Is Celeste up yet?'

'Did I hear my name?'

Damn. She always went barefoot in the house so he could never hear her coming.

His wife sashayed into the room, her white silk dressing gown short enough to show off her toned, tanned legs, her ebony hair pulled up into a high ponytail. If any cosmetic aesthetician wanted a great advert for its business, Celeste would be a top pick.

Like him, she was in her mid-forties, but only according to her birth certificate. Her cheekbones were like carved alabaster, her feline eyes devoid of all but barely discernible crow's feet and she visited the top clinic in the city once a month to tweak whatever element of her Botox, fillers, lasers, oxygen facials, lip plumping and neck tightening regime that needed work. It took a whole lot of money, time and effort to stay exactly the same, but Celeste maintained that it was worth it. Shallow as it was, when he was out with a wife who still turned heads, he tended to agree.

She applied the same dedication to her body maintenance. Not for her, the thumping round the streets in the morning, but thanks to daily yoga and Pilates sessions, and a pathological avoidance of carbohydrates, her body had barely changed since they'd got together. The only marked difference was the breast enhancement, her fortieth birthday present to herself. 'It's an investment in myself and in my business,' she'd told him. He didn't argue. But neither did he chide Isla when she heard the news and responded with mutterings of, 'Didn't realise huge knockers were essential to run an events company.'

While nothing much had changed on the outside in ten years, on the inside, however, it was a very different story. Back then, she'd adored him so much he'd risked everything for her. Now? Sometimes he felt like their marriage was more of a business transaction. And he was getting short changed. He just wanted to know why.

She pressed the buttons on the coffee machine to produce a steaming Americano, then filled a glass from the filtered water dispenser on the front of their brushed chrome, American fridge freezer.

'I'm just going to take these back upstairs,' she announced, clearly too busy to pass the time with them.

Mitchell cleared his throat before Celeste left the room. 'Do you have anything on today? I thought maybe we could grab lunch? Skye is going over to her mum's.'

There it was. The hesitation. Not exactly a rabbit in the headlights – Celeste was far too smart and could think on her feet faster than anyone he knew – but there was definitely a flicker that told him a lie was about to come out of her mouth.

Stretching up on her tiptoes, she kissed him on the cheek. Another diversionary tactic. He didn't remember the last time they'd had an actual meaningful exchange.

'I already have plans, darling.' She managed to sound regretful. 'Yoga at 10.30 and then I'm meeting a potential new client for lunch.'

'On a Saturday?'

'Only day he could make it. Packed schedule. It's like the yuppie years all over again. Big demands and they want everything on their terms.'

Mitchell couldn't help the thought. *Pot. Lycra-clad kettle.*

'We could grab a coffee on the terrace when I get home though, if the sun's still shining.'

There was no way that was happening, he knew. Celeste hadn't allowed sun on her face since the nineties.

'Yeah, sure. I've got some work to catch up with. Give me a shout when you get back.'

He could almost feel the relief oozing from her pores at the prospect of escape, when Skye chimed in. 'Celeste, you haven't forgotten that it's my Mum's surprise party tonight, have you?'

Another flinch. Another fake smile. If Skye noticed, she let it pass. She'd always been the more circumspect of the twins and Mitchell was grateful that she maintained a polite relationship with Celeste because it made life easier. Isla's restraint would already have left the building and she'd be calling Celeste out on her bullshit by now.

If his wife's eyebrows had been capable of movement, she'd have raised them. 'Of course not, darling. Although I still think it's a crazy idea. Your mother hates surprises. Anyway, I'm looking forward to it.' Another lie.

If Celeste had a choice between a night celebrating Agnetha and a cold sore, she'd chose the herpes virus every time.

'Actually, that's given me a thought – I might go shopping and pick up something new to wear after lunch, so I'm not sure when I'll be back.' Celeste's eyes didn't reach his.

Wow. Had she just grasped on to another excuse to stay out of the house and tell him another lie?

Some people might say he deserved it. After all, the woman he was married to now had been his ex-wife's best friend. His current suspicions that Celeste had new interests elsewhere would suggest that karma had come back to bite him on the arse.

'I'll be in my dressing room if anyone needs me,' she said, in a tone of reluctance that made it obvious she didn't want to be disturbed. Celeste's dressing room-come-sitting room was the one area that was off limits to everyone else. She'd converted a full double bedroom and bathroom into an area that had more square footage than the master bedroom. In it, there were copious wardrobes, an en suite bathroom, make-up and hairdressing stations, and a large TV that could be viewed from both the free-standing clawfoot bath and the overstuffed sofa in the middle of the room. She'd designed every inch of it and in the beginning, it had been just another glamourous achievement to brag about on social media, rather than somewhere she sought refuge. Over the last few months, though, she'd spent more time in there than in any other room in the house, including their own bedroom. Actually, *especially* their own bedroom.

After she'd gone, a few silent moments passed before Mitchell dropped his cup into the sink and headed to the shower, decision made. He definitely wouldn't be getting any work done today. Nor would there be any relaxation. If she wasn't going to be straight with him, then he was going to have to find out the truth for himself, and if that required a bit of subterfuge, then so be it.

Today was the day that Mitchell McMaster was going to follow his wife and find out if she was having an affair.

3

AGNETHA AND CELESTE – 1997

Agnetha stretched her naked body across the cool white sheets and let the breeze from the window glide over her. She'd barely taken a second breath when she felt Aaron's hand brush along her thigh, a soft sleepy moan accompanying his touch.

'Happy birthday, baby,' he murmured, leaning over and giving her a slow, sultry kiss. His Californian accent was unfailingly sexy and she'd been intoxicated by it since she met him, three months ago, on the day they'd arrived in LA.

Agnetha groaned, with both pleasure and pain. The prospect of spending her twenty-third birthday with Aaron made her deliciously happy, but the hangover caused by last night's celebrations had a steel band using the inside of her skull for practice. And she really needed to brush her teeth. 'Am I dreaming the bit where I danced on the bar in that nightclub and the manager offered me a job?'

'Nope. He's expecting you at 8 p.m. tonight. He's providing the sequinned bikini.'

Agnetha's chuckle was low and husky. Too much singing in the clubs last night too. It had been a pretty special introduction to Vegas. This was the first time she'd been, and they'd come on a whim – actually Aaron's whim – to celebrate her birthday.

Unfortunately, she wouldn't be claiming the sequinned bikini because this was a short visit. They were all heading back to LA the following morning and then she and Celeste would be flying home to Glasgow, via London, in a few days' time.

Reluctantly, she pushed herself up on the bed, to an immediate objection.

'Woah! Where do you think you're going?'

'To get showered and ready. I'd like to see a bit of Vegas before we go back to LA tomorrow.'

'Screw it. Forget going home tomorrow.' The way he said 'home' gave her goosebumps, because they both knew that LA wasn't her home. It was only his. Yet, it sounded so right, it set off a flurry of tingles in her stomach. 'There's another bus the day after... and the day after... and the day after,' he insisted, as his lips found hers, the need for dental hygiene temporarily forgotten.

'Bus' was probably a bit of an understatement for the luxury coach that had transported them here from LA. It had picked them up at a plush hotel in West Hollywood, a few blocks from Aaron and Zac's apartment. She'd stared out of the window the whole way, loving the transition from the beach, to the desert, to the kaleidoscopic extravaganza that was Las Vegas. At his insistence, they'd checked into Caesars Palace, courtesy of Aaron's credit card. Unlike the card that she'd put this holiday on, she was fairly sure Aaron could more than afford to pay it back.

Not that she'd worry about her burgeoning credit balance for a single moment. Not while she was here, in a gorgeous hotel room in one of the most exciting cities on the planet with a breath-takingly gorgeous man whose hand still appeared to be wandering up the inside of her thigh.

This trip had definitely taken an unexpected turn for the incredible. She'd landed almost twelve weeks ago at LAX with her best friend, Celeste, intent on experiencing everything Tinsel Town had to offer two twenty-something Scottish girls with a thirst for adventure. They'd checked into a chain motel off Santa Monica Boulevard, then showered, thrown on dresses and heels, and headed out to explore.

It was pure chance, serendipity, that Aaron and his mate Zac were sitting at the bar in the Chateau Marmont. Agnetha had dragged Celeste in there because she'd once seen it mentioned in a Jackie Collins novel and wanted to see it for herself. It didn't take long to get chatting to the two handsome guys at the next seats.

'So, actors, models or musicians?' Celeste struck up the conversation with a coy seductive smile. 'I'm thinking models?'

Agnetha could see she was flirting, but then, it was a standing joke that Celeste would flirt with a bamboo plant just for practice. She couldn't help herself. It was her natural default setting. However, it had got them into more clubs than they could count, got them out of more sticky situations than they wished to remember, and led to some memorable nights with unforgettable fun, so Agnetha had long ago learned to roll with it.

'None of the above. I work at CAA. I'm the assistant to an agent that represents TV and movie talent,' Zac had replied. He was the shorter of the two, and gave off an unusual vibe of stockbroker crossed with surfer in his white dress shirt with his tie loose, smart dark trousers and long blond hair pulled back into a messy ponytail.

Celeste's reaction made it obvious that she liked that answer. Anything less than five degrees of separation from someone who'd actually met a movie star and she was all over it. Last year she'd made them stand outside Robert De Niro's block in New York for two hours in the hope that he'd nip out for a newspaper. All they'd got was an enquiry from an agitated doorman as to why they were there and several small New York dogs barking in their direction.

'And you?' Agnetha had asked breezily, the combination of happiness, a little jet lag and her second bourbon and Coke making her feel both chilled and giddy at the same time.

The other guy was much more her type. Taller. More casually dressed in jeans and a white T-shirt. Brown hair cut so short she wouldn't have been surprised if he'd been in the armed forces. 'Construction. Family business,' he said. So the biceps and the wide, muscular shoulders that shaped and stretched the white cotton fabric hadn't come from a gym.

That night, they'd chatted for a couple of hours, then wandered down to Sunset, where they'd let the guys take them to a couple of bars, then on to a club. At every one of them, Zac and Aaron seemed to know someone on the door or behind the bar, and Agnetha loved the party atmosphere. This is what she lived for. She slogged her heart out for weeks and months on temporary catering jobs and in the family café back in Glasgow, working day and night, so she could escape to fabulous places and live wild and free for weeks at a time. Thankfully, her parents were understanding of her wanderlust and positively encouraged it, keeping her job open every time. It was an unconventional way to live, but she loved it, especially when her childhood friend, Celeste, who'd moved to London a couple of years ago, could get time off from her bar and part-time modelling work to join her. That's when the really wild stuff tended to happen. Like checking out of their hotel and moving into Zac and Aaron's West Hollywood apartment after their first week there. Like postponing their return home three times now, because they were making the money they saved on hotel bills last as long as possible. Like waking up naked in Vegas on the morning of her birthday with an utterly captivating man who was clearly intent on doing all kinds of blissful things to her. Maybe the sights of Vegas could wait.

The thought was interrupted by a knock at the door. Aaron grabbed a towel that he'd dropped on the floor after his shower last night and wrapped it around his waist. Agnetha pulled the sheet up to her neck and enjoyed the view. Every muscle in his back rippled as he walked. There was a sight she'd never get sick of looking at and one that was going to be tough to say goodbye to, but she had to go. The money was now running out and so was the time on their tourist visa.

The wheels of the room service trolley clanked quietly as it was trundled into the room by an impeccably uniformed waiter.

Aaron tipped the waiter, then lifted the lids of the two silver cloches on the table. Pancakes. Bacon. Maple syrup. Strawberries. With orange juice and coffee to wash it all down.

Tucking the sheet around her body like a sarong, Agnetha got up and padded over to the dining area at the window, watching as Aaron transferred the food from the trolley to the small round table. She poured two coffees from a tall silver pot, then two glasses of orange juice.

For the first few moments, they sat in comfortable silence. Agnetha, knees pulled up in front of her, nursing her coffee with both hands, stared out of the window.

Aaron tossed up a strawberry and caught it in his mouth. 'What are you thinking?'

'I'm thinking that this is so far away from my normal life that it all feels completely unreal,' she answered honestly.

'What would you be doing at home right now?' he asked, genuinely curious.

She'd already told him the bones of her life in Glasgow. Lovely mum and dad. Only child. Lived above the West End café in Hyndland that her grandparents had passed down to her parents. Went to catering school. Became a qualified pastry chef. Now worked in the café, as well as for a temping agency, taking short-term catering and cooking jobs because she wanted the flexibility to travel and enjoy life.

'Depends, if I had a temp job. If so, I'd be there already, prepping the food for the day. If not, then I'd have opened up the café with my dad, and I'd be up to my elbows in bread dough and cake mix.'

'Is it wrong that I find that mental image completely sexy?'

Agnetha's chuckle was low and throaty. 'Completely wrong. I refuse to associate with a man who gets turned on by carrot cake.'

'It's not the carrot cake,' he answered, his eyes locked on hers, his smile still there.

'Ginger sponge?' she asked innocently.

God, she was rubbish at sexy. She much preferred funny. Thankfully, Aaron seemed to feel the same. She was going to miss this guy more than she wanted to think about right now.

'Yep, definitely the ginger sponge.' He leaned over, his hand curving around the side of her neck, his thumb stroking her cheek, as he pulled her towards him and kissed her slowly, sexily... 'I think we're going to have to hold off going out for a little while longer,' he murmured.

'I think you're right.' There was no tourist spot in Vegas that would feel better than this.

His other hand was in her hair now, his tongue probing hers and she was just about to slip over on to his knee when there was another knock on the door.

'Ignore it,' she whispered, still kissing him.

'I'm going to,' he replied, his fingertips working their way down her neck, across her collarbone, to her...

Another bang on the bloody door. Louder this time. Insistent.

It was enough to make Agnetha break the lip lock and grin. 'That's one stroppy housekeeper. We'd better answer before they storm in.'

'It's not housekeeping. I put the "Do Not Disturb" on.'

'Then what else have you organised? A brass band? Personal shoppers? The Chippendales?'

Aaron shook his head, his laughter revealing his slightly crooked but pearly white smile. 'Nope. Not setting myself up for that kind of competition.' He rose, then paused. Lifted her chin. 'I meant it, you know. I really don't want you to leave.'

Agnetha's stomach swirled as the realisation dawned. She didn't want to leave either. Right from that first night, when they'd ended up sitting in a layby off Mulholland at dawn, watching the sunrise, she'd known this was different from the holiday flings she'd had before. There had been romances in Paris. In New York. In Thailand. On a skiing trip to Austria. But much as she fell hard and fast and enjoyed every moment of them, she always knew she wanted to leave them in the magical place they belonged and not drag them back into the real world. But this time...

Aaron barely had the door open a few inches when Celeste barged through, her gleaming mane of Cindy Crawford dark waves falling down to cover the top of her silver bikini, the rest of her tanned torso tucked into a tiny pair of Daisy Duke denim shorts.

'Have you seen Zac this morning?' she blurted, brittle fury clipping every word.

Agnetha and Aaron glanced at each other, then back at the room's source of irritated energy.

Aaron answered for both of them. 'No. Isn't he with you?'

Celeste's hands were on her hips now. 'Eh, that would be a definite no. The bastard got a phone call in the middle of the night, snuck out and hasn't come back yet. Honestly, I could kill him. How rude is that?' Without waiting for an answer, she plonked down on the chair vacated by Aaron and picked up a rasher of bacon. 'Well, his loss. Anyway, Happy Birthday Aggs. What have we got planned for today, then?'

Years later, Agnetha would always remember that moment as being the start of the unravelling of the day that changed her life.

4

HOPE MCTEER

'Hope, are you absolutely, positively, completely sure you don't want me to come with you?' Maisie asked, eyes wide and pleading. 'I mean, he could be a complete fraud after your money. Or a serial killer. Or one of those catfish guys.'

Hope stopped applying her mascara at the mirror on the kitchen wall and responded with pursed lips of cynicism that eventually broke into a smile.

'First, I'm twenty-two, not twelve. That makes me a grown-up who is allowed out on her own. Secondly, he's not a fraud because it was me who tracked him down, not the other way around. And even if he was, all he'd get from me is my shoe collection and a payment plan for my student loan. Same goes for the catfish stuff. And he may be a serial killer, but if that's the case, it's better that I know before I start shelling out for Christmas cards.'

Over at the white IKEA dining table, a shadow crossed Maisie's face. 'Fine. But if you don't come back, I'll hunt him down. And I want a call or a text every hour.'

'Deal. I'll also keep my phone on so you can track me. And if you get a text that says SOS, you can commando crawl in and get me out.'

Maisie nodded. 'I'm on it.'

Hope went back to applying her make-up. Not that there was much of it. A coat of mascara, a bit of blusher so that she didn't look like the walking dead, and a clear lip gloss to finish it off. Growing up with her mousy brown hair and pale skin, she'd always been beyond jealous of Maisie's dark complexion and thick ebony hair. They'd got used to the raised eyebrows of surprise when they told people they were sisters. Mum and Dad had equipped them with all sorts of answers when they were younger, but they'd soon realised that it was far more effective to throw back a defiant stare and watch the curiosity turn to an embarrassed squirm.

They were sisters. Adopted a couple of years apart, but sisters in every sense of the word that mattered. The fact that they didn't share the same DNA was irrelevant and always would be, regardless of what happened today.

Maisie reached over to the biscuit tin in the centre of the table and liberated a chocolate digestive, just as her mobile phone rang. 'It's Mum.'

Hope felt another explosion of butterflies in her stomach. Her mum had been supportive from the start of this journey, but that didn't mean that it had been easy to navigate the emotions of such a difficult and complicated situation.

'Hey, Mamma,' Maisie said, with a sigh, unable to mask her mood as always. 'Yep, she's just getting ready to leave.'

Hope chimed in from the other side of the room. 'Tell Mum I'll buzz her on the way there.'

'Did you get that, Mum? Hope will call you on the way. She won't let me go with her. I mean, what if she gets kidnapped?'

Hope could only hear one side of the conversation, but she

could guess what her mum was saying. 'Don't be ridiculous. She'll be fine. She needs to do this.'

Always the voice of reason. Their dad had been the same. Both teachers, her mum, Dora, in English and dad, Tim, in Chemistry, neither of them were prone to drama or over-anxiety. That was Maisie's role in the family. Handy, given that she'd been a jobbing actress since she came back to Scotland after studying at RADA for four years. It had made perfect sense for her to move into the spare room in Hope's flat. She contributed to the rent when she was work-ing, and when she wasn't, Hope's wages from her job at the hospital and her student loan made up the slack until Maisie paid her back when she landed another job. Hope didn't mind. Studying at university for the fourth year of her medical degree while moon-lighting as a part-time care assistant on a paediatric ward at Glasgow Central didn't leave her enough time to spend her money on a social life any way.

Mum had offered to come with her today too, but Hope had declined. This was something she had to do on her own. There was no plan. No script. She wasn't even sure how much she'd tell him or whether this was going to be a twenty-minute meeting with a full stop and no further contact at the end. All she knew was that she had to try.

'Mum, I have to go,' Maisie said into the handset. 'Stay near a phone in case we need you to identify her body.'

That actually made Hope giggle. 'You are shameless, do you know that?'

Maisie disconnected the call and tossed her phone on the table. 'I do.'

'Fine. I see you trying to get Mum onside and I raise you this.' Hope opened the kitchen drawer, the one below the cutlery that was full of miscellaneous stuff like batteries, bulbs, Sellotape and pens, and pulled out a small white box. Crossing the room, she placed it in front of Maisie. 'Here's the perfect thing to distract you while I'm gone. Get this done.'

Her sister stared at the box. 'Man, you fight dirty.'

Hope shrugged then snaked her arms around Maisie's neck and leaned down to kiss her on the cheek. 'Yup. Only because I know you want to, but it's only fear that's holding you back.'

They both stared at the box for a few seconds. The logo on the front said 'Ancestry'.

They'd both received them on their twenty-first birthdays from Mum – her way of telling them that if they ever wanted to track down their biological families, she supported their decision. They both knew Dad would have too. His passing the year before had devastated them all.

Neither of them had done the test immediately. They'd lain in the drawer until the day, a couple of months ago, when Hope learned just how important it was that she find someone with a genetic link.

Doing the test was easy – just a case of spitting into a tube, then sending it off for analysis. Getting Maisie to do the test proved more difficult. Hope tried to persuade her to do it at the same time, but her sister resolutely refused, claiming that she had no desire to know more about her heritage. Realising she was fighting a losing battle, Hope went ahead and did it by herself. Last weekend that decision paid off.

On Sunday, she'd just got home after a twelve hour shift at the hospital and all she needed was her bed and to sleep. Trying to combine studies with work was exhausting, but she was determined not to live off her mum, especially now that her dad was gone. She was so tired, she was tempted to ignore the ping of an email dropping into the inbox on her phone. A quick glance had changed everything. The headline read:

Your Ancestry results are in!'

Suddenly awake, she'd grabbed her laptop and opened it on the kitchen table, fingers trembling as she logged on.

The first result she clicked on was her 'Ethnicity Estimate' and her eyebrows had immediately knitted together in confusion. She'd expected to see the Scottish heritage. It was where she'd been born and raised. But the shock? 44 per cent North American.

What?

She was almost half American?

As far as she knew, her only connection with the USA was a couple of trips to Disney World when she was a kid. The revelation took her breath away for a moment, as her chest had tightened with anxiety, while her brain had refused to send her hand the signal to click on the next category: DNA Matches. This was it. The people on the database with whom she shared a genetic link.

Breathe. Breathe. Click.

She'd read that it wasn't uncommon to have up to half a million fifth to eighth cousins, so she was hoping for something a bit closer than that. A starting point. Maybe an aunt. Or a great-grandparent. Just some place to begin the search. She hadn't dared to hope that there would be anything closer in there. After all, her adoption had been a closed one and there were no clues to go on, no background information, only the emphatic stipulation on her adoption file that the mother wished for no contact at any time in the future and requested that no information ever be released to Hope or her new family.

She'd grown up thinking she'd never have answers, had come to terms with that, but the advent of easily available DNA testing had changed everything.

Now it was a possibility. A chance.

Click.

One close match.

Her yelp had roused a sleeping Maisie from the couch in the lounge and she had charged through, hair wild, eyes blazing, ready to attack. 'What? What is it?'

'My DNA results,' Hope had whispered.

Maisie had immediately sagged, adrenalin dissipating. 'Holy shit, I thought you were getting mutilated in the kitchen by a masked intruder.'

'Did you fall asleep watching *Criminal Minds* again?'

'Yep.'

Just as the ridiculousness of the situation helped Hope's heartbeat come down from the beat of a speeding train, Maisie had switched on to the gravity of the situation.

'Oh my God, your results. What do they say?'

Hope had turned the laptop towards Maisie as she crossed the room. 'Meet my biological link.'

'Oh God. Oh God. Oh God.' Every word was punctuated by a step towards the screen.

Hope's hands were over her mouth as she'd watched Maisie read. There was just a name. Then the word FATHER.

'Click on his profile!' Maisie had gasped.

'Argh, I didn't even notice that bit. My brain shut down right about the same time as I screamed.'

With a shaky hand, Hope had clicked on the blank circle next to his name and was taken to another page, but there were no further details on there. No family tree. No other matches. Nothing. Except...

'There's a message button.' Hope was staring at it as if it had the potential to self-detonate.

Maisie had slid onto the bench at the other side of the table. 'How are you feeling?'

Hope had slowly shaken her head. 'I've no idea. Gobsmacked. Happy. Excited. Fricking terrified. Anxious. Did I say gobsmacked?'

Maisie had nodded. 'You did. Bugger, why did I have to give up smoking? I could so do with a cig right now. Sod it, Prosecco will have to do.' In the few minutes it took for Maisie to retrieve a bottle of wine from the fridge, uncork it, pour generous measures into two glasses, and return to the table, Hope had simply stared at the screen in silence.

Maisie had grimaced a little as the large gulp of wine went down. 'Right then, what are you going to do?'

'I don't know. I mean, I know I need to send him a message, but I just don't know if I'm ready.'

'You are!'

Hope had rolled her eyes, then settled into a rueful glare. 'This comes from the woman who won't even do the test.'

'But I'm a born coward,' Maisie had conceded. 'You're much, much braver than me. That's why we send you in to get the spiders out of the bath. And, you know, to do medical stuff, like cut people up and fix broken folk. I'm here for entertainment and cocktails – nothing that requires balls of steel.'

'Well, my balls of steel are having a think about this before doing anything rash,' Hope had admitted, her voice uncertain.

'Nope, do it now. If you put it off, you'll psyche yourself out. And besides... not to pee on your parade, but you don't really have a choice, do you?'

That had focused Hope's mind. Nope. There was too much riding on this to let it go now. She had to see it through, had to try.

That's what she was telling herself now, two weeks later, when she was getting ready to leave for Glasgow Airport, to meet the man whose name was on that DNA match.

Her fingers shook a little as she tied the laces on her white

Samba trainers, then slung a denim jacket over her pale blue sundress. Layers helped add a bit of a shape to her frame.

Her stomach was rumbling, but she'd been too nervous to eat. His flight was due in just after 10 a.m., and it would take her around twenty minutes to drive to the airport from their Shawlands flat, on the south side of Glasgow, so she'd be there in plenty of time to pop into the Starbucks at the arrivals area for a coffee and something to eat, if she thought she could get anything past the huge lump in her throat.

She kissed Maisie, hugged her tight. 'I love you, sis.'

'I love you too. And I'll be ready to rescue you.'

The front door clicked as Hope closed it behind her. She stopped, took a breath of warm summer air, let the sun soothe the frown lines between her eyebrows, then she started walking towards her Mini. She had so many questions, so many blanks to fill. And now she was closer than she'd ever been.

Today was the day Hope McTeer was going to meet her biological father for the first time. And she was praying that he'd be able, and willing, to save her life.

10 A.M. – NOON

5

AGNETHA

Aggs took a long, leisurely shower in the new gloss white en suite bathroom, a conversion of the old cupboard next door to her bedroom that had been home to decades of accumulated junk owned by her grandparents and parents before her. Usually, she'd just blast her hair with the dryer, then pull it up into a messy bun, from which more and more tendrils would escape throughout the day. But not today. Today she was going to make an effort.

Liberating the box from the bottom of her wardrobe, she took out the huge blow-drying brush that the girls had bought her for Christmas. She'd never tried to use it before, but how hard could it be?

It took a few false starts and a tangle situation that required five minutes of picking trapped hairs out of the brush using the metal handle of her comb, but eventually she got the hang of it.

Hair done, not exactly a smooth salon finish, but passable, she reached for the make-up bag. Another first. She wore make-up so infrequently that she was fairly sure she'd bought that Avon plum lipstick in the nineties.

Five minutes to eleven. She hadn't taken an hour to get ready since the girls were born. But then, lots of things were changing now. She picked up the phone and looked at the text again.

Happy birthday gorgeous. Have you told them yet?

She should reply but... not yet. Soon.

The butterflies in her stomach were in full force, just like they were on that day a few months ago, when she'd realised that her grief over the loss of her mum and dad wasn't something she could deal with on her own. It had taken her weeks to pluck up the courage to go to her first meeting with the group that had helped her topple the first domino on the trail that had led her to here and now.

As soon as she'd walked in the door of the anonymous room that hosted The Wednesday Club in Glasgow Central Hospital, the delight on Yvie's face had de-escalated her trepidation. 'Agnetha, you came!'

'I came,' she'd said needlessly, just to check she could still get words out past the boulder that had yet to dislodge itself from her windpipe.

'Come, come, sit,' Yvie had beckoned, gesturing to one of the ten or so chairs around a long oak table in the centre of the room. Aggs had realised she'd been watching too many TV shows, where these groups met and sat in a circle of chairs, with no barriers between them and the other participants, an open void in the middle to pour their story into.

The room was probably like most others in the hospital – white walled, greyish-green rubbery floor and lighting panes inset into the ceiling. There were already six people at the table, their voices a low hum, a couple of them glancing up at her with smiles that sat somewhere between reassuring and sad.

That made sense.

A woman at the end of one side of the table had yelped as she pulled a blue mug from her mouth before exclaiming a pained, 'Jesus, Yvie, you'd need lips made of asbestos to drink that tea. You're going to be able to suction me to a window by the time I've finished it.'

Yvie had given her a cheeky smile. 'Then keep going, Val – voluptuous lips are all the fashion these days.'

The woman – Val, Yvie had called her – had emitted the most deliciously warm laugh, the eyes that were outlined in mug matching pale blue twinkling as they left Yvie and landed on Aggs.

'Come sit beside me, love. Especially if yer any good at first aid.'

Val had bumped along one seat to free up hers for Aggs. She took it gratefully, but before she could introduce herself, Yvie had pushed a mug in front of her and poured steaming tea from a large steel teapot.

'I'm so glad you're here,' Yvie had whispered, and Aggs could hear the sincerity in every word. Their eyes met for a second of mutual understanding, before Yvie switched up to a lighter, louder tone to address the group. 'Right, you lovelies, we'll get started in a few minutes. Let's just give everyone time to get settled and give a minute for Val to get some ice on her gob.'

That had raised a roomful of smiles and an eye roll from Val, and Aggs had felt herself relax just a little. She caught a conspiratorial look passing between Yvie and Val and realised this banter was deliberate, a bit of levity to put everyone at ease, to lift the mood before the inevitable.

In the centre of the table there was a large box of tissues. Around it, there were a few red-ringed eyes. The man in his forties opposite her sat hunched over his mug, gaze downwards. Next to him, another guy, perhaps fifties, chatted animatedly to two elderly ladies at the end of the table.

Aggs didn't get a chance to really observe any more, because

Val's platinum blonde bob turned to face her. It was a daunting sight. Not a hair of it moved independently and she was immediately transported back to her childhood, watching her mother spray half a can of Elnett on her perm before she left the house.

'I'm Val.'

'Agnetha,' she'd responded. She could see Val's brain working, the same effect her name had had on countless people she'd met over the years. Agnetha wasn't a common moniker in Glasgow. In fact, in all of her forty-five years she'd never met another one. She'd got in first to put Val out of her misery. 'My mother was a huge Abba fan,' she'd explained, churning out the all too familiar explanation. 'She named me after the blonde one.'

Val's pencilled eyebrows had raised in obvious admiration. 'Oh, that's brilliant. Although, thank Christ she didn't name you after one of their songs. Waterloo might have caused a bit of a stir in primary school.'

'Right, I think that's everyone here now,' Yvie's voice had interjected and Aggs was immediately grateful. She was fairly sure this wasn't the place for hilarity and with her nervous anxiety already running high, Val's comment was in danger of setting her off on a fit of mildly hysterical giggles that was likely to get her expelled on her first day. Yvie had sat down in the empty seat on the other side of Val. 'Welcome, everyone,' she'd said, pouring her own mug of tea while she spoke.

Over months of close contact with Yvie, Aggs had realised that she operated on the high-grade fuel of tea and chocolate Hobnobs, both of which she was always happy to share.

'Thank you all for coming. We have a couple of new faces today,' she'd said gently, 'so I think we'll just run round the table and make some introductions. You can tell us as much or as little as you're comfortable sharing. No pressure. And if you don't want to say anything at all, that's fine too,' she'd offered, with a caring glance at the hunched man, still staring downwards at the table in front of him.

'I'll kick things off. I'm Yvie and I started this bereavement group for a few reasons. As you all know, I'm a nurse here in the geriatric ward, so I wanted to create something to help the families of the patients I nursed towards the end of their lives.' The knowing gazes that passed between Yvie and a few of the people round the table hinted that, like Aggs, that was how they'd first encountered the lovely Senior Charge Nurse, Yvie Danton, too.

'But this is also personal for me. My dad passed away when I was eleven and last year I started having panic attacks. After a while, I realised it was because I'd never really dealt with the loss of my dad or talked it through. So here I am. And although this is for each one of you, it really helps me too. I called it The Wednesday Club to remind everyone what day to be here...' There were smiles at that. 'But also because I didn't want you to feel the hurt of the word "bereavement" every time you talked about coming here.

'You should know that there's no judgement, no opinions, and we don't think there's a right or wrong way to grieve. It's important that you feel this is a safe space where you can let out whatever feelings or thoughts you're having. Because no matter whether they feel right, or make sense, they're your feelings and they're valid. Sorry if that sounded all a bit too psychobabble touchy-feely,' she added, with an apologetic grin. 'I'm trying my best to sound like I know what I'm talking about when really I just want to say we're here to listen and offer all the support that we can.'

Lots of nodding. Aggs had started to feel a swirling storm brewing in her stomach and a recurring mantra in her head. *Please don't ask me to say anything. Please don't.* This had just all got very real, very quickly.

Her eyes had flown to the exits, wondering if she could commando crawl that far.

'Val, why don't you go next?' Yvie had suggested.

Aggs got the feeling that Val was probably the go-to person in this situation as she didn't flinch, just took a deep breath, her fingers twirling the gold and red wrapper of a Caramel Log.

'I'm Val,' she began. 'And I come here for the cakes.' The joke had made the corners of several mouths turn upwards, because it was so obviously meant to be a gentle ice breaker. 'But also because it helps me deal with some of the things that I've been through in my life. Several years ago,' she went on, 'my daughter, Dee, was killed by a drugged-up driver. She ran into the road to save a little kid who was about to be hit by the scumbag's out-of-control car and it got her instead.' There was a discernible anger in her voice as she'd said it and she took a moment to steady herself.

'That's the kind of lass my Dee was. For a long, long time, I thought I'd never breathe without pain again. But somehow I did.' She'd paused and Aggs could see that she was determined to hold it together. 'One of the people who got me through it was my best pal, Josie. Och, she was a cracker, but then, last year, she passed away too. One minute we were drinking champagne and having a right old laugh in a hotel room after a wedding, and then she was gone. And since then... well, our Josie is a big, loud hole to fill. When Dee died, I used to walk the aisles of supermarkets all night long just to have somewhere to go. This time, I come here and talk and listen and it makes me feel a bit less... sore.'

More nods of recognition and empathy. In the pause after Val had finished, Aggs took a sip of tea, hoping beyond words that it wasn't her turn to speak.

'Agnetha?' Yvie had prodded softly.

Bugger.

Get it over with. Just say your name. Cut it short.

'I'm... I'm... Ag-Agnetha.' Damn. First time she'd ever actually stuttered over saying her own name.

She'd slipped her hands under her thighs so it wouldn't be obvious to everyone how much she was physically shaking at the prospect of speaking here. Put her in a café and load her up with a Victoria sponge and a tray of brownies and she could talk the socks off anyone. Ask her to get real and bare her soul? No thanks. That involved dealing with emotions, it required the ability to think about herself, to be publicly vulnerable and open and she was way, way out of practice on all counts.

'Most people call me Aggs.'

Okay, move along. Nothing to see here.

Silence. Her toes had clenched inside her biker boots as she prayed to the gods of mortification for a bloody big hole to swallow her.

They were waiting for something more, while she knew without an iota of doubt that she had no more to give without risking a full-scale watershed. How ridiculous was that? It had been months. She knew she should be more together. More composed. But that's one of the things she'd learned about grief. She could discuss what happened with her family and no longer dissolve into pieces. She could talk about it with friends without crumbling. But no one tells you that the first time you break the news to someone new, whether you know them or not, the reality of it can catch you unawares and make it hurt just as much as it did the very first time you ever uttered the words. He's dead. She's dead. They're gone.

All around her, they were still waiting.

Aggs had heard Yvie take a breath and realised she was about to jump in to save her and, in that split second, something inside had her compelled her to rip off the plaster.

'I met Yvie when she looked after my dad before he passed away a few years ago. He'd been pretty much bed bound for years after his last stroke. He had three strokes altogether over twenty years or so and each one left its mark.' Her eyes had caught Yvie's and she could see the encouragement there. It was enough for her to give just a little bit more. 'And then we met again when Mum was admitted to the geriatric ward last year before she... she... died. Bowel cancer. She'd been battling it for many years, but still, the shock...'

As a river of tears had swelled and made their way to her eyes, a triffid of pain had tangled itself around her throat and begun to tighten, slowed only by the touch of Val's hand, which was now on hers.

'I lived with them and I cared for both of them for the last ten years. So now, I'm forty-five, and both my parents are dead. Taking care of them, and raising my children, took up every minute I had, so now my daughters are adults and my parents are gone, and I've no idea how to fill the void that they've left. That's why I'm here. I feel like my life has belonged to other people for over twenty years, and now that I can have it back, I've no idea what to do with it.'

Back in the present, a knock her bedroom door interrupted the memory and snapped her back to the real world. She put the cold coffee down, aware she'd been daydreaming for ages. How far she'd come since that day. Yvie and Val were now two of her closest friends. And as for the others... well, they'd all become a gang of survivors, there for each other through every tear and the bitter-sweet laughter of the grieving process.

'Right, Mother, your enforced chill is over. Wow, you look fab! You'll be putting selfies on Insta next.'

'I'd rather poke my eye with a fork,' Aggs retorted, pleased though, that Isla noticed the effort she'd put in.

Isla grinned at the standard response to any mention of social media. Aggs had successfully avoided the social media revolution, leaving it to Isla to set up Facebook, Twitter and Instagram accounts for the café.

'Come on then. We've got loads of surprises for you today,' Isla gushed.

Aggs held her breath. She wasn't great with surprises and she really hated being the centre of attention or anyone making a fuss. However, it was a different thought that had the stomach butterflies on spin setting again.

Her family and friends might have a few surprises for her. But she had a few shocks of her own to deliver.

6

MITCHELL

Mitchell was back in the kitchen, showered, dressed in sweatpants and a T-shirt, and making a protein shake, when Celeste appeared in her workout gear, carrying a suit hanger which she hung on the back of the door. 'I'm just going to go straight to lunch from the studio. No point me coming home to change when it's on the way.'

Mitchell shook the plastic bottle to mix the chocolate flavoured gunk that was a part of his daily diet now. 'Okay, darling. Makes sense. Where's the lunch?'

'City centre,' she answered curtly, and he considered probing further, but she was making it obvious she was in a hurry, so he let it go.

Polite. Civil. Non-confrontational. When had they become so fucking pedestrian?

Once upon a time they hadn't been able to keep their hands off each other. Weekend-morning sex was a must, and then they'd spend the rest of the day together, desperate to milk every minute with each other.

Karma. Was that what this was?

He didn't have time to finish the thought because she reached up and kissed him on the cheek. 'See you later.'

Skye came back from the bathroom and interrupted them before he could reply with another banality.

'Well, that's a statement,' his daughter said, eyes wide, as she took in her stepmother's outfit.

She had a point. White yoga pants that sat low on the hips, with a matching Lycra crop top worn very obviously braless, showing off a taut rack of abs. The fact that Celeste was now pulling on a tiny cotton, off the shoulder sweatshirt over it made little difference.

Celeste unhooked her suit hanger. 'Worked hard for it. Deserve to show it off. Bye, sweetie.' With an unapologetic wave, she was gone.

Skye picked up her pen and went back to her books with a nonchalant shrug. 'Could be worse. At least she doesn't post daily selfies on Insta. One a week on Facebook is enough to make sure everyone over thirty she's ever met knows that she's got an arse like a rock.'

Mitchell barely heard over the noise of his internal dialogue. This was the moment of truth. Was he really going to do this? Was he actually going to follow his wife like some weirdo stalker husband? Had they really sunk that low?

He picked up his car keys. 'I'm heading over to the boxing gym to get a couple of rounds in.' Hello, gutter.

Skye barely glanced up at him. 'Cool. Go and be a middle-aged man who hits another bloke for fun. Perfectly normal pastime for a forty-five year old lawyer. If you took up archery, you could maybe spear a few people in the street as well.'

Mitchell didn't rise to it – just kissed her on the head as he passed on his way out. Both his daughters had been blessed with Agnetha's dry sense of humour and they weren't afraid to use it, usually at his expense. Not that he minded. He wanted his girls to be able to stand up for themselves in this world.

Maybe that was what he was doing now. Fighting his own corner. It was the thought he needed to get him out of the door and to his Merc GLE, parked at the bottom of the steps up to their townhouse. In his twenties and thirties, he'd gone for sports cars, but now it was all about space and comfort. Yet another sign of getting older. Maybe it was time for a midlife crisis flip back to Ferrari central. Not exactly unobtrusive when following the wife though.

Her car – a white Porsche 911 – was just pulling out of the end of the street, turning left, with a few cars in between them. He hung back, wary of being spotted.

This was ridiculous. He could still stop and go back, redeem the day and his opinion of himself. Yet his foot felt like it was made of lead and was refusing to leave the accelerator.

He followed her for ten minutes as she snaked through the West End, finally stopping outside a glass fronted studio on Hyndland Road, not far from The Ginger Sponge.

The Bends. A yoga studio.

Fuck. She was doing exactly what she said she was going to do.

Okay, this was his chance to go home. Forget this. Swallow the shame and put it down to an error of judgement that no one ever had to know about.

But then…

An orange Volkswagen Beetle pulled out of a parking space right in front of him. Was this a sign that he should just wait it out? And why was he, the most pragmatic, non-superstitious man, suddenly thinking that complete coincidences were anything more than that? Christ, this was all messing with his mind and sending him batshit crazy.

With a jerking action that made the driver in the car behind him furiously beep their horn, he pulled in, parked, and leaned his head back against the seat, heart racing faster than it was after this morning's five kilometres.

Across the road, about fifty metres ahead, he could see Celeste climb out of the car and take her kit bag and suit carrier into the yoga studio.

He switched off the engine. Needed to think. Go over the facts. Weigh up the evidence. Wasn't that his area of expertise in his career?

He took note of the time – just after 10.30 a.m. – and closed his eyes, rewinding to the day, about six months ago, that he first suspected Celeste had checked out of their marriage and checked into someone else's life.

The charity ball at the Glasgow Hilton was one of her recurring annual events. The Derek Evans Charity for Young Athletes. A former football player for a Scottish premier league team, who went on to play for a couple of top European clubs before finishing his career in Barcelona, Derek Evans was the local Glasgow boy done good. If you didn't count years of tabloid headlines about his high profile affairs, which led to more headlines about his three divorces. Or was it four? Now he was living back in Glasgow and raised money every year for grass-roots football, supplying kits and upgrading facilities across the country, most of it funded by the annual shindig that brought the football glitterati, past and present, to the linen covered tables of ten with their chequebooks open.

Of course, since Celeste was organising the event, Mitchell supported it by buying a table on behalf of his company and he and his partner, Leo Oswald, had taken along eight of their top clients. Never hurt to inject a bit of social glamour into a professional relationship.

Halfway through the night, he'd begun to get an uncharacteristic feeling of unease. A couple of rows away, at the front, middle, VIP table, he could see Celeste sitting on Derek Evans' left and they were deep in conversation. He'd shrugged it off. He'd never been the jealous type and had no reason to feel insecure. Yet...

His eyes were drawn back, time and time again, as he'd realised that to anyone in the room, Celeste and Derek looked like a couple, constantly in conversation, laughing, casually tactile and paying very little attention to anyone else.

Back then, he had a thought that felt like a sucker punch to the gut. Is that what Aggs had seen when he and Celeste began seeing each other behind his wife's back?

There it was again. The karma. And the worst thing of all was that, despite a million pathetic excuses of justification, he deserved it.

The rest of the night had passed in a fake smiling, anxiety whirling, blur. He had to talk to her. And he had to choose his moment.

It came the next morning. When he'd woken, he'd reached over, tenderly traced a finger along her cheek as she'd roused from her sleep. 'Morning, darling.'

She'd flinched. Pulled away. Rolled over. Ouch.

Later that evening, he'd gone for the direct approach. 'You and Derek Evens were pretty chummy last night,' he'd said over a late supper of steak and asparagus, delivered in because Celeste refused to cook at the weekend. Or any other night for that matter. Skye was at her mum's, so they had the house to themselves.

Celeste had responded with a flippant dismissal. 'He's a client and it's my job to keep him happy.'

'How happy?' Jesus, he'd hated himself for sounding like a jealous teenager.

That one brought out his wife's death stare. 'Seriously? What are you implying, Mitch? You think I'm having an affair?'

'Are you?'

She'd picked up her wine glass and taken a sip. 'Well, wouldn't that be ironic?'

They had both let the truth of that sit for a moment before she'd uttered a sigh that oozed irritation.

'No, I'm not having an affair. Derek is good fun, he's a client, and trust me, if I wanted to look elsewhere, I'd tell you first.'

They'd had that agreement right from the start and it was hard to argue. Celeste was the most upfront woman he'd ever met. She saw what she wanted and went after it every time. If she wanted someone else, wouldn't she already be out of here?

He'd braced himself for an argument, but suddenly her shoulders had relaxed down a couple of inches and she'd purred, 'Ooh, it's a bit sexy that you're jealous though. I kinda like it.'

Pushing her plate away, she'd wrapped her perfect manicure around his neck, kissed him, her tongue probing and teasing, and his concerns were instantly silenced. Aggs once accused him of being controlled by his dick, and in that moment, she was 100 per cent accurate. As he'd lifted Celeste up, she'd curled her legs around his waist and he took a few steps to the kitchen island, where they made love on the Carrara marble top. Actually 'made love' didn't quite cover it. It was pure physical passion – hot, frantic and fuelled by the kind of lust that came from jealousy and desperate need. It was the best sex they'd had in months.

Afterwards, they'd showered together, watched some TV in bed.

'Sorry, I was a tit,' he'd told her, trying to make light of it. 'Think it's some kind of midlife crisis.'

Celeste had groaned. 'Great. Although, it would probably be better for our marriage if you just bought a bomber jacket and a motorbike.'

That should have been it. End of suspicion. Case closed. Nothing to see here.

But the senses that made him a great mitigator in court, that gut instinct for lies and weaknesses, the ability to feel when danger was coming, to predict an ambush, just wouldn't let it drop.

Then there was the factual evidence. The dropped phone calls. The late-night dinners that stretched until the early hours of the morning. The weekend trips, supposedly to scout event locations. The spa breaks that she insisted on going to on her own, despite offers from him or Skye to tag along. There was a separation, a feeling of a fork in the road and they were both now going on separate paths.

Most of this he could put down to familiarity and to the length of their relationship. The biggest change of all, though, was the one that made the hair on the back of his neck bristle. He loved his wife, but there was no denying that Celeste was emotionally high maintenance. She needed to know that she was valued and adored. He'd once thought it was a beautiful vulnerability, and he'd been happy to give her the attention she needed, but in the last few months she'd been almost low-key. Wanted nothing from him. And if she wasn't getting the ego strokes from him, were they coming from somewhere else?

Unaccustomed to practising patience, he fidgeted in his seat of his Mercedes as the minutes continued to tick by with no sign of Celeste, until eventually, a knock on his window snapped him out of his thoughts. Bloody traffic warden.

Mitchell rolled down his window just as the small-eyed, pinched face of a man who loved his uniform contorted into a sneer.

'You planning on buying a ticket any time soon? You've already been here an hour.'

Mitchell immediately went into bluff mode. 'Sorry, mate. The wife said she was popping into the shop for five minutes. But, you know, once she gets talking...'

The traffic warden didn't look impressed, but before he could react, Mitchell spotted a figure in a stunning white jacket and pencil skirt, huge shades adding to the glamour, alighting from the studio. Celeste had obviously changed in there, and now she was sliding into the front seat of her car.

'Actually, you know what? Stuff it. I'm not waiting any longer,' Mitchell shrugged, 'She can walk home.'

With that, he indicated, then swerved out of the space, leaving a slack-jawed jobsworth staring after him.

He was pretty sure his heart rate was on the rise again as he navigated the traffic in pursuit of his wife, a new observation adding to his feeling of dread that he might actually be on to something here.

The suit. The gleaming hair. The Chanel bag. The heels.

Even for a first lunch with a potential new client, she'd gone way above and beyond on her look. Celeste McMaster clearly made a huge effort for someone today and Mitchell knew he had to find out if it really was a business meeting, or was it the kind of pleasure that led to a division of property and expensive legal bills?

As he pressed his foot on the accelerator, he had a sinking feeling that it was too close to call.

7

'She's not shy, is she?' Aaron drawled, putting his bottle of Budweiser down on the table on his side of their double sunlounger.

Agnetha followed his eyeline, to see Celeste, on some guy's shoulders in the pool, playing an impromptu game of pool volley-ball with a crowd she'd introduced herself to about twenty minutes ago. They were a group of graduates from UCLA, here celebrating the end of term, and very happy to welcome the gorgeous tourist into their celebrations. All plans for seeing the Vegas sights had been postponed after Celeste's bottom lip had shot out at the very mention of an open-top bus tour. 'What are we, like sixty? This is Vegas and it's your birthday! We should be drinking, partying, meeting people, not traipsing around looking at things we can see on postcards in the fricking gift shop.'

Lying here at the side of the pool, snuggled in a cabana with Aaron, Agnetha conceded that she had a point. Sometimes going with the flow took you to exactly where you were meant to be. And right now, she couldn't think of anywhere more perfect.

Aaron nodded his head in Celeste's direction. 'Has she always been like that?'

Agnetha took a sip of her pina colada, then winced, her buttocks instinctively clenching when she rested the ice-cold glass on her bare stomach. 'Pretty much. She likes to enjoy herself. It's great now, but it used to get us into all sorts of trouble when we were at school. When we were fifteen, she got us suspended because she persuaded me to sneak out to the pub at lunchtime to celebrate my birthday. We walked in and four of our teachers were already there. Caught red-handed.'

His face melted into the sexiest grin as he rolled towards her, so that he was lying on his side facing her, resting his chin on his beer, the contours of his muscular torso glistening in the heat.

'Don't laugh. My parents grounded us for a month.'

'Us? She lived with you?'

Agnetha nodded, surprised that they were only having this discussion now. In the three months since they'd met, they'd spent every night and weekend together. Sometimes they were a four-some, other times in separate couples. At weekends, they'd jump in the car and head to Malibu, where they'd sneak on to the private beach at the Colony and chill in front of some of the most expensive houses in the country. During the week, they'd head to bed early, because Aaron had to be up at 6 a.m. every morning to go to work on the construction of a mega mansion in the Hollywood Hills. Agnetha would get up with him and, leaving Celeste to sleep, she would use the time to explore the area on foot, sometimes covering miles before Aaron got home around 5 p.m.. They'd have dinner on the roof terrace of the apartment, then catch an early night, while Zac and Celeste hit the hotels and clubs up and down Sunset.

'She had a pretty crap life at home. Her parents split up, her dad took off and her mum loved the single life and the party scene, so even as a kid, she was left alone all the time. I knew her from school, but we were in different crowds. Then my dad gave her a Saturday job in the café when she was fourteen, and she pretty much moved in and didn't go home. Best friends ever since.'

The pamphlet version of the story would do for now. Aaron didn't need to know that Celeste's mum had left her alone on Christmas Day to go to Gleneagles with her new boyfriend. And for weeks at a time while she swanned off on holiday with her latest man. Or that her dad had barely spoken to her since the day he left. Or that Agnetha's mum and dad, Alex and Ella, had been so worried about Celeste going off the rails that they had welcomed her into their home for the whole of the last two years of school and Celeste's mum hadn't complained or questioned it, delighted to be free of the constraints of motherhood. None of that mattered now. They were both happy and getting on with their lives, and Agnetha was grateful that Celeste's thirst for enjoyment had rubbed off on her and given her an appetite for adventure too. They'd had almost ten fantastic years of friendship and she treasured her friend like a sister. An unpredictable, wild, hilarious sister who was probably going to land them in jail, but she loved every crazy bone of her anyway.

Aaron reached over and pushed a red curl off her cheek. 'So your parents are as nice as you then?'

Her smile was automatic. 'Much nicer. You'll love them.' It was out before she even realised she was saying it. Damn it. Where had that come from? This was a holiday romance, not a preamble to marriage and two-point-two kids. Bugger, he was probably totally freaked out now. He'd have his stuff packed and be waiting for that bus to leave first thing tomorrow.

Face flushed, and not from the heat, Agnetha was about to backpedal furiously when he leaned forward and kissed her. 'I think I will,' he murmured, before their lips met again.

The noise from the pool, the scent of sun cream, the searing heat; everything faded as his fingertips cupped her face and every nerve and bone in her body responded to him.

'Urgh, you two really need to, like, get a room.'

Agnetha could feel Aaron's lips break into a smile even before he pulled back and held his hand up to the new arrival. Zac was wearing the same grey suit he'd had on last night, the top buttons of his black shirt open.

Aaron squinted against the sun. 'Man, you look like crap.'

Zac appeared to find this amusing. 'Cheers, bud. I may look like crap, but I'm a fucking hero at the office, so I'll take it.'

Zac plonked down on the end of Agnetha's sunlounger, completely unaware that he'd just taken a wrecking ball to an incredibly special moment. Agnetha tried really hard not to mind. For all his cocky bluster, Zac made her laugh and she could see that there was a really close bond between the two men. They'd met in college, and Zac had moved to LA from New York, sharing a flat with Aaron while trying to find a way into the entertainment industry. He'd eventually landed the CAA job and he was determined that nothing was getting in the way of him rising through the ranks.

Agnetha glanced over and saw that Celeste was still in the pool, oblivious to Zac's arrival. 'Tell us all about it. And make it quick before Celeste decks you for running out on her last night.'

Zac had the decency to squirm a little uncomfortably. 'Listen, Aggs, I need to talk to you about Celeste.'

'Here it comes,' Aaron whistled knowingly, shaking his head. 'He's usually got a six week attention span. We're now at twelve. It was only a matter of time.'

Agnetha felt a clenching sensation in her stomach. Bollocks. Zac's lack of denial told her where he was going with this and Celeste would not take it well. She didn't do rejection. It didn't take a psychologist to understand that underneath all that riotous zest for life, her childhood had left its scars and for Celeste, it was a lightning reaction to any sense of abandonment. She hoped beyond words that Aaron was wrong...

Zac sighed. 'I need to call it a day. It's not her, it's just that... well, this work thing.'

Aaron wasn't wrong.

'I need you guys to run interference. Look, she's a nice girl and all that, and we had a good time, but the whole steady relationship isn't my deal right now.'

'Come on, Zac. We're heading back to the UK in a few days. Can't you let it ride for now?' Even as she was saying it, Agnetha could hear how wrong it sounded.

The repetitive tapping of Zac's foot on the tile floor was a definite tell that there wasn't going to be an agreeable reply to the question. He ran his tanned fingers through his long blond hair, a gesture Agnetha had seen him make many times when he was on a work call and hustling or pressing for something.

'That's the problem. Last night Jilly Jones had a meltdown. Dived into the Bellagio Fountains naked in front of dozens of tourists and some paps.'

'You're joking!' Agnetha gasped. Jilly Jones was her favourite romcom actress. America's Southern sweetheart, she had a squeaky-clean reputation, perpetuated in the kind of movies that you watched after a break-up to restore your faith in love.

Zac glanced around to make sure no one could overhear, then lowered his voice to make extra sure the conversation was just between them. 'She was off her head on coke. It's been a problem for a while.'

Now Agnetha's chin was next to Zac's tapping foot on the floor.

'My boss represents her and he called me last night. I had to go get her, salvage the situation, call a doctor in and get her on lockdown until a private jet could be arranged back to LA. We're leaving in an hour.'

Aaron's abs visibly rolled as he effortlessly pulled himself up to a sitting position on the sunlounger. 'So, what... you're going too?'

Zac shrugged, with no hint of an apology. 'I need to, man. This is a big opportunity for me. Like, up close and personal with Jilly. If I handle this, it could be what I need to take the next step up.'

On one hand, Agnetha could understand. But on the other...

'Where the fuck have you been?' They'd all been too deep in discussion to notice that Celeste had climbed out of the pool, and was now standing, in a leopard bikini, hands on hips, looking like a bronzed Amazonian goddess who was about to go to war.

Zac went for the direct approach. 'Look, I'm sorry about last night, but I need to split. It's a work thing. I'm needed back in LA.'

'And you think you can just snap your fingers and I'll jump?' Celeste folded her arms, clearly not getting a full read on the situation.

'No, I, eh, I need to head back on my own. My boss hired a jet. I just came back to get my stuff.'

The pin was out of the grenade and it had just been tossed into the middle of the conversation. It was all Agnetha could do not to put her fingers in her ears and crouch low.

'Fuck you. Fuck. You,' Celeste spat, before spinning round. The splash she made as she dived back into the pool soaked Zac's shoes.

It was a small price to pay, Agnetha decided. Her heart hurt for her friend. Celeste put on a tough shell, but Agnetha knew that underneath there was a good person that just needed to be loved. She was about to follow her, when Celeste climbed back up on to the shoulders of the UCLA hunk, and gave Zac the middle finger. Perhaps later would be a better time to check how she was feeling.

'I guess that got the message across then,' Zac deadpanned,

shaking his damp feet as he stood up. 'I'll catch you guys back in LA. Just do me a favour...'

'Shoot.' The corners of Aaron's mouth were turning up at the edges.

'Make sure she doesn't buy a baseball bat on the way back to LA.'

'Can't promise anything,' Agnetha teased. He deserved it. He'd just dumped her best friend, so Girl Code demanded it.

'Man, tough crowd.' Zac was still shaking his head as he disappeared through the loungers to retrieve his things from his room.

Aaron lay back down and rolled over on his side to face her again. 'Guess we've something else in common.'

'What's that?'

'Seriously unpredictable friends.'

'No arguments here,' Agnetha smiled, kissing him again. God, she could not get enough of this guy. He was absolutely intoxicating. She loved a romance, adored the early stages of a relationship and had fallen fast before, but this felt different. This was...

'I really hope we've got something else in common,' he whispered, making her stomach flip.

'What's that?' she answered, enjoying the game.

He was watching her face now, studying her reaction.

'I'm falling in love with you. And I was just kinda wondering if you felt the same?'

8

HOPE

Hi,

I'm not really sure how to start this email or what to say. I guess, first of all, I need to apologise if this comes as a shock to you. I'm unaware of the circumstances of my birth, so if you weren't aware of my existence, I'm sorry to break the news this way.

My name is Hope McTeer, and according to the results of my DNA test, I'm your daughter (I didn't want to be presumptuous or freak you out by referring to you as 'Dad' at the start of this email).

I'm twenty-two and I assume I was born in Scotland, as this is where my adoption was formalised. I have had no access to my adoption records, so I know no more than that. As you can imagine, it was quite a surprise to discover my biological father is American, but I am, quite honestly, intrigued to learn more.

I also want you to know that I'm very grateful to have been adopted by two wonderful parents who have loved and supported me every day since I became their daughter. I'm now studying medicine at university and live with my adoptive sister in Glasgow.

It goes without saying that I would very much like to meet you. I understand if this takes time to process, so please be assured that I will not pester or badger you with more emails. I'll wait in the hope that you will feel the same way and that I will hear from you soon.

Yours,

Hope

The digital clock at the top of the arrivals board said 10.05 a.m.. Hope scanned the lists of incoming flights, searching for one from Heathrow. He'd arrived there from LA at 7 a.m., so hopefully he made his 8.45 a.m. connection to Glasgow and would right now be touching down on a runway on the other side of this building.

She wondered if everyone around her could see that she was actually trembling with nerves and about as light-headed as it was possible to be without keeling over. She couldn't faint now. Not here. He could come right out of there and step over her, not realising that she was the welcoming committee.

Heathrow. There it was. Delayed. Now arriving at 11 a.m.. Crap. She should have checked for delays before she left the house, but between her anxiety and her outraged sister, it had completely slipped her mind. Now she had to try not to faint for at least another hour. She couldn't guarantee that it was possible.

For years, she'd watched family reunion shows with obsessive interest, and wondered how she would feel when and if the moment came. Now she knew. She'd be absolutely terrified, yet incredibly excited too. This was the point at the start of the roller coaster that was equal parts fear, adrenalin and desperation to get going.

There was no point standing here for an hour. Behind her, Starbucks was busy, but there were a few single seats at the high bar counter from where she would have a view of the arrivals board and the doors.

10.15 a.m.. She bought a latte that she probably wouldn't be able to drink, and a lemon muffin that she probably wouldn't be able to eat, and climbed up on the bar stool, eyes trained on the sliding doors that were constantly opening and closing, each movement bringing through people pulling suitcases, businessmen clutching briefcases, cabin crew with relaxed expressions, happy to be off duty. Every now and then, someone would break from the crowd and run towards a new arrival, making everyone around them smile. And making Hope's heart hammer so loudly in her chest she was sure it could crack a rib at any moment.

10.35 a.m.. Coffee still not touched. Muffin still not eaten. Hope picked up her phone and called her mum as promised. She answered on the first ring with, 'Are you okay?' It was unusual to hear anxiety in her mum's voice. Dora was the calmest woman that Hope had ever known, even in times of adversity and heartache. It was a strength that had been tested many times over the years.

'I'm fine, Mum. I'm at the airport. His flight is delayed until 11 o'clock, so he should be here just after that.'

'How are you feeling, my love?' Dora's voice was calmer now, more like herself.

'Nervous. Terrified. What if he's horrible? What if he doesn't like me?'

'He'll like you. And you're far too lovely to have horrible genes.' Joking now, and Hope was so grateful. Her mum always knew exactly what to say to make her feel better.

'Thanks, Mum. I'd better go and phone Maisie before she puts out a bulletin on Radio Clyde saying I'm missing, possibly abducted.'

'Good idea. Just keep us posted, love. We'll both be by our phones all day and can be with you in no time if you need us.'

'I know. I love you.'

'I love you too, darling. Big hugs.'

10.45 a.m.. Hope took a sip of the latte and tried not to grimace. The muffin was still a step too far.

She decided she couldn't face speaking to Maisie, so she opted for a text.

His flight is delayed. Coming in at 11 a.m.. Just waiting in Starbucks.

Have you eaten?

Yes.

You're lying.

That made Hope smile.

I am. But I've got a muffin.

Trying really hard not to make inappropriate jokes right now.

You're so immature.

I know. Sorry. Text me as soon as you can to let me know what he's like. And if there's a problem, use the pepper spray.

I don't have pepper spray. Pretty sure it's illegal.

Bought one on the internet. I slipped it in your bag.

A feeling of cold dread worked its way up from Hope's gut. Surely not... She picked up her backpack and unzipped the main compartment. Yep, there it was. A small silver can nestled between her iPad and the latest Dorothy Koomson novel. She was suddenly very aware of the two armed policemen just metres away, patrolling the terminal. There she was, in an airport, with a weapon she was fairly sure was illegal. Christ Almighty.

You're a fkn maniac!

You won't be saying that if you need it.

Hope closed her eyes and inhaled, trying not to panic. As if today wasn't stressful enough. Now she could add possible arrest to the list of things that could go wrong. Great. Smashing. But then, she knew that Maisie was only behaving like this because she loved her.

She felt the anger dissipate and picked up her phone again.

Need to go. Will buzz you later. Love you.

Love you too. Stay safe.

Xx

She put the phone back down on the counter in front of her and exhaled, trying to channel her mum's energy as opposed to her sister's. She had this. She could do it. She'd faced worse and survived.

10.55 a.m.. Another sip of latte. One bite of muffin that felt like it took five minutes to chew and swallow. This was excruciating. She was a planner by nature, always had been. She liked to know the facts, to think things through, analyse from every angle, prepare for every outcome. This one was out of her control though. It was all down to him and she had no idea what to expect.

Picking up her phone again, she flicked on to her Ancestry account and clicked on the inbox. His reply had come in the day after she'd contacted him.

Dear Hope,

Like you, I don't know what to say. I had no idea that I had fathered a child during that time and I'm stunned. Stunned, but so grateful that you've found me. There's so much to say, but I want to do it in person. I'm in LA but will come to you if you want to meet? I can get there Saturday. Please say yes?

Of course, she'd agreed. She'd crammed her studies all week so that she could take the weekend off, and she'd managed to juggle her hospital shifts around so she didn't need to be back in work until Monday night. A whole weekend to get to know the father who was a complete stranger to her. That's if he even planned on staying that long.

He'd sent his flight arrival details an hour or so after she agreed to meet him and that had been the last contact other than exchanging mobile numbers.

11.04 a.m.. Flight Landed. Coffee and muffin discarded. Hope left Starbucks and went to the front of the crowd that was waiting a few metres back from the doors. There were several men in suits there, holding up cards with names on them, and Hope suddenly realised that she had no way of recognising him. Why hadn't she thought of that before? Dammit.

She texted his mobile.

I'm in arrivals. White dress. Blue jacket.

Send.

She stared at the screen. Three moving dots. He was replying.

On way. I'll find you.

Oh God. Her heart was racing again as the doors opened. Closed. Opened. Closed.

Don't faint. Do not faint. The cops will find the pepper spray and his first act as father will be to bail you out. Do. Not. Faint.

Doors opened.

Was that him? A grey haired, forty something hipster type in a suit seemed to be searching for someone. Hope was about to step forward when he spotted one of the signs and gestured to the driver holding it. Nope. Not him.

Another guy. Mid forties. Dad chinos. Brogues. Corporate haircut. He paused, scanned the crowd, then turned to the left and seemed to continue his search as he walked out of the area. Was that him? It could be. He'd be completely unfamiliar with this airport so he may think the arrivals area stretched along the corridor.

She was still staring at the man disappearing from view when someone much closer spoke. 'Hope?'

Her head spun back and there he was, right in front of her. She knew. Just knew.

Eyes wide, she managed to nod and stammer out a reply. 'Y... y... yes. Hi.'

It was the strangest sensation she'd ever experienced. When she was a little girl, she would wonder if she looked like anyone. Sometimes she'd search the faces of people in the street, in the library, in airports, to see if there was anything there that she recognised, any sign of who she belonged to. There never was. Until now.

Same colouring. Same shade of hair, although his was flecked with salt and pepper strands. But the most striking thing of all was the eyes. Grey. A shade of steel that she'd never seen before except when she looked in a mirror.

'I'm not sure what I should do,' he said, his smile revealing the kind of white teeth that were natural and not the result of an expensive set of veneers. 'Is it okay to give you a hug?'

Slowly, wordlessly, Hope nodded and was immediately enfolded in the broad, muscular arms of a man who was at least six inches taller than her, definitely over six feet tall.

The most surprising thing was that he was handsome. That wasn't something she'd even considered before now, assuming he'd just be like most other dads of that age. Maybe he was – if the dads in question had a square jawline and an outdoor tan that creased into attractive lines at the side of his eyes when he smiled. His clothes helped too. A black T-shirt and black jeans, with leather boots that stopped on just the right fashion side of cowboy.

After seconds that felt like minutes, he pulled back. 'Your eyes, they're...'

He paused, and she finished for him. 'They're yours.'

It was the moment that all doubt was blown away. This man was her dad. And now she just needed to find out so many things. Who was her mum? How did he not know she existed? And the biggest question of all... did they have something much more important in common than the colour of their eyes?

NOON – 2 P.M

'Happy birthday!' The cheer went up as soon as Aggs opened the door that led from the back stairs to the café, the riot of noise bringing on a mortified case of the giggles. The café's white brick walls had been decorated with balloons and streamers, and there was a 'Happy Birthday, Agnetha' banner hanging from the ceiling that stretched the whole length of the serving counter. However, it was the grinning faces in front of her that were the greatest thrill. She'd known that Val and Yvie were here, and that Skye was popping round to have lunch with them, but the rest of the friends she'd made at The Wednesday Club were beaming at her too.

'We invited a few others. We hope you don't mind,' Isla whispered into her ear as she hugged her.

'I'm delighted,' Aggs said honestly. Several months of weekly sessions had brought them all so close and it felt so right to be sharing such a big day with the people who'd been by her side as she worked through this transition of her life. It was perfect. Marge and Myra were there, two septuagenarian sisters who'd lost their older sister, Maggie. There was Jonathan, whose wife had passed away in a drowning accident in Thailand last year. And Colin, whose partner of thirty years, Jason, had suffered a fatal heart attack at Christmas. A room of heartbreak. Of sadness and struggle. And yet, here they were, all happy for her, all laughing and cheering through sunny smiles.

All except... Where was he?

As she hugged everyone in turn, Aggs scanned the room again to see if he was hiding behind someone, but no, he definitely wasn't there.

Ignoring the little tug of disappointment, she nipped over to say hello to a group of regular mums and tots who were sitting at the tables in the windows. Their round of applause showed they were delighted that they'd inadvertently stumbled on such a happy occasion.

She was on the way back to join her own party when the door opened. Her heart stopped. There he was. Rushing in at the last minute, Will Hamilton was in the building.

He came straight over, kissed her on the cheek, hugged her. Nothing untoward there. Just a friend, cuddling another friend on her birthday. At least, that's what she hoped the others would think. Meanwhile, her insides were tumbling like a teenager on her first date.

'Happy birthday, you,' he whispered.

'Thank you.' Her reply was a bit strangled, aware that from the corner of her eye she could see Val, Yvie and Skye watching with interest.

It could have been her imagination, but she was sure she could feel the heat of his body as he added, 'You look incredible.'

Her internal organs took another spin around her insides, while her brain sent urgent orders to her face. Act natural. Act nonchalant. Smile. Be cool.

'You didn't answer my text this morning,' he murmured close to her ear, so that only she could hear. 'Have you told them?'

She shook her head. 'Soon. At the right moment.'

A flash of something crossed his face – what was it? Disappointment? Annoyance? Aggs wasn't sure, but she couldn't talk it out here and now without making it all too obvious, and this wasn't the time or the place.

Whatever it was, he recovered quickly. 'I've got a pressie for you, but I'll give it to you later.'

Before she could reply, they were interrupted.

'Will, you handsome big devil, come flirt with me and I'll reward you with a bloody great chunk of carrot cake,' Val bellowed, her arms out wide, as she welcomed him to the party.

Aggs breathed a silent sigh of thanks for the intervention. It had taken the heat off her and given her a moment to regroup and settle her inner turmoil.

Will Hamilton. Member of The Wednesday Club. And so much more.

They'd met on that first day, and her initial response to this tall, stoic man had been heart wrenching sympathy.

He'd been sitting across from her at the wooden table. Around the same age as her, she'd guessed, his body language screaming exhaustion, maybe defeat, as he'd stared into the mug in front of him. He'd been the next to speak after her. 'I'm Will,' he'd said, in a quiet voice that was husky with emotion. 'My boy, Barney, my only kid, passed a year ago. One of those freak things. A fight outside a pub. He was out with some mates, the night before his twenty-first birthday and ended up in the wrong place at the wrong time. It was nothing to do with him. Some maniac threw a punch, he went down, banged his head and...' The words had caught in his throat. 'We lost him. Just like that.'

He'd paused for a moment, visibly swallowing back tears. 'After that, everything changed. My missus and I couldn't cope with it. I guess that kind of thing either makes you stronger as a couple or tears you apart. Carol couldn't look at me without seeing Barney, and I couldn't change that, so we called it a day. For the first few months, I was a mess, to be honest, but then my doctor suggested I come here and it took a bit of time, but it's helped me see things a bit differently. I realise now that I still have to get up. And what honour am I showing to my boy's memory if I wreck my life, when he wasn't even allowed to live his? So now I get out of bed, I go to work – I'm an engineer at the airport – I come here, I go to the gym, I go on holiday... And I miss him every day, but I can't give up because now I have to live for Barney too.'

His very visible pain had chipped a piece off Aggs' heart right there and then. This lovely man had experienced so much loss and yet here he was, still getting up in the morning, still trying to find joy, talking about his feelings instead of locking himself away. There was a lesson to be learned there. Inspiration to be drawn.

After that, their friendship had built gradually. He'd started popping into the café before work. Sometimes at weekends too. Their conversations always flowed effortlessly – two kindred spirits who'd suffered loss, both bereavement and their closest relationship.

Aggs understood that. Hadn't her own marriage crumbled when life threw a curveball? Although, there was a former best friend shaped influence in there that had blindsided her. That experience had left her scarred and wary of trusting people, but with Will, she'd instinctively known that he would be gentle with her heart. So far, she'd been right.

Hopefully, no one noticed her blushes as she headed to the table in front of the counter. There were glass jars with lilac peonies, her favourite flowers, all the way along the silver jacquard runner in the centre and matching silver charger plates at every place.

'Mum, you're a stunner today. Your seat's here, between me and your less attractive daughter,' Skye laughed, ducking to avoid the teaspoon that came flying over the counter in her direction. 'She's far more violent too,' Skye added, with a casual nonchalance.

Isla came around from behind the counter, carrying two long platters of nibbles. 'That may be true, but people love café cooks much more than they love lawyers.'

Isla put the platters of chicken skewers, haddock goujons, mini quiche, tiny steak pies and buffalo mozzarella balls on the table, just as Val and Yvie followed with a huge focaccia and a big bowl of salad.

Aggs felt a soaring wave of gratitude. She hated surprises, but this was one she could definitely live with.

'Sandra and Nasim are here all day,' Isla said, nodding to the two teenagers who usually worked Saturdays with Aggs, and who were now taking trays of coffees over to the mums' group. 'So relax and enjoy yourself.'

Skye passed the salad bowl to her. 'We were going to take you out somewhere, but we knew you'd prefer to be here.'

'You know me too well,' Aggs agreed, feeling herself fill up with pure contentment. This was her home. And, yes, it was work, but it was also the place she loved more than any other, so to be in The Ginger Sponge, with people she loved, no big fuss or spectacle, was perfect. She could get back to work in a couple of hours and get on with the day, happily looking forward to a quiet dinner with Isla and Skye tonight.

'Right then, Aggs, tell us your plans for this year then.' Val couldn't have known just how much Aggs wanted to answer that question honestly, but she couldn't, not yet.

She and Will had talked this through. She was going to tell the girls about their relationship first, on their own, just to make sure they were comfortable with it all. God knows, it had taken Skye and Isla a long time to accept that their dad had moved on, especially with someone so close to them all, but they'd been much younger then. Aggs didn't expect her news to be an issue, but she wanted it handled in a sensitive way. She'd tell them soon. Maybe later tonight when they were out for dinner, just her and the girls.

'And we want to know your birthday wishes too,' Val pressed her, putting her on the spot as everyone at the table immediately halted their own conversations to listen.

A searing red heat rose up her neck. This was why she hated being the centre of attention. Her body just wasn't built for it.

'Oh Val, you know I'm rubbish at this kind of stuff. I always sound like one of those pageant queens, but without the posh frock and perfect body. I just want... erm... happiness. For all of us.' She met Will's eyes across the table and returned his grin. 'And to save the world from poverty, cure disease and find a way to make calorie-free cakes. I mean, not too much to ask, is it?'

'I'd settle for the calorie-free cakes,' Yvie offered. A curvy size 18, Yvie's relationship with her weight yoyoed depending on her frame of mind. In the last few months, she'd been working on embracing her curves and it showed in her glowing, beautiful face, but she made no secret of her love of food. It was a passion she shared with her boyfriend, Carlo, who worked in his dad's Italian restaurant. They were a match made in gastronomic heaven.

'What about a new romance, Mum?' Of course, that came from Isla, who had zero filter when it came to talking about personal lives. Aggs blamed it on that bloody *Love Island* programme. 'Don't you want to get back out there on the dating scene?'

All seventy-eight years of Marge piped in on that one. 'Oh, you should, dear. Everyone needs a bit of romance and excitement in their lives. I'd do it myself, only I'd be worried about my osteo-porosis.'

Her seventy-six year old sister, Myra, couldn't resist chiming in.

'Aye, Marge. One false move and you'd be in the fracture clinic. I couldn't be pushing you in a wheelchair with my chest.'

Aggs tried to divert attention from the question, and from the fact that Will's eyes were looking at her questioningly, by going along with the joke. 'I'd push you, Marge, don't you worry.'

'No, you're fine, love. I'll stick to bingo. More exciting and you don't have to pick up socks.'

Marge's indignant retort set off unanimous amusement, and by the time they all settled back into conversations and enjoying their lunch, Isla's question was thankfully long forgotten.

Aggs could hear snippets of the discussions.

Jonathan, who'd lost his wife, Jayne, when she'd got dragged down by a riptide in Thailand the year before, was talking about the fund he'd set up to pay for swimming lessons for primary school age kids in his village. Colin had decided to sell the time-share he'd owned with Jason and go on a group hiking tour of Nepal with some of the proceeds. Everyone was finding a way to deal with their loss, to move on, and Aggs knew that it was time she did the same. Living here, taking care of her parents for the last ten years while bringing up the girls had been her choice and she didn't regret it. But it was time. Time for her.

When Isla, Val, Skye and Yvie refused her offer to help with clearing away the empty platters and plates, Aggs excused herself. 'Back in a sec,' she said, before nipping through the side door to the corridor the loos were in. After washing her hands with the rose scented soap she provided for her customers, she opened the door to see Will waiting for her. 'You'll get arrested for loitering outside women's toilets,' she teased.

He shrugged, laughing. 'You're worth doing the time. Would it be crazy to kiss you right now?'

'Completely. But I'll let you,' she said, going up on her tiptoes so that her mouth met his. At well over six feet, he towered over her, even in heels.

The first time he'd kissed her had taken her by complete surprise. It had been a month or so before, and the café had been open for a private function on a Friday night. Will had been on a late shift, his job as an aircraft engineer wasn't nine to five, and he'd stopped in on the way back. Isla had just left, off to a club to meet her mates, and Aggs was about to lock the door when it opened.

'Any coffee going?'

Her yelp had been instinctive. 'There would have been if you hadn't just terrified the life out of me. I was about to burst out my karate moves.'

'You do karate?' There was no concealing his surprise.

'Er, no, but I did a self-defence course in 1998 and I'm pretty sure I can still remember the gist of it.'

The coffee had turned into a bottle of wine from the fridge, and they'd sat on the window bench watching the late night Glasgow world go by. Dog walkers. Pub goers. And later, after they'd been chatting for a couple of hours, young women in weather defying miniskirts and heels, arms linked with guys in T-shirts and no jackets, swaying and singing as they headed home from clubs. Time seemed to have a fast forward button when she was talking to Will Hamilton. Or maybe it was just that this was the first guy she'd got to know in a long time. It helped that they had so much in common, both trying to find their way back to some kind of normality.

'Isla will be back soon,' Aggs had said, surprisingly wide awake, despite a sixteen hour shift and three hours of conversation with Will.

'I'd better be going then,' he'd replied, picking up his phone and his glasses from the table. He began to rise, then paused, mid-movement. 'Except...'

'What?' Woah, what was happening? And why did she suddenly

have a rush of something she hadn't experienced in so long, she barely recognised it? She was... attracted to him. Actually attracted. The hormones that she was sure had deserted her sometime around Mitchell buggering off with her best mate had apparently sprung back to life in a deserted café in the middle of the night.

'Except... Sod it, I need to say it. I want to kiss you. I'm sorry. I know we're friends and I'm probably crossing all kinds of boundaries here, and please don't think that I came here tonight planning to do this because I didn't, but the thing is...'

'Kiss me, Will. Just kiss...'

He didn't need to be asked twice.

The kiss had been thrilling and, even now, in the decidedly unglamorous setting of the corridor outside the toilets, it still felt as exciting as it had that night, and every time she'd seen him since. Always in private, of course, and kissing was all that had happened so far. It had taken ten years for her to kiss another man. She wanted to get used to the idea before they let anyone else know about it or took it further. God, even the thought of that made her feel queasy with nerves. It had been twenty years and a couple of stones since she'd slept with someone new. Much as Will made her ovaries contract, she was still going to have to work up to anything involving nudity.

They unlocked lips. 'I think I love birthdays,' Aggs said.

'I think I could probably get used to them too,' he replied, nuzzling her neck.

Aggs playfully pushed him away. 'Calm down there, Romeo. If Marge and Myra see this, it could set off their pacemakers. Right, better get back in. Hopefully, they haven't even realised we're both gone.'

As soon as she opened the door back to the café, she saw she'd miscalculated.

'Happy birthday to you, happy birthday to you...' Every pair of eyes in the room were on them, as Isla stood at the end of the table holding up a huge birthday cake. The chorus of song got louder as everyone in the café joined in, thrilling the toddlers that were over with the mums' group.

The only thing to do was to brazen it out with a wide smile and act like there was nothing amiss. Just two people returning from the toilets at the same time. Nothing to see here. Nothing suspicious at all.

As the candles flickered and the chorus rose to a crescendo on the last 'Happy birthday to yooooooooou', Aggs slipped back into her place and then gasped as she saw the design on the large square cake. It was a photograph, transposed on to the icing. Another one that the girls must have found when they were clearing out her bedroom and the upstairs cupboard before decorating them both. Agnetha. Las Vegas. 1997. Her skin was glowing, every inch of her body taut and tanned, her hair flying behind her as she lay on a sunlounger in a white bikini, oozing youth and vitality and pure happiness, laughing at the person who was taking the picture.

Over twenty years later, she still remembered the very moment it was taken. For a split second, the birthday chorus faded into the background, everyone else in the room disappeared and it was just her with her younger self, and an overwhelming feeling that she'd give anything to go back and live that moment again.

10

MITCHELL

Mitchell felt his chest tighten with indigestion as Celeste's car slipped into a parking space outside the Malmaison Hotel in the Blythswood Square area of the city centre. Directly across from the iconic Blythswood Square Hotel, Mitchell had always thought the Malmaison had an air of decadence about it – the bigger, grander hotel's more rock and roll, rebellious little brother.

'Shit,' he exhaled, as he drove around the square before claiming a space further along the same street as Celeste's Porsche, but mostly obscured by the Range Rover Discovery that hogged the next space. From there, he could see the front of Celeste's car, he could see the entrance to the Malmaison, and he could see his wife strutting like a catwalk model across the road, her expensive outfit, edgy black bob, huge shades and bright red lipstick giving her a celebrity aura. She'd love that. There was nothing that Celeste enjoyed more than causing interest and intrigue.

So what now? The acid reflux made him wince again and he opened the glovebox and popped a couple of antacids from the stash he kept there for the days when he was facing the occupational hazard of high stress situations. He'd take a convoluted corporate fraud case over suspected infidelity any day of the week.

He pushed the car seat back and flexed his legs to stretch them out. What was his next move? He saw now that he'd messed up by dressing so casually. He'd look pretty conspicuous if he wandered into the hotel dressed in sweats and a T-shirt. And what if Celeste was in the lobby? How would he explain his arrival? 'Hi honey, fancy meeting you here? What a coincidence? I was just popping in to make a reservation to bring you here for our, erm, anniversary. Yes, I know it's not until October.'

Never had he felt more of an urge to bang his head off a steering wheel. His ringtone cut through the thought. Skye.

He flicked the steering wheel button to accept the call on hands-free.

'Hey honey!' He'd aimed for 'breezy', but it came out way too enthusiastic so he sounded like a daytime TV presenter on helium.

'Eh, how many coffees have you had today, Dad? You sound wired.'

'Probably too many,' he admitted, happy to go along with her assumption. It was better than 'I've turned into the kind of stalker they make documentaries about. Bail me out if I get arrested for suspicious behaviour.' *Act normal. ACT NORMAL.* 'What's up, sweetheart. All okay?' He could hear laughter and chat and clinking glasses in the background. Sounded like there was a bit of revelry going on there.

'Yeah. I'm at The Ginger Sponge for Mum's lunch. Did I see you driving past the window about fifteen minutes ago? Are you going to pop in?'

Bloody hell. She must have eyes like a fricking hawk. The Ginger Sponge was on the same street as the yoga studio, so, yes, he'd gone past it.

'No, love, I'm not coming in. I was...' *Think. Think.* What else was on that street? 'I was just picking up some dry-cleaning.'

'Oh. I thought you were going to the boxing gym?'

'I am. I'm here now.' He could almost hear the siren of a lie detector wailing above him.

'Cool. Okay. If you change your mind, we'll be here for a couple of hours and I know Mum would be happy to see you.'

He wasn't entirely sure that was the case. After the split, and the bitter fallout afterwards, he and Aggs had found their way back to a civil friendship for the sake of the girls. And, yes, they celebrated big occasions together – Christmas, family birthday parties, New Year – but that was different from him casually gate-crashing her lunch.

'I don't think I'll be back in time, darling, but thank you for the invitation. Wish your mum a happy birthday for me.'

'I will, Dad. Have to go. Isla's giving me the death stare because I'm supposed to be helping her get drinks. If I don't get home, check the café's wheelie bins for my body.'

With that, she was gone. Mitchell only realised he was grinning when a woman walking past the car gave him a strange look and veered further to the inside of the pavement so that even if he opened the door she was too far away to be snatched in broad daylight. He rapidly straightened his face, lifted his phone up to his ear and faked speaking into the handset until she was out of sight. Never had he felt more ridiculous.

What was it the young ones said? FML. Yep, fuck my life. And fuck the stupid decisions that he'd made to get him to this point. When it came to his marriages, he had enough self-awareness to admit that he'd made mistakes – and in moments of introspective brutal honesty, he had to concede that sometimes he thought that if he could go back and replay everything, he wasn't sure he'd take the same path. The old saying about hindsight being 20/20 vision definitely applied here. In his case, he'd long accepted that hindsight was also proof that he'd been an utter tit. Actually, make that a cheating tit. Maybe payback was exactly what he deserved.

The roar of an exhaust snapped him out of his self-flagellation. It was the stuff of a *Top Gear* host's wet dreams, the unmistakable sound of a Maserati rumbling past him and pulling up at the entrance to the hotel. He didn't even have to look, but of course he did, and, yep, there he was. Derek fucking Evans.

Evans got out, abandoning the car on a double yellow line (where were the bloody traffic wardens now?), and swaggered towards the entrance. Mitchell couldn't miss the contrast. Who was winning in life today? Him, sitting in a car in the midday heat, sweating his bollocks off while staking out his wife, or Derek Evans, climbing out of his hundred grand car, dressed in a suit that probably cost more than a few pairs of those Louboutin shoes Celeste was so fond of.

Mitchell switched the engine back on so that he could turn up the air con. Okay, think this through. Arguments for the defence. Maybe it was just lunch with a client. And perhaps Celeste didn't want to say it was Evans because Mitchell had got a bit arsey and jealous after the fundraiser. Or maybe he'd called and asked to meet after she left the house this morning and she'd ditched the other meeting to come here instead. All plausible. At a stretch.

Arguments for the prosecution? She'd lied for illicit reasons. She knew the whole time that she was coming here because she's been shagging Derek Evans behind his back for an indeterminate length of time. She was never planning to meet a new client and then go shopping, because if she was, she wouldn't have come dressed like she'd just walked off the pages of a power lunch spread in a magazine. In fact...

Another scenario began to play out in full colour in his mind. Celeste, in a luxury bedroom with Evans. There was no way she'd let him rip her clothes off, she'd always been far too concerned about damaging her designer wear. Instead, she was gradually discarding each item of her clothing, while Evans lay on a bed, a leer of enjoyment on his smug face. No amount of antacids could settle his stomach until he knew the answer to the question that was burning his insides. What was this – lunch or something far more?

One way to find out. He flicked another button on the steering wheel, bringing up the favourites list on his speed dial. He might have to redefine that term after today. There were only five names on there. Isla. Skye. His secretary, Catherine. Agnetha. Celeste.

He scrolled and hit 'call' on Celeste's name.

It rang. It rang again. It stopped.

Shit, she'd rejected the call.

But then, if it was a business meeting, he wouldn't expect her to answer.

This was getting him nowhere. Reaching back into the glove compartment, he popped another couple of antacids, then made a decision. He'd been in the hotel a few times before and vaguely remembered the layout. He wasn't sure if he could pull off what he needed to do, but it was worth a try.

Switching off the engine, he jumped out of the car and jogged along the road and into the hotel. A smiling receptionist greeted him and he just hoped that she hadn't been on all morning without a break. 'Hi, I'm staying in the hotel and just realised I didn't take my key when I went out for a run. I think my wife's in the restaurant. I know I'm not dressed for it, but do you mind if I just pop in and grab the key from her?'

'Of course not, sir. Just through there to the left.'

'Great, thanks.'

This was stupid. Fraught with risk. But if he was both careful and a bit lucky...

The restaurant was in the basement with an internal staircase that would allow him to look around. As long as Celeste didn't look up and spot him, he just might get the answers he needed without looking like a complete tool.

A couple, holding hands and both radiating the kind of happiness he only had faint memories of feeling, were coming out of the door as he approached it and they held it open for him. He nodded thanks as he passed them, then pretended to look at his phone as if he'd just received a text, so they wouldn't wonder why he didn't carry on down the stairs into the restaurant. As soon as they were out of sight, he edged in, scanning the tables below. No sign of them. There was a problem though. The restaurant stretched round a corner so he couldn't see all the tables. Shit. Stay or go? Should he take the risk? It would be crazy. He'd have to go down there and somehow peek round the corner and...

Sod it. He went for it. Ignoring a couple of curious glances, he went downstairs and surreptitiously scoped out the whole restaurant, gradually edging around corners to ensure he didn't bang straight into them.

No sign of them.

He repeated the same cautious investigation in the bar. Nothing. They weren't here.

At least, they weren't downstairs. So that could only mean one thing, couldn't it?

They had to be upstairs in a bedroom. Fuck.

If there was an upside to the nausea that was now bubbling inside him, at least it was taking his mind of the searing pain of the indigestion.

There was no next move to make here. He wasn't going to go upstairs and storm the room, even if he knew where they were. He'd spent the last ten minutes hiding behind plant pots in a hotel restaurant and bar – hadn't he sunk low enough?

As he passed her, he reacted to the receptionist's confused expression with a cheery 'Thanks, bye!' and then jogged back to the car. This required serious thought. Knee-jerk reactions weren't his style. He needed a strategy. Needed a plan. But, first, he needed to understand and there was only one place he knew that he'd find help with that.

Mitchell McMaster slipped on his Prada sunglasses, switched on the engine, and headed for The Ginger Sponge.

11

AGNETHA AND CELESTE – 1997

'I'm falling in love with you. And I was just kinda wondering if you felt the same?' Aaron's words were hanging in the air, just waiting for a response, and Agnetha paused, temporarily robbed of speech by the tendrils of excitement that were furling around her vocal cords. The rest of the world, the waiters circulating with drinks, the pool lifeguards in the wooden seats at the top of their stations, the crowds of revellers on sunloungers and splashing in the water, the pool speakers blaring TLC's 'Waterfalls', all of it just faded away. It was just Aaron. And her. And he'd just told her he loved her.

A heartbeat. Then another. Aaron's expression was melting from adoration to something closer to concern, then to abject relief when she finally responded with a giggly, 'Yes. Yes!'

'Holy crap, you had me worried there. I think I just aged a few years.'

'It just took my breath for a moment...' Agnetha stretched across to kiss him, then yelped as he somehow managed to flip her up so she was lying on top of him, their lips sealing the deal until Agnetha pulled back. 'Hang on, I need to check... Are you sure?

Nobody's spiked your drink? You've not just been watching too many romcoms since I got here? Under hypnosis?'

Feigning outrage, he playfully bumped her off him, so she rolled back down onto the canvas top of the double lounger, both of them creasing with giggles. He held his arm out straight, palm on her shoulder, so that their faces were an arm's length apart. 'I love you, Agnetha Crazy Lady. Just so you know, I've never said that to anyone before. Well, apart from my cousin and we were six, so it doesn't count. You're sure you feel the same?'

'I do. Although I'm now worried your cousin may hunt me down. Could I take her?'

'I'd bet on you.'

'Excellent. I feel much better about it all now.' Even with the excitement and sheer fricking joy of the moment, Agnetha hoped he didn't ask her if she'd said that before. The truth was that she had, three times – one was a teenage romance and the other two occasions were short-lived but passionate relationships that blew out as quickly as they'd started.

Yes, sometimes she was guilty of getting swept up in the moment, but that wasn't what this was, she was sure of it. The truth was she'd been feeling the same thing for days now and the thought of leaving him made her want to sob. And now... now he was saying he felt the same. She'd proclaim her happiness to the world if she wasn't fairly sure that Celeste would react by launching the water polo ball at her head.

'Tell me,' Aaron was coaxing now, his voice equally tender and teasing.

She went for innocence. 'Tell you what?'

'Tell me you love me. I want to see your face when you say it.'

'You're very odd.' She was playing with him. 'But okay. Since we're here and there's nothing on the telly...' That came with a nod to the blank TV screen on the wall of the cabana. 'Aaron Ward, I love you. It's bonkers, but I don't care, because I'm so frigging happy. I love you.'

He punched the air. 'Yassssss! Christ, you're beautiful. Do you know that?'

'Now I'm sure your drink has been spiked.' Accepting compliments had never been her strong point and he shushed her by kissing her again. She had a feeling there would be a lot of that today.

This time, he pulled away first, and reached over her to pick up her camera from the table at the side of the lounger. 'I want to take a picture of you, so you'll see how beautiful you are. And we'll know forever that this was the moment you told me you loved me.'

'We can't ever show the grandkids. My boobs are falling out of this bikini.' She feigned suspicion. 'Is that why you said you love me? You've got a thing for public indecency?'

His exasperated eye roll set her off on another fit of the giggles and that was the moment the shutter of the camera clicked.

Great. Now the whole of the Boots photography department was going to see her in an obscenely tiny bikini, face a shade of tomato from the heat, hair a wild mane of red curls, when she put this in to be developed. She'd never be able to show her face in that shop ever again.

'What did I miss?' Celeste asked, as she appeared at Agnetha's side and shook her body so the drips from the pool soaked her friends, making Agnetha shriek and Aaron groan in protest.

She pushed her wet hair back from her face and Agnetha could absolutely see why she was picking up more and more modelling jobs as every month passed. If Celeste had been in George Michael's 'Freedom' video, she'd have been Linda Evangelista's ebony haired sister, the one who shared her insanely gorgeous eyes and cheekbones like speed bumps. Not to mention the body that was as close to perfection as it got without medical intervention.

Another thought, and it didn't come from smugness, more abso-lute gratitude and incredulity. How lucky was she that Aaron was in love with her, and hadn't gone after Celeste, who was always the most beautiful woman in any room?

Aaron climbed off the lounger, tenderly trailing his hand along hers as he moved away. 'I'm just going to go cool off.' He slipped into the pool, his back to them now, his shoulders and arms stretched along the pool edge, every muscle defined and hard.

Celeste clicked her fingers in front of Agnetha's face. 'Earth call-ing, Aggs, come in, you soppy cow.'

Agnetha shrugged. 'Guilty as charged.' She shook it off, not wanting to rub salt in Celeste's gooseberry wound. 'How you doing, honey? Pissed off about Zac?'

Celeste lay down on Aaron's side of the lounger, adjusting her bikini so that it sat perfectly on her flat stomach, and batted away the question. 'Nah, not at all.'

Agnetha could sense that there was a large slice of bravado in there, but she didn't say anything, just let Celeste reframe the reality in whatever way she needed to.

'It was always just a bit of a fling. To be honest, it probably blew itself out for me a couple of weeks ago, but the guy had VIP access to every club in town so I was having waaaaay too much fun with that to end it. It's only a few days until we go home though, so I think I'll cope without free entry into the Viper Room for the rest of the week.'

Agnetha took a sip of her drink. 'I'm glad, hon. He's clearly a tit anyway. There isn't a guy at this pool who would get out of bed with you in the middle of the night and take off. He's obviously got issues.'

'Exactly what I was thinking,' Celeste grinned, before rolling over and flopping on top of Aggs, cuddling her. 'This is why you're my friend. You're completely biased and you don't mind that I take daily bitch pills.'

Agnetha laughed. 'Yeah, you might want to cut down the dosage. Zac's worried you're going to come back to LA and pummel him with a baseball bat while he sleeps.'

Celeste popped her head up off Agnetha's shoulder. 'He really shouldn't give me ideas like that.' She sat up and stretched over to the bag she'd left on top of the cabana's mini fridge. Pulling out a packet of Marlboro Lights, she lit one, took a long drag and then gestured to the back of Aaron's head, just a couple of metres away. 'How come you always pick the nice one and I always pick the one who turns out to be a complete prick?'

Agnetha knew the answer to that, but this wasn't the time to volunteer it. Celeste always went for the guy with the edge, with the glint of trouble in his eye, the one with a thirst for danger and excitement that matched hers. It was like two positive electrodes meeting – they created sparks but burnt out really quickly. Case in point, the hunky UCLA football player who was now beckoning her back into the pool.

Agnetha grabbed the chance to go for an answer to Celeste's question that didn't cut to the core of her psychologic make-up. 'Maybe because you're blinded by a fine set of pecs and an arse like two rugby balls in a windsock?'

Celeste's cackle was contagious. 'You're so right. And I do believe that those pecs are demanding attention.' She took another long drag of her cigarette, then stubbed it out and climbed off the sunlounger, her glorious long tanned legs rippling as she moved. She took a step, then suddenly stopped, turned back, leaned down and kissed Agnetha on the cheek, 'I love you, Agnetha Sanders. Promise me it'll always be you and me against the world.'

The unaccustomed show of vulnerability made Agnetha's reply catch in her throat. 'Of course it will.'

A wide smile broke across Celeste's beautiful face, before she turned and dived right over Aaron's head into the pool, only surfacing when she'd located the rugby ball arse of her new friend.

Agnetha followed her to the pool edge, slipping into the cool blue water beside Aaron, feeling her body temperature cool but her heart heat up as she wrapped her arms around his neck and her lips found his. This was heaven.

Ignoring the shrieks and splashes of the new game of water polo that had broken out at the other end of the pool, she nuzzled into his neck and playfully bit his ear. 'Hey, handsome. What were you thinking all alone in here?'

His sigh threw her. Not what she was expecting. Had he changed his mind already? Had the cool water shocked him back to his senses? Bollocks. It had been so good while it lasted, but this had to be the fastest heartbreak in history.

His arms tightened around her. 'I'm thinking I want you to stay here.'

Oh, thank God. He was still in this. His words erased the fracture line that had just formed on her heart, but at the same time they opened a new one caused by the thought of leaving him.

'I know, me too. Maybe we can just extend our reservations here indefinitely and hide from the world. We could do a John and Yoko and stay in bed for weeks.'

'Aggs, I'm serious.' Wow. He actually was. This was a new look for him – furrowed brow, jaw tight with tension. 'I meant what I said about never feeling this way before and I can't stand the thought of you leaving. I want you to stay.'

'Where?' It could have been the heat, the change of mood, or the two pina coladas she'd already knocked back, but Aggs wasn't sure exactly what he was saying.

'Here. Or, I mean, in LA. With me.'

Wow, this was big. Too big. He wanted her to move here? A

storm of thoughts kicked up in her head. She had a life back in Scotland, a family there. And, okay, it wasn't like her mum and dad couldn't live without her, but for all she loved to travel, she adored her family and had never pictured a life where she didn't see them or speak to them every day. Since she got here, she'd only been calling them once a week because it was so expensive. And, no, she didn't have a full time job back in the UK, but that was her choice and she loved the set up she had, working alongside her dad some days, out on temp jobs on other days. Chatting to her mum in the kitchen before she went to bed every night. Mum and Dad had moved into Gran and Grandad's flat above the café, so that they could take care of the grandparents as they got older, and now that they'd both passed away in the last couple of years it was just the three of them. Could she really leave them behind?

A familiar squeal permeated her thoughts and she turned to see Celeste being thrown up and then tumbling in mid-air, only being caught by the muscular arms of the UCLA guy a fraction of a second before she hit the water. The squeal turned to laughter and then fell silent as Celeste went in for a kiss and they were suddenly locked in a long, passionate snog.

Hadn't she just promised Celeste that it was them against the world? How was she going to carry out that promise from thousands of miles away?

Yet...

The thought of leaving this man made her heart clench. They had something. More than something. Sure, it had been quick, but she didn't doubt how she felt for a second. This was it. The love of her life. Or maybe technically it was the third or fourth, but this was the first real one, the first man that made her feel the way she did now, that she could only breathe when he was beside her. In three months, he'd become her life-support system, her oxygen, and she couldn't switch that off.

Only a tug of pain made her realise she was biting her bottom lip.

'I don't want to leave either.' As each word rolled off her tongue, she knew it was true. 'But I have to go, because my visa runs out the day after our flight leaves.' They'd already extended their trip as long as their ninety day tourist visa would allow.

It was hopeless. She couldn't stay. Without a visa, she'd be here illegally. She couldn't work. She couldn't support herself. And she couldn't go back to visit her mum and dad, because if she left, she wouldn't get back into the country.

'Maybe I can go home, and then come back when I've saved again...'

He shook his head. 'Long-distance relationship?' He sighed. 'I love you. I want to wake up in the morning and see your face lying next to me.'

'I do too, but...'

He lifted her up so she was sitting on the edge of the pool, her legs dangling in the water, his arms leaning on her thighs as he looked up at her.

'No buts. If we could find a way that you can stay, would you do it?'

Would she? Would she really leave her whole life for a guy that she'd only known for eighty-five days?

A burst of emotion answered for her. 'Yes. Yes, I would.'

12

HOPE

Hope indicated and turned left into the street outside the Malmaison Hotel, then braked sharply to avoid a bright yellow Maserati that screeched to a halt right in front of her. Idiot. Did he think a car like that was a licence to drive like a tit?

She stopped herself from vocalising that thought. Probably not the best impression to give her new dad. Her dad. It was surreal to even think of him as her father, never mind call him Dad. She wasn't sure that would ever come naturally.

'Good catch there,' her passenger whistled. 'Man, everything feels strange when you're driving on the wrong side of the road.'

'Eh, I think you'll find this is the right side of the road. It's you lot that have it wrong.'

That made him laugh, a gorgeous low chuckle that Hope knew she could listen to all day.

She turned left at the end of the road, then immediately pulled into a free space just along from the entrance to the Dakota hotel, a modern charcoal grey stone and glass building that was just off the square, on West Regent Street.

She'd wondered if the half-hour journey from Glasgow Airport would be awkward, but it hadn't been at all. Aaron had made sure of that by breaking the ice as soon as they'd got into the car in the airport parking lot. He'd turned to face her, smiled as he put out his hand. 'I think we missed the introduction bit back there in the terminal. I'm Aaron Ward.'

Hope had automatically returned his grin. 'Hope McTeer.'

'Pleased to meet you, Hope McTeer. I can't tell you how much I mean that.'

To her surprise, she'd noticed that his eyes had misted over. Wow. The juxtaposition between his muscular, macho appearance and the tears that were threatening to fall got her right in the feels.

'And I need you to know right off the bat that I'm so, so sorry I'm only getting to tell you this now. I had no idea.' His voice had been so emotional, Hope knew that he meant every word.

'Me too. But we got here. That's all that matters.' Hope had taken a deep breath to steady herself. *Don't cry. Do not cry.* She had a horrible feeling that if she started, it would unblock a dam that might never stop flowing. *Hold it together. You've got this.*

Aaron had cleared his throat. 'I'm not usually a crier, but it's not every day that I find my daughter.'

'Likewise. I can't wait to find out what other genes I got from you.'

On the centre console between the two seats, his hand had fallen on hers and Hope had realised that they were just grinning inanely at each other, drinking in the moment, memorising every curve and line of each other's faces.

Hope had broken the spell first. 'Okay, so we'd better move otherwise I'll have to sell a kidney to get out of this car park because it's extortionate. Shall we go to your hotel and you can ditch your stuff and then maybe we could grab lunch? Are you hungry?' He'd asked about hotels when he'd emailed her about his flights, and she'd suggested the Dakota. She'd been at a medical conference there and it had looked impressive and modern, but not over-the-top grand. She wasn't sure what his style would be, so she figured that was a safe bet.

'I could eat. Sounds like a plan to me. And how about we just chat about the small stuff on the way there and save the big stuff for when we're sitting across from each other and we can talk properly?'

Hope had nodded. Thank God. It wasn't that she doubted her driving, but she wanted to concentrate on every word he had to say, and if there were any shocks, she didn't want to be veering across the M8 into the path of an articulated lorry. It would obviously be preferable not to accidentally kill her father on the day that they finally met. 'I just need to text my sister first, otherwise there's every chance a police helicopter will suddenly appear over us at some point. She's a bit overprotective.'

'I like that,' he'd replied warmly.

Hope had fired off a text.

Still alive. On way to his hotel. No need for pepper spray as yet. Xx

The reply had been instant.

I NEED DETAILS!!!!! XX

Soon. About to drive. Will call when I can. xx

AAAAAAARGH!!!!! (also, keep pepper spray handy – serial killers are always charming at the start) xx

Hope had slipped her phone into the side pocket on the door, then pulled out of the space and drove them, with very deliberate concentration, out of the car park.

They'd made it on to the motorway and the conversation had flowed easily as they'd chatted about surface stuff, just as they'd agreed. Hope had racked her brain to come up with questions that didn't delve deep into his relationships and past – plenty of time for that later. Instead, she'd stuck to geography, work and hobbies. He'd always lived in LA. He was in construction. Family business that he and his brother had taken over when he was in his late twenties. Hope didn't ask if that meant his father had passed away, realising that he was her grandfather too. That was too close to an emotional question, so she'd skipped back on to lighter stuff. No, he wasn't much of a fan of celebrity haunts, preferring to lay low at his house in Santa Monica. Yes, it was at the beach. And, yes, he surfed. Hope had a vague thought that a beach house in LA must be mega-expensive, but it drifted away as quickly as it came. No, he'd never been to Glasgow. In fact, he hadn't travelled to Europe at all. He tended to go to Canada for his holidays – up to Vancouver Island – or he'd do a road trip up the west coast to Monterey or San Francisco. Good vibes there, he said.

It wasn't all one way traffic though. He was equally as inquisitive about her life, and they'd slipped into asking alternate questions. He'd seemed interested to learn that she had an adoptive sister and that Maisie was twenty-four and an actress and that her adoptive parents were teachers. She'd been to America a couple of times, but only to Disney World and Epcot in Florida, never the West Coast. She was studying to be a doctor and working part time in a hospital and yes, it was hard, but it was everything she'd always known it would be. And, no, that left zero time for relationships, so she wasn't seeing anyone at the moment. Oh, and yes, it did rain a lot here and this was an unseasonably warm day for May.

The chat had ebbed and flowed and got them all the way into the city, right up to the point where they had almost rear-ended that bright yellow Maserati.

'Home sweet home,' Hope chirped when they reached the entrance to the Dakota, just round the corner from the Malmaison and the Blythswood Square Hotel.

A very efficient receptionist checked him in. 'Would you like me to book you a table for lunch in the restaurant, sir?'

Aaron turned questioningly to Hope.

'Sure,' she nodded, glad of the suggestion. The less she had to think about the logistics of today, the more she could take in everything else.

'I'll just go up and dump my stuff and get a quick change. Do you want to come up or wait here?'

A tug of awkwardness caused her to pause. Was it too familiar to go to his room? Would it be weird? In the end, she decided she didn't care. If this was the father she'd grown up with she wouldn't hesitate, so why treat her biological dad differently?

Her casual shrug made it seem like it was no big deal. 'I'll come up – that way you don't need to rush.'

They made more small talk as they went upstairs in the lift. He'd booked a one bedroom suite with a separate living space, a riot of greys, purples and browns that shouldn't work together but somehow did. She sat on the L-shaped leather sofa while he had a quick shower and changed. She flicked the TV on, more for the noise rather than because she wanted to watch something. Sitting there waiting for him should feel strange, she decided. Maybe even uncomfortable. But, oddly, it really didn't.

He was ready in fifteen minutes, charcoal jeans this time and a white T-shirt. There was no need for a jacket, so the only things he picked up were his phone and wallet. Hope had a thought. He hadn't called or texted anyone to say he'd landed. Did he not have anyone who was waiting for news? Or perhaps he did it on his way through baggage before he reached her? So many questions, but she didn't want to bombard him with them all at once.

There was a lively buzz in the busy restaurant, mostly, Hope guessed, tourists in town for a concert or an exhibition. It was a relief when they were shown to a corner table, out of earshot of the other diners. They were going to be having the kind of conversation that she wasn't comfortable with anyone else overhearing, so it was perfect. For a moment she wondered if they should have had their first proper chat in private in his room, but this seemed more relaxed. Less pressure.

She was touched when he pulled her chair out for her before taking his own.

'Cool place,' he said, as he glanced around the room at the eclectic combination of dark exposed brick walls, solid wood tables, and leather studded chairs, mixed with opaque glass accents and rustic art on the walls.

Aaron ordered a steak, Hope went for a monkfish curry that, once again, she was fairly sure she wouldn't be able to eat. He'd put her at ease, but she still didn't think that the butterflies in her stomach had calmed enough to accept incoming nutrition.

'Do you mind if I have a beer?' he asked.

'Of course not. I'll have a glass of wine, if that's how it's going down,' she told him, laughing. Even if this was just a random guy she'd met by chance, she already had the feeling that she'd like him.

As the waiter discussed the beer and wine choices and then jotted down their orders, Hope wondered what the server was thinking. Older guy, younger woman. Did he think they were a couple? Or did he realise they were father and daughter?

It was all still so surreal that she almost wanted to shout it out to help it sink in. *That's my father*, she wanted to yell. *My biological dad. This guy. Right here. I found him. And yes, it still feels bizarre to call him that.*

When their drinks arrived, he held up his beer. 'To new discoveries,' he offered warmly.

'New discoveries. I like that.' Hope clinked her glass against his beer bottle, then took a sip, resisting the urge to build up a bit of Dutch courage by downing it in one. It wouldn't do for him to think he'd fathered a wild child. Instead, she put the goblet back on the table, and went with what she hoped was a gentle opening. 'So, are you married? Do you have kids?'

Aaron took a sip of his beer and Hope guessed that this wasn't going to be straightforward. 'I was married for fifteen years, divorced a couple of years ago. No big drama. My ex-wife, Jen, is a great lady, but we just grew apart, wanted different lives. We have two boys. Mack and Sonny. They're sixteen and fifteen and already taller than me and smarter than me.'

Hope loved the self-deprecating way he told the story, as well as the respect he showed for his ex-wife and the way his face lit up when he mentioned his boys. Would that happen in future when he talked about her?

'Wow. I have brothers. Well, half-brothers. Did you tell them about me?'

He nodded. 'The night before I came. I ain't gonna lie, they were pretty shocked, but pretty excited too. They were both up for coming along for the ride. Although, that might just have been an excuse for getting out of school.' He laughed, obviously remembering something else. 'Mack also loved the opportunity to scold me for getting a girl pregnant. He pretty much repeated word for word the contraception conversation I've been having with them for the last couple of years. The two of them thought it was hilarious.'

Was this it? Was this the opening to ask about her mum? No. Not yet. Too soon. She wasn't ready. And if it was a painful memory for him, it might make him defensive or uncomfortable. Best to stick to neutral territory for now.

'Do you have a picture of your boys?' Ridiculous as it sounded, up until now, she'd only given real thought to her biological parents, not any potential siblings that this search would throw up. She couldn't imagine she'd have much in common with two teenage American boys, but DNA was probably a good starting point.

'Here they are. That's Mack, and that's Sonny.' Aaron handed his phone over and Hope gasped. The older one, Mack, was the epitome of a California blond, his long hair tucked behind his ears, his 'Ride or die' surfing T-shirt the same colour as his pale blue eyes. But the younger one, Sonny... She could have picked him out in a line-up. They shared the same colouring and his eyes were identical in shape and shade to hers.

Aaron snatched the thought right out of her mind. 'You look so like Sonny.'

'Oh my God, I do. This is so crazy. I've never had a resemblance to anyone before and now I look like two other people on this earth. That's so bizarre to me.'

Aaron nodded, clearly relating to the overwhelming reality of it all. 'Yep, it's a lot.'

Hope took a sip of wine. 'What made you do the DNA test?'

She'd been curious about that right from the start.

A flicker of something new made him frown – sadness, maybe? Before he could respond, the waiter arrived with their food, and Hope wondered if he was glad of the interruption to prepare his answer.

'Both my parents have passed now...' he began.

'I'm sorry,' Hope replied, feeling a twinge of sadness for the grandparents that she would never meet.

'Thank you. They were both in their eighties, had great lives, and didn't regret a minute. They'd come to LA together from Oregon when they were barely out of high school and they were married sixty years. They spent the first decade or so working their butts off, building my dad's construction firm, so my mum was well into her thirties by the time she had us. Time had passed, and they'd let their relationships with their families drift, so it was really just the four of us my whole life. After they were gone, and it was just my brother, Sly, and me left, I got to thinking that I'd like to have more than that for my boys, a bigger family, more people looking out for them, you know? So I did the DNA test. Found more cousins, aunts and uncles that I could round up in a rodeo pen.' His eyes lit up as he said that, and Hope could feel how much it meant to him. 'But I sure didn't expect this. Didn't see it coming at all, but I'm mighty glad it did.'

Hope's insides melted. He was so sincere. So genuine. How lucky was she that he'd reacted in this way? And how much longer was her luck going to hold out when he learned the truth about why she'd tracked him down?

2 P.M. – 4 P.M

13

AGNETHA

'Right, my love, you enjoy the rest of the day. I'll expect to hear that you got drunk and sang in the street before having a wild night of passion with a man with abs like a toast rack,' Val told Aggs as she hugged her goodbye. Marge, Myra, Jonathan and Colin had already left, and Isla and Skye were in the kitchen clearing up, so it was just Val, Yvie, and Will who were still at the table and now the two women were getting up to leave too.

Yvie came around from the other side and hugged her next, while Val moved on to her goodbyes with the others. 'Are you sure you're okay? The first ones are always the hardest, but you're doing great.'

Aggs knew exactly what she was referring to and she tried her hardest not to let her mind go there again. Her first birthday without her mum. And, yes, she'd give anything to have her here, but she was still determined not to wallow, not when the girls had put in so much effort. Besides, as she'd discussed with Isla earlier, her mum would be furious if Aggs moped. She heard her mum's voice again, but this time it was in her head and not Isla's perfect impersonation. *Get on with it, love. Nothing else for it.*

On her last birthday, she'd sat with her mum all day in hospital, feeding her yoghurt, brushing the wisps that were left of her hair, rubbing moisturiser on her arms and hands, trying desperately to repair some of the damage that the chemo had wreaked on her mum's body. For the years before that, other things had been more of a priority than the number of candles on her cake. So while the first birthday without Mum made her heart a little sore, she knew, without a single doubt, that both her parents would want her to live, to love again and to be happy. Especially today.

'Thanks, Yvie,' Aggs murmured, before roping Val back into a group hug. 'I love you both. I'd never have got here without you.'

'Oh, you would have, lass,' Val argued. 'And you wouldn't have had to feed us all so many cakes. I've put on half a stone since you joined us.'

It was the perfect retort, and both women were still laughing when they hugged Will and then disappeared out of the door.

'Would you think I was losing it if I told you I'm fairly sure my mum sent those two into my life to make me laugh, even when things are crap?'

Will shook his head. 'Nope. You know I think the people that aren't with us any more are still around. Makes sense that they might give the fates a nudge sometimes.'

They'd talked about this so many times. Will absolutely chose to believe that Barney was still with him, watching over him. Aggs hoped it was true, otherwise, the daily conversations she had with her mum were just her talking to herself while making a cup of tea every morning.

She slipped into the seat next to him and had a quick look over her shoulder to see if Isla or Skye were eavesdropping. No sign of either of them. They must be in the kitchen now, clearing up, or chatting, or declaring war on each other. It could be any of the above.

'I was thinking that I was going to tell the girls tonight. We're going out for dinner, just the three of us.'

Will frowned, then recovered quickly, a reaction that Aggs didn't understand. Had he changed his mind in the last half-hour, somewhere between the tête-à-tête outside the loos and here?

'Is everything okay?' she asked, puzzled.

'Totally fine.' He didn't sound totally fine, but maybe it was just because he was a bit nervous about what they'd say. He went on, 'I was just thinking that maybe you'll be too busy chatting about other stuff to tell them tonight. Maybe today would be better? I could wait and tell them with you, if you like? Give you a bit of moral support?'

Aggs thought about that for a moment. 'You're lovely to offer, but I'd rather do that on my own.' Maybe he had a point on the timing though. The girls were both here, so if the opportunity arose this afternoon, perhaps they could have the conversation then and get it over with, instead of waiting until later. A twinge of anxiety made her lips purse, but she pushed it back down. She was forty-five years old. A grown woman. She'd been divorced for ten years. If she wanted to have a relationship with a new man she was perfectly entitled to. In fact, it was long bloody overdue.

'No worries. When do I get to give you your birthday present?' Will asked, now sporting the kind of grin that hinted at something more than a little flirtatious.

Aggs raised her eyebrows. 'Is it illegal? Or a framed picture of you in Speedos?'

His laugh made a couple of the mums at the window table look over and smile.

'Bugger, how did you know? I thought I'd managed to keep it a secret.'

'Call it intuition. And, you know, a manifestation of the kind of images I see in my nightmares.'

He leaned forward, his eyes glistening with amusement and lowered his voice. 'I'm so glad I met you, Agnetha McMaster. You've no idea how good it feels to have someone to laugh with again.'

Agnetha didn't correct him, but the truth was she knew only too well. She just smiled and let her fingers quickly graze his. It was all they needed. A connection. She glanced around again, making sure the girls were still nowhere to be seen. Coast was clear.

'Maybe I can just tell you about your present then?' he suggested. 'Perhaps show you a picture?'

'Oh God, I knew it was the Speedos.'

Will pulled his phone from his pocket and flicked to his Apple wallet, then showed her a boarding pass for...

She peered at the screen. Damn. It was fuzzy without her glasses, but that looked like her name. And a flight ticket to...

'Paris?'

'Oui.'

'You speak French?' she asked, shocked, not yet taking in the element of this equation that she should actually be gobsmacked about.

'Non,' he admitted with a Gallic shrug. 'That's all I had. So, what do you think?'

'Will, I...'

'Please don't say no. Come. To Paris. With me.'

'But... but...'

'Don't say "but",' he pleaded.

Aggs was still too shocked to formulate anything as elaborate as a sentence, so she went with, 'When?'

That made him smile. 'Tomorrow morning. Two days and one overnight stay. Back Monday night.'

'But...' she stopped when he gently interrupted her.

'It's an early flight tomorrow, and you're off anyway, so you'd only need to find cover for Monday and I'm sure Isla could rope someone in to help her. Val would do it if you're stuck.'

Wow, he'd thought all this through. And he was still talking.

'You once told me that travelling was like nectar for your soul when you were younger, and that you used to love to be spontaneous. Well, I know you're out of practice, but come and be spontaneous with me, Aggs.'

Aggs knew her mouth was open, but words appeared to be elusive. This was the kindest, sweetest thing that anyone had done for her in a long, long time. And what made it even more touching was that he'd obviously really listened to her when they'd had all those late night chats, because everything he said was absolutely correct. Paris was one of her favourite cities and taking off for a couple of days there was exactly the kind of thing she'd done on a whim many times when she was younger. The patisseries, the pavement cafés, the Louvre, the left bank of the Seine, the romance...

Oh dear God, the romance! She immediately felt a state of panic originate on her unshaved legs, spread up through her cellulite, over her wobbly stomach, up past her droopy boobs and land in the creases on her neck. Had he booked a double room? WOULD HE EXPECT TO HAVE SEX???

The last time she'd showed her body to a man was ten years ago, and even then it was only to Mitchell and they'd been married for over a decade by then.

Breathe, Aggs, she told herself, trying desperately to climb down from DEFCON 1. Would it really be so bad? In fact, wasn't there a possibility that it could actually be lovely? Will Hamilton was a thoroughly decent, kind, caring guy and, yes, there was no denying the physical attraction either. He'd had a terrible time and he was putting in a huge effort to make her happy. How often did something like this come along? And didn't they both deserve to have a bit of fun?

She thought back to this morning and her plans for a new start and reclaiming her life. *Well, Aggs*, she told herself, *here's your chance, love.*

'Okay,' she whispered.

'Okay? As in yes?'

'Yes. I'll come to Paris, and yes, I think you're bloody magnificent, Will Hamilton. I'd snog you now, but it's a public place and PDAs make me a bit queasy, so I'd rather do it when we're alone. But just know that I'm thinking about it and planning to make it the kind of long, slow kiss that you'll want to remember.'

'I like the sound of that,' he said, his face splitting into a gorgeous grin. It struck Aggs that right now he looked years younger than he did when she'd first met him. Maybe that's what a bit of happiness could do for the soul.

A buzz from the table interrupted the two of them just staring at each other with stupidly goofy gazes.

Will lifted his phone and tore his eyes from hers to read what it said on the screen.

Aggs' gaze went to the clock on the wall. Almost 3 p.m.. It had been such a perfect day – a truly lovely, magical birthday.

'Shit.' It was one of those involuntary exclamations that he probably didn't even realise he'd uttered. At the same time, like a balloon deflating, he seemed to shrink into himself, his shoulders hunched, his face settling back into the creases of heartache that weren't there just a few minutes ago.

'Something wrong?' There was no need to ask. It radiated from his every pore.

'It's a text from Carol.'

Carol. Will's ex-wife.

'Is she okay?' Aggs had never met her, but Will talked about her and he hadn't hidden his feelings about how their divorce had broken his already shattered heart yet again. They'd shared something that Aggs knew would bond them for ever and even though it had torn their marriage apart, he spoke of her with nothing but respect and a sad, almost wistful affection.

Will shrugged. 'I don't know. She's asking me to go over. Says it's important and she needs to talk to me.'

'When?'

'Now,' he said, clearly flummoxed. 'I don't get it. I haven't heard from her for months.'

Aggs felt something inside her sink too, but she immediately chided herself. The poor woman. Grief didn't have a time limit or follow a rulebook. Of course there would be moments when Carol would need to talk to the man who'd shared their son's life, and death, and of course he should go.

'Maybe she needs you,' Aggs prompted gently. 'I think you need to go. It's the right thing to do.'

Will met her gaze. 'I'm sorry. This is such bad timing. Did I just take the edge off Paris?'

Aggs smiled. 'Not at all. You go and see Carol and I'll go and look out my berets.'

His eyes flicked around the room and Aggs could see that he was checking no one was watching him. Satisfied, he leaned over and kissed her, lingering just long enough for her heart to thunder so loudly she didn't hear the bell of the door opening.

It was only when it banged closed that she tore away from Will's kiss and turned to see who'd come in.

Her face flushed beetroot as she realised who was standing there and what he'd just seen. Not that she should give a toss what he thought.

'Aggs?' Will probed, picking up on her reaction.

Aggs felt a giggle starting and cleared her throat to stop it. This was ridiculous.

'Will,' she said, as calmly as possible. 'This is Mitchell. My ex-husband. Mitchell, meet Will.'

14

Mitchell froze. Shit. Talk about terrible timing. In the background, the cuckoo clock on the café wall chiming three o'clock sounded like it was laughing at him. Here he was, in the pits of angst about Celeste, and he walks in on Aggs in full lip lock with some guy. And he knew Aggs; she wasn't one for casual dating, so this had to be something special.

Damn it.

Why had he even thought that coming here to talk to Aggs could be a good idea? He'd driven around for the last hour, bottling out of coming, changing his mind a dozen more times. He'd even gone home, had a coffee, and tried to settle to watch some footie on TV, but his mind was racing. So now he was here and right at that moment he'd pay good money for a hole to open up on the tiled floor and swallow him.

After a pause that was on the wrong side of awkward, Aggs' questioning expression snapped him into action and he stepped forward, just as Will rose from his seat and did the same. Now that he was on his feet, Mitchell could see that Will was taller than him, well over six feet, and had the wide shoulders and lean frame of someone who worked out.

The two of them shook hands. 'How're you doing?' Mitchell said out of habit.

The answer wasn't necessary. Given what he'd just seen, Will was doing pretty bloody well.

'Good, yeah. Pleased to meet you. Look, I'm just leaving...'

'Don't leave on my account,' Mitchell blurted.

Will put his hands up in a reassuring gesture. 'No, not at all. I was just about to go.' He leaned down, kissed Aggs on the cheek. 'I'll give you a buzz later about...' He paused, clearly not wanting to mention something in front of an audience.

Was it Mitchell's imagination or did Aggs look a bit flushed as she replied, 'Yeah, that's... erm... yeah, talk to you then.'

Mitchell's toes were curling. This couldn't be more awkward if he was standing there in his pants. Nothing else for it, but to bluff his way through and act like this was perfectly normal.

'Good to meet you,' he said as Will passed him, heading for the door.

'You, too,' Will answered easily.

Seemed like a friendly guy and he and Aggs were obviously a thing. Mitchell wondered why Skye had never mentioned him. He glanced around for his girls, but neither were there. Must be in the kitchen. That wasn't a bad thing – would give him time to talk to Aggs – but the problem was that now he was so thrown he wasn't sure if he could go through with it.

'Well, this is a surprise,' Aggs said, her smile warm. They'd become good at congeniality over the years. No choice. They'd both been so determined that the girls wouldn't be scarred or emotionally damaged by their split that they agreed to put on a united front. He would always be grateful to Aggs for that, because he was under no illusion she'd had the worst end of that deal, having to be kind to the man and woman who had betrayed her in the worst possible way.

'Come and sit down,' Aggs beckoned, gesturing to a whole table of empty seats around her. Given the glasses, the cake, the pile of gifts and cards, there had clearly been quite a party.

Mitchell gave her a kiss on each cheek, then took the seat across from her, as opposed to the one next to her recently vacated by Will.

'I just thought I'd pop in and wish you a happy birthday.' Shit. Even as it was coming out of his mouth, he realised that if he was going with that line, he should at least have brought a card and a bottle of bubbly. They didn't normally do gifts, but then, he didn't usually come and see her on her birthday either.

'Would you like something to eat? There's loads of cake left and I think the girls are in the kitchen – they could rustle something up for you.'

'No, I'm fine, thanks, I've eaten.' He hadn't, but he couldn't face anything right now. The indigestion in his gut was making him wince. 'A coffee would be great though.'

Aggs turned to the young guy at the counter. 'Nasim, would you mind making a couple of Americanos for us please?'

He responded with a wink and a thumbs up, making Aggs laugh.

If Mitchell was a witness in a legal case and the lawyer asked him to sum up how Aggs seemed right now, he'd have to go with happy, relaxed, carefree, chilled. It was a long, long, time since he'd seen her like that. In fact, it reminded him of the Aggs he'd first met. She was twenty-four and doing the catering for an evening retirement function at the legal firm he'd been working for since he left uni. They'd got chatting at the end of the night and he'd been completely captivated by this young woman, who ran her family's café during the day and then did freelance catering in the evenings. She was funny. Optimistic. A bright light that was the perfect contrast to his serious, stressful work in the legal system. Their romance had been a whirlwind. They'd met in the February and, in the June, Aggs fell pregnant. They married in a West End church and had the reception right here in the café. Back then it was called The Sanders, after her family name. Years ago, she'd given the place a major overhaul and changed the name to The Ginger Sponge and it was the perfect moniker for the warm, cosy haven she'd created.

The place had such a comfortable, chilled atmosphere that Mitchell felt his shoulders drop a tiny notch. 'Sorry if I interrupted something there.'

'That's okay. You didn't really. He's a... friend.'

He chose not to air his observation that their actions made it abundantly clear they were more than just casual pals. 'You don't have to explain anything to me.'

Aggs' smile came with a pointed raise of the eyebrows. 'I'm perfectly well aware of that, thank you.' She was teasing him now and he realised he'd sounded like a pretentious arse. Fuck. Thankfully, she didn't seem in the least bit bothered. 'I'm going to tell the girls about him tonight though, so I'd appreciate if you didn't say anything to them before I do.'

Tonight? It was almost out of his mouth to ask why she was going to tell them at her party, but just in time, he caught himself. The celebration this evening was still a surprise. She thought she was going out with the girls for dinner.

'Of course. I'm sure they'll be happy for you.'

'I think so too. And it'll get Isla off my case about joining one of those dating apps. She keeps threatening to set me up on something called Your Next Date. I'm verging on terrified that she'll go ahead and do it.'

He found himself mirroring her smile, a defence mechanism to cover a fleeting, unexpected tug of surprise and protectiveness. When they'd first divorced, he'd told anyone who'd listen that he wanted Aggs to meet someone else. Now... well, it might just take a little bit of getting used to, that was all.

There was a pause as Nasim delivered their coffees, and Aggs was the one to restart the conversation.

'So tell me then...' she said, her smile a little rueful, expectation lacing her words.

He was caught off guard. 'Tell you what?'

She'd taken a sip of her coffee and was now cradling her cup under her chin. 'Mitchell, you haven't come here on my birthday for years, so either you have big news or there's something you want to discuss about one of the girls. But I doubt it's the latter, because you know they're both here, and if it's something awful I don't think you'd have come on my birthday. Even you have a little more emotional intelligence than that.'

She was teasing him again, but he let it go. In fact, if it wasn't for the stress of the situation, he might even be enjoying the banter.

He capitulated immediately. It was the reason he'd come, although up until that moment he'd no idea if he'd actually go through with telling her. Now his need to confide in someone he trusted was overwhelming and, yes, he completely grasped the irony of that thought. 'I'm pretty sure Celeste is having an affair.'

Her eyes widened. 'I'm going to need more than coffee for this.' She reached over and picked up a bottle of Prosecco from the middle of the table and refilled her glass. 'Do you want some?' she said, holding the bottle up.

'No, I'm good. If I start, I might not stop and I need to drive today.'

There was a pause as she absorbed the enormity of what he'd said. 'I can't believe it, Mitch. I mean, obviously I know she's capable of it...' Ouch, shots fired. He took the blow. It was the least he deserved. 'But, well, to be honest, I can't imagine her leaving you or your lifestyle.'

Again, a truth, and again, it was deserved. Aggs had never cared about the financial benefits of his success. When they'd met, he was skint and knee deep in loans he'd taken out to get him through university. For several years they'd been paying them off, raising the kids, and they'd scraped together enough to buy a three bedroomed terrace house that might only have been half a mile away from where he lived now, but cost about £300,000 less, thanks to the less desirable postcode. Then he'd set up his company and there were a couple of lean years while he built it up. It was only in the last few years of his marriage that the big financial rewards had started to come in. Coincidentally, around the same time that a spark ignited between him and Celeste. And, no, he wasn't foolish enough to believe there was no connection there, but back then he'd been in way too deep to see it.

'What makes you think this?' Aggs went on, and for a second he had to marvel at this woman's capacity to care. She would be perfectly within her rights to laugh and tell him he deserved it, but that wasn't Aggs. She put other people first, every time.

He would never have a good excuse for the way he'd treated her, and there was absolutely no defence for his betrayal, but even Aggs would acknowledge that she was so busy caring for her mum, her dad, the girls, the café, that their marriage had ceased to be a priority. She looked at the situation as doing the best she could for the people she loved and she was absolutely right. Unfortunately, he'd been so shallow and self-centred that he'd viewed her lack of attention to him as a frustrating rejection and a blow to his ego that made him seek attention elsewhere. Unfortunately, he found it with his wife's best friend. Back then it had actually pleased him that Celeste didn't want kids because he knew he'd always come first. What a vile excuse for a human being he'd been.

'I think she emotionally checked out of the marriage a while ago. Stopped taking an interest, started being a bit more secretive.

She started staying out, going away for weekends... it was like a gradual withdrawal from us as a couple.' He suddenly felt like a prize dick for relaying a list that could equally have applied to him when his marriage to Aggs was crumbling. 'Look, is this okay, me telling you about it?' he asked anxiously. 'I know it's messed up, but I feel like you're the only person who would understand. And obviously it could affect the girls.' He added the last one as a bit of an afterthought, but that didn't make it less true.

'No, it's fine,' she said with a kindness that he didn't deserve. 'But, you know, all that, it could be down to other things. Midlife crisis. Changing interests. Could even be the menopause and all the changes that come with that.'

He shrugged, unconvincingly. 'Could be...'

'But?'

Time to put all his cards on the table. 'I know this is going to sound nuts, but I was at a function and she was on another table and the way she was behaving with the guy sitting next to her set off alarm bells.'

'In what way?'

Mitchell sighed, ran his fingers through his hair, torn about whether to spill it all and then doing it anyway. 'The same way she acted towards me when I was married to you.'

'Ouch,' Aggs winced. 'I want it known that I'm trying really hard to be non-judgemental here. The wine is helping.'

'And then I followed her.'

Aggs nearly choked on her Prosecco. 'YOU WHAT?'

Mitchell had never felt lower or more ridiculous. 'This morning, I followed her. She told me she was going to yoga and then to a meeting with a new client, but she came out after her workout looking like she was ready for a catwalk and then went to a flash hotel...'

'She has meetings in hotels all the time,' Aggs interjected.

'Yes, but then the same guy from the function turned up. Couldn't miss him. He drives a neon yellow Maserati. Attention seeking much?'

Aggs groaned, and he barrelled on.

'It gets worse. Look, I'm not proud, but I had a look in the hotel restaurant and bar...'

'What, like commando crawled round the place searching for them?' Every word was steeped in incredulity.

'Pretty much.'

'Oh, Mitch...' The incredulity turned to sympathy. Or maybe it was pity over how pathetic he'd become. He didn't always get this stuff right, hence their divorce.

'And there was no sign of them, so I'm pretty sure they must have been up in one of the bedrooms.'

'You don't know that for sure,' she offered, unconvincingly.

A rueful laugh escaped him. 'Call it intuition.'

'So what are you going to do?' Not a trace of triumph or smugness there and a shocking thought flashed to the front of his mind. What the fuck had he been thinking when he left this woman for someone who wasn't a patch on her?

'I don't know. I'm not going to go storming in and confront her yet. She'll deny it and I'll be no further forward. I think I need to take a more strategic view. Gather a bit more proof.' This was his marriage and he was talking about it like it was one of his cases. Perhaps that was the only way he could deal with it. 'I just wanted to know what you thought.'

Aggs took another sip of her wine and then matched his gaze. 'Because I've been where you are now?'

His whole body sagged. 'I'm sorry, Aggs. For this, for everything. What I did to you was unforgivable and I know how lucky I am that you've found a way to make our fractured family work all these years...'

'I did that for the girls,' she said calmly. 'And by imagining you with electric probes on your man bits.'

He didn't know whether to laugh because she was funny, or cry because she was being so fricking decent by trying to lighten the moment. 'But I'm here because I trust you, and because... because, to be honest, you're my oldest friend and I needed to get an outside opinion from someone who knows both of us well. So what do you think? Am I being a paranoid stalker, or could she be having an affair?'

Aggs pushed her wine glass forward, then flopped her head on the table. 'Aaaaargh!'

Emotionally intelligent or not, even he could sense that probably wasn't good.

A few seconds passed before she raised her head again.

'Look, I don't want to get in the middle of you two and it's none of my business...'

'I know...'

'And if you tell her you spoke to me about this I'll be on Amazon and ordering those electric probes before you can say "smouldering pubes"...'

'I hear you,' he said, involuntarily crossing his legs.

'But, given what you've told me, I'd say it's a definite possibility.'

He let out a low, painful, 'Fuck.'

'I'm sorry,' and, to her credit, she genuinely did look like she was concerned for him. 'I really hope I'm wrong,' she went on. 'But, to be honest, when it comes to Celeste, you had me at the neon yellow Maserati.'

15

Celeste opened the washroom stall door, checked that no one was outside at the sinks, then stepped aside to let Mr UCLA sneak out before he was spotted loitering in the ladies' toilets. She'd already forgotten his name. It had been a quick shag and she'd orgasmed, so she was perfectly satisfied, but she was done with it now. Over it. In fact, she was done with this whole Vegas trip. What a blowout Zac had turned out to be. How fucking dare he ditch her like that? One minute he was all over her, introducing her as his 'model girl-friend from the UK' like she was Kate bloody Moss or something, and the next he was blowing her off because some actress snapped her fingers.

Meanwhile, she was having to deal with love's young dream, who were probably still in that cabana sucking the faces off each other. How boring was that? They were going home in a few days and Agnetha would never see that guy again, yet she was wasting every minute they had left in Sin City by sticking to him like glue instead of doing stuff with her.

Celeste washed her hands, threw water on her face, then ran her fingers through her hair, pushing it back so that it was off her face. It was a good look on her. Highlighted her bone structure and her eyes. Several years of modelling had taught her how to maximise her assets and they definitely worked for her.

She turned to the side to check her profile and the silhouette of her body. Boobs a natural 34D, stomach completely flat, ass round, the perfect size for lingerie, swimwear and catalogue work. That's what a balanced diet of Marlboro lights, black coffee, Diet Coke and vodka tonic did for you.

The thought of her job made her smile. Since she'd moved to London she'd been working in a bar while trying to make it on the modelling circuit. At the start it was slow, but in the last year it had picked up some momentum and she was getting put forward for some fairly decent jobs now. On Tuesday, the day before they'd travelled from LA to Vegas, she'd called her agency in London to say that she'd soon be back, and the head booker, Valeria, had practically screamed down the phone at her.

'Celeste, where the FUCK have you been?'

Celeste had temporarily been struck dumb. Russian by birth, Valeria was loud, she was brash, and she could swear in several different languages, but Celeste had never heard her so wound up.

'I'm in LA on holiday. Well, an extended holiday actually. But if I can tear myself away, I'll be back in London next week.'

'I don't actually care where the fuck you are! We have a callback for you next week for the Next campaign. It's down to you and one other and you disappear! Do you not care about me, Celeste? Because if you did, you wouldn't be trying to give me a fucking stroke!'

Celeste had tuned out everything except 'Next campaign'. Oh. Holy. Crap. Not that she was prone to self-doubt, but she hadn't thought for a minute that she stood a chance with that one, expecting them to go with a recognisable face, instead of an unknown with nothing but catalogue shoots, a few women's maga-

zine fashion spreads and a white-moustached billboard for the
'Drink Milk' crusade.

'Valeria, calm your jets, you fricking wonderful woman,' she
exclaimed. 'I swear to God, if you were here right now, I'd shag you.'

That made Valeria cackle. 'Not my type, darling. I prefer the
kind with the penis, but thanks for the offer and you're forgiven,
okay? Just be here, next Friday, 10 a.m.. The campaign doesn't
launch until October, but it's TV, print and billboards, so they want
the face locked down now so that they know what they're working
with.' The phone clicked then went dead.

Even now, in a Vegas bathroom, replaying the call in her mind
gave Celeste a visceral thrill. Next Friday. Almost a week away, and
the day after she landed back in London. Aggs would then catch a
connecting flight back up to Glasgow, so they'd always planned to
say goodbye at Heathrow.

Celeste's mind starting whirring. They'd be back in LA
tomorrow night, so that meant she'd have five days there before
going back to London. It was perfect. She'd get her teeth whitened
and spend a couple of days nude sunbathing on the roof to get rid
of any tan lines from this weekend. Then she could do her waxing,
manicure, pedicure, eyebrows and facials there too, and hit the gym
in Zac's apartment block every day.

Sure, they'd apparently split up, but there was no way that Zac
would kick her out, especially with Aaron and Aggs there. Besides,
he would probably be guarding Jilly Jones in rehab for the foresee-
able future so he wouldn't be around anyway. Yep, this was all
perfect. Finally, after years of disappointments and sheer hard graft,
she was going to get the break she deserved. This was it.

In fact, this could be everything. If she got the job, she could
move out of the cupboard she was renting in Earls Court into a
bigger flat, and she planned to persuade Aggs to come down and
live with her. The truth was, London was a great city, but there was

no one there that she really connected with. Aggs could pick up temp jobs anywhere and she loved an adventure, so surely she'd be up for giving London life a try for a while? If she came down, the two of them could have an absolute riot together. Great friend. Great job. Great life. It would be perfect.

Feeling her spirits swelling more from the thought of her and Aggs in London than from the shag she'd just had on the cistern of the middle loo, Celeste blew herself a kiss in the mirror, threw her shoulders back and opened the door. Time for more sun, more pool, more alcohol and more fun. And she planned to prise Aggs away from Aaron and have some girl time too. Maybe they could go and do a bit of shopping for a killer outfit for her call-back.

Out at the pool, the DJ was revving up the tunes and Montell Jordan's 'This Is How We Do It' was blaring from the speakers. Gorgeous, lithe, twenty-something women were holding their cocktails high as they danced on the deck, while guys in the pool were busting their moves. Celeste spotted Aggs, still lying in the shade in the cabana at the other side of the pool. With her red hair, she went straight from pale white to third-degree sunburn if she spent time in the sun, so she always stuck to shade, while Celeste slapped on baby oil and let herself fry to a deep golden brown.

As she got closer, she could see Aggs was on her own. Yes! They could ditch Aaron and she could steal her away now to go shopping. Maybe even broach the idea about Agnetha moving to London too and get that sorted. Celeste didn't doubt for a second that it would happen. She was getting the job, they'd live together and it would all be fantastic.

Feeling the heat from the tiles burning her feet, Celeste upped her speed as she made her way along the length of the pool.

The music faded out and the DJ's voice came over the microphone.

'People in the house!' A roar went up. 'I've got something a bit special here and I'm gonna hand the microphone over to my man, Aaron!'

Celeste frowned. She was sure the DJ just said, 'Aaron'. How bizarre. There must be two of them here at the pool.

She put her hand up to her eyes to shield them from the sun, and zeroed in on the DJ box, down at the end of the row of cabanas and there she saw... Holy shit, that was their Aaron. And he was holding the mic. What was this, karaoke? Some kind of stupid game?

Whatever it was, he must be drunk because it was totally out of character. Zac was the attention seeking, limelight loving guy and Aaron was the one who preferred to stay in the background. Budweiser had a lot to answer for.

'Hey guys, thanks for letting me cut in here,' he said into the mic, eliciting another roaring cheer from a pool deck of revellers who were up for anything. It didn't harm his case that working as a builder had given him an incredible body, and he was standing there like a bronzed god in his swim shorts. Maybe if she'd seen that body first, she'd have chosen Aaron over Zac, but then Zac was the one with the contacts, the one who liked to live it up and party like a rock star. No amount of muscle could make up for the fact that she'd have been over Aaron's low key personality in a week.

Around the pool, everyone had stopped to listen, and it was now impossible to get past them all, so Celeste slipped down and perched on the edge of the water, giving her a full view of the action. She switched her gaze from Aaron to Aggs, who had stood up now and stepped out of the cabana, her hand over her mouth, obviously just as shocked that her boyfriend had hijacked the party.

'I'm here with my girlfriend, Agnetha, who is over here from the UK...'

Another chorus of cheers. Bloody hell, this lot would applaud anything.

'That's her, right there!' He pointed to Aggs, who put two hands over her face.

Celeste knew she'd be hating this. Being the centre of attention was Agnetha's worst nightmare. Still, that was the shopping trip sorted – Aggs would be happy to ditch Aaron after this.

While another roar went up, Aaron crossed the thirty feet or so to Agnetha, and stood in front of her. 'And it's her birthday today, so...'

He started singing 'Happy Birthday' and a couple of hundred sun worshipping party people joined in.

Celeste wondered if she could drown herself in the shallow end of the pool to make it stop.

When it finally subsided, she expected Aaron to hand back the mic, but he didn't. Instead, he moved over to Aggs and stood right in front of her. Wait a minute, what was going on here?

Despite the heat, Celeste began to feel a cold tingle of dread.

He lifted the wireless mic to his mouth. 'We've only known each other for a couple of months, but I love you, Miss Agnetha...'

Another fucking cheer. What was wrong with these people? Urgh, this was awful. It was almost like one of those pathetically cheesy proposals that...

Celeste hadn't even finished the thought, when Aaron dropped down on to one knee, unleashing a horrified howl of 'Noooooooooo' in her head.

'And I want to know...' he went on, 'if you'll marry me, right here in Vegas, today.'

Oh God. Oh God. Oh God. Celeste couldn't take this in. This couldn't be happening. Was this some kind of out-of-body experience? Had she banged her head on the toilet wall when Mr Muscles was shagging her on the cistern?

Her eyes shot daggers as she tried to communicate with Aggs, but her friend wasn't receiving her glares of warning. Oh, she'd be mortified. Celeste had to get her out of there, to save her from this, but how did she do that without looking like a maniac? She could hardly run over there and rugby tackle Aaron to the ground.

The crowd's roar had subsided to a hush now as everyone waited to hear Aggs' reply.

Celeste tried again to send subliminal messages. *Just say no, Aggs. Get it over with. Shake your head, and sure, it'll be embarrassing, but it'll all blow over by the time the next song is finished and nobody knows you here anyway, so what does it matter?*

Aggs said something, but because Aaron was kneeling, the mic was too far away from her to pick it up.

'What was that?' Aaron asked, this time lifting the mic aloft, so that Aggs could speak into it.

Aggs threw her head back for a second and Celeste wondered if she was praying to the heavens to get her out of here.

Hold on, was she laughing? She was! Christ, she must be pissed too.

The cold dread was spreading now, giving Celeste goosebumps from head to toe as Aggs leaned forward until her mouth was only inches from the microphone. 'Yes,' she giggled.

No. She wouldn't. Surely not...

'Yes,' she repeated louder this time. 'I'll marry you.'

The crowd went crazy, Aaron jumped up, threw his arms around Aggs and swung her round, both of them clearly ecstatic.

But that's not what Celeste saw. She didn't see romance. Or happiness.

She just saw her whole vision of the future crumble in front of her eyes.

16

HOPE

Hope surprised herself. When her lunch came, something switched on her appetite for the first time in days, and she realised she was ravenous. It helped that the monkfish curry was delicious, and the second glass of wine definitely took the edge off her anxiety. She desperately wanted to cut to the big question, but she forced herself to slow down, worried about opening a box that could be filled with pain or confusion for the father she'd just met.

Relax, she told herself. *Go easy. You're here now. Plenty of time for everything you need to know. Just let this happen organically and see where it goes.*

Aaron made it so much easier because he wanted to know everything about her life, her family, her likes, her dislikes. The elephant was definitely in the room, but it was sitting quietly in the corner, biding its time.

When the waiter cleared their plates, Hope asked for a black coffee and Aaron went for a flat white.

Hope excused herself and nipped to the loo. In the cubicle, she pulled her phone out of her bag.

In hotel restaurant. Had lunch. He's soooooo lovely. Can't believe it. xx

WHERE THE HELL HAVE YOU BEEN??? I'VE BEEN WORRIED SICK!!!! I
AM GOING TO KILL YOU WHEN YOU GET HOME.

Hope rolled her eyes in amusement, picturing Maisie pacing the
kitchen, punctuating her steps with dramatic sighs.

I'm sorry. It's a bit intense. Can't stop convo to keep texting. Can you let
Mum know I'm good and it's going okay?

Yes. Can I come and hide behind a pot plant to spy?

Definitely not!

D'oh! Have you told him yet?

No. Waiting for right time. Soon.

Hope felt her grip tighten on the phone just thinking about
what had to come.

Okay ma darlin. You've got this. Love you. Xx

Thanks sis. Love you too. Will call when I can. Xx

Hope rested her head in her hands for moment. Maisie was
right, she had this. Didn't she?
Her phone buzzed again.

Just checking – still a hard no on the pot plant?

If there was anyone else in these loos, they be wondering why there was a giggle from one of the cubicles.

A definite hard no.

Sigh. xx

Out at the basins, Hope washed her hands and then brushed her hair, taking in her reflection in the mirror. Hope McTeer, Aaron Ward's biological daughter. That's who she was now.

Have you met my dad? This is Aaron Ward.

Nope, she still couldn't imagine saying it. It was difficult to pin down the emotions that were crashing around inside her.

She popped her brush and phone back into her bag and returned to the table just as the coffees were arriving. The restaurant had almost emptied now, only a few other diners at a couple of tables across the other side of the room, so it felt like just the two of them, in a corner, the whole world locked away somewhere else.

She took a deep breath, fired up by Maisie's support. Time for truths from both of them. Something told her that Aaron sensed it too.

'I can't stop staring at you,' he said, with a tenderness that made Hope smile. 'I'm so grateful to be sitting here, but it's like none of this is real.'

'I know. But is it weird that it feels... right?'

He shook his head. 'Not weird at all. But...' He paused, picking his words. 'I'm trying to take this at your pace. Fast or slow. Up to you. I guess there's some stuff that you want to know about that we haven't covered yet. I promise I'll be honest about everything you ask me.'

The tension that had been blown away by his easy manner and his acceptance of her began to ratchet back up again. It was time.

She'd thought about these questions a million times, but now that the moment was here, she couldn't remember what order the words should come out in.

Come on, Hope. You can do this.

He was still staring at her, waiting for her to be ready.

'My mum.' That was all she could manage at first.

She regrouped, took another breath, tried again, terrified of the answer. If it was a 'no' she was in trouble.

'Do you know who my biological mother is?' She'd asked it that way because for all she knew he could have been a rampant one-night-stand kind of guy back then. Maybe he had no idea who he'd slept with twenty-three years ago. Perhaps it was all a blur. Obviously, she'd been born in the UK, so maybe it was a holiday fling and he couldn't remember her name.

Aaron leaned forward so that his elbows were on the table, then swung his hand over and took hers. The skin-to-skin contact was warm, comforting.

'Yeah. Do you want me to tell you about her?'

The sheer relief made tears spring to Hope's eyes and she wiped them away with the heel of her free hand.

'Now don't you go starting or I'll be right there with you, and I'm trying to keep it together here,' Aaron said, laughing despite the tears he was now blinking away too.

Hope choked out a chuckle. 'Sorry! Oh my God, I'm a mess.' Her tears were falling freely now and she used her napkin to stem them. It took a few seconds, then she inhaled deeply, cleared her throat and looked him in the eye again, smiling. 'Okay, I'm good.'

He took both her hands, met her gaze, and began to speak.

'Back in 1997, I was twenty-five and just living my regular life in LA, working construction, hanging with my buds. One night I was in a bar with my buddy, Zac, and we got chatting to two girls. Scottish girls.'

Hope's stomach flipped. Her mum was Scottish. That explained her being born in Edinburgh. She resisted the urge to butt in with questions. Was she the product of a one night stand after a hook-up in a bar after all? Or a holiday fling?

She bit her tongue, determined to let him tell her in his own way. Aaron's voice was thick with emotion and she could see that this wasn't easy.

'I don't want to say it was love at first sight, but it was close. They were there on holiday, supposed to be for a month. We started hanging out, and then they moved into our apartment – my buddy was hooking up with her friend too so it kinda made sense. The month got longer and... I guess she didn't want to go home, and that suited me just fine.'

That brought the tears back, but Hope just let them fall. They'd been in love. Or as much in love as you could be after a few weeks. Somehow, the thought of that made her happy.

'What was her name?'

'Agnetha.'

'Agnetha,' Hope repeated it, letting it roll on her tongue. It wasn't exactly a common Scottish moniker. Maybe her mum's parents were from somewhere else? 'And Agnetha was definitely Scottish? From where?' Her resolve not to ask questions went right out of the window as curiosity climbed into the driver's seat.

'That's the thing, she was from here. From Glasgow.'

'Oh my God,' Hope murmured. Her mum might have been in the same city as her for her whole life. All those childhood thoughts were spot on. She used to wonder if she'd ever walked past her in the street. Or sat next to her on a bus. Now she knew for sure that could have been a possibility. More than that, it gave her hope that there was a chance to find her and that was so important because...

'Are you doing okay?' he asked, squeezing her hand.

She had to tell him. She couldn't keep this to herself for a minute longer.

'I need to find her,' she blurted, feeling a crushing weight descend on her as she said it. This was the moment that could wreck everything, that could make him question her motives, feel he was being used, change his mind about having a relationship.

And he didn't even realise it. 'I get that,' he said, oblivious to the motivations behind her words. 'It's only natural that you'd want to track her down, hear her story. To be honest, I've a few questions myself.' It was said with no malice or resentment, just... sorrow? Sadness?

Tell him. Tell him. Get it out there. You have to do it. Channel Maisie.

'It's not just because I have questions. There's something else I need to tell you.'

He was still holding on to her hands, his curiosity all over his face.

'It's just...' she paused, then decided to go with full disclosure. 'This is going so much better than I ever dared to dream, and I'm really scared that you'll be upset with me, that it'll change the way you're feeling about meeting me.'

'Whatever it is, nothing will change how I feel. I'm an all-in kind of guy, Hope. You're my girl. Nothing you can say will make me want to change that.'

Right there, in that moment, she believed him.

Do it. Just do it.

'I wanted to be a doctor ever since I was a teenager. You see, I spent a lot of time in hospital because, when I was fourteen years old, I was diagnosed with Hodgkin lymphoma.'

Aaron reeled like he'd been slapped. 'Cancer?'

Hope nodded. 'Yeah. Bummer, right?' She'd had a lifetime of talking about it, dealing with it, so she knew that if she stayed strong and steady as she was telling him, with a bit of black humour too, then he'd find it easier to discuss.

'Shit.' He sagged as if he'd been winded. 'I'm so sorry. That must have been tough. Breaks my heart that I wasn't here for you.'

She could see that he meant every word. 'It's okay, really,' she reassured him. 'My parents were great...' She wondered if the mention of her parents would jar with him, but there was no reaction on his face, only concern. 'And we got through it. I was in and out of hospital for a couple of years, and then back and forward for a few years after that for checks and tests to make sure it was gone.'

Relief perked him up a little. 'Thank God it was, Hope. And I'm so glad that your mom and dad were there for you. They sound like real good people. I'm grateful.'

'Me too.' The anxiety was making her heart hammer again. This had to be done. 'The thing is, a couple of years ago, it came back. Which was a bit of a shock, because most recurrences happen within five years and I was just outside that timeframe.'

His skin paled, his mouth opened, but no words came out, so she carried on, knowing that if she stopped, she would crumble.

'I had to have more treatment, more chemo, more radiotherapy. The best option for me would have been a stem cell transplant, and there's a national data base for that called the Anthony Nolan register, but no-one on there was a match. It was touch and go for a while, but we think we got it.'

'So you're cured? You're okay?' The desperation for reassurance made her feel like her heart would burst.

'For now. I get tested every year and it might come back, or it might not. I just need to live in hope. Pardon the pun,' she added with a smile, which he returned with bells on. She went on, 'Now there are so many new treatments and pioneering trials, though. That's the field of medicine I plan to go into. I want to specialise in oncology.'

'Jeez, girl. Is it wrong that I'm so proud of you? I know that I had nothing to do with the woman that you've become, but, damn, you're spectacular.' He spoke calmly, with real sincerity, and there were new tears for both of them.

Hope felt a swell of gratitude. Maybe this was going to be okay. *Keep going...*

'The thing is, if it does reoccur this year, next year, any time in the future, then more than ever, my best chance of survival will still be a stem cell transplant and I still haven't found a suitable donor.'

Time to say it. Get it out. She paused, plucking up the courage. 'The highest chance of a match would be a biological parent.'

She didn't add that a biological sibling could also be a match, terrified of scaring him even further at the thought of involving his other kids. Instead, she let that hang in the air, let him absorb what she was saying. Yes, she wanted to find her parents, but not just so that she understood her background and heritage. The truth was, her life could depend on it. And if that was too much for Aaron to deal with, she'd understand. It was a lot. This wasn't the hearts and flowers perfect ending he'd probably been hoping for. This was complicated. She was a biological child that came with baggage and she knew from experience that not everyone could deal with the tough stuff.

'Let me get this...' he said, his brow furrowed in concentration. 'The cancer could come back. And if it does, I might be able to help you by giving you my...' he stopped.

She helped him out. 'Stem cells. If they're a match.' It was close enough. He didn't need to have the medical terminology or the specifics down pat. The general gist would do.

Her top teeth dug deep into her bottom lip again, as she waited for him to finish processing that. He was taking too long. Fuck. Bugger.

'I'm sorry,' she blurted. 'I know this is a shock and I hope you don't hate me because I didn't tell you this up front. If you think I got you here under false pretences, I totally understand and if you want to leave...'

'Hope!' His interruption was calm but firm. 'Let me tell you this, I'm not leaving.' He was leaning forward now. 'It doesn't matter what you need, or when you need it, I'll be there and you can have everything I've got to give. I owe you twenty-three years of love and everything else that goes with it, so you can collect in any way, any time.'

He lifted her hand, kissed it, then put it back down on the table. It was such a pure, loving gesture.

"Thank you," she whispered.

'And we'll find your mom too. We weren't together for long, but I knew her heart and the kind of person she was, and I have to believe she'd do anything for you too.'

This was all too much. Hope wanted to flop on the table, the emotional turmoil giving way to exhaustion that was now seeping into her bones.

A thought. She'd cut him off before he told her how their relationship had ended.

'You haven't said what happened with you and my mother. Did she just come home from her holiday and you never heard from her again? You didn't keep in contact?'

His sigh came from the soles of his leather boots. 'It was a bit more complicated than that.'

4 P.M. – 6 P.M

17

'Dad, what are you doing here? And where's Cruella?'

'Isla!' Aggs chided her daughter.

Skye and Celeste had a good relationship and Aggs was glad about that because she didn't want any discord in the girls' lives. Unfortunately, Isla had never quite got the memo. 'Materialistic, shallow tart,' was Isla's general opinion of her stepmother, but that was only expressed to Aggs, and only on the mutual agreement that her feelings were kept between them. Thus, Isla tolerated Celeste and was perfectly civil to her on a superficial level, but couldn't resist the odd dig when she wasn't around.

On any other day, Mitchell would throw back a disapproving rebuke, but, thankfully, today he just rolled his eyes and stood up to give his daughter a hug.

'Good to see you too, darling. And Celeste had a meeting today so I'm flying solo.'

Aggs winced a little inside. Poor bugger. She knew she should feel smug about his predicament, but the truth was she didn't have the energy for bad feelings. She'd made her peace with what happened years ago and there was no point going back to the darkness. Her shiny new life was going to be lived in the light.

She was mentally congratulating herself on her positivity when Skye wandered through from the kitchen too. 'Dad!' she echoed her sister, then, 'See,' she side-mouthed to Isla. 'He can't keep away from me. I'm definitely his favourite.'

Aggs tried to supress a chortle. Mitchell was one of the top lawyers in the city, he was good looking, successful, wealthy, driven, a man of accomplishment and a pillar of the community... but his daughters definitely kept him humble and on his toes.

'So what are you doing here then?' Isla pressed.

Sympathy rising, Aggs decided to pitch in and help him out. 'He just popped in to wish me a happy birthday. Is that okay with you two madams?

Mitchell threw her a grateful glance, then soon discovered he wasn't out of the woods yet.

'What, no flowers? No pressie? You didn't even bring her a card?' Isla demanded, her eyes darting across the table. 'Oh, Dad,' she said wearily. 'No wonder you two are divorced.'

She was obviously teasing, but Aggs couldn't deny there was an element of truth in there. Mitchell had never been the most romantic of men, but then, when they were together, they didn't have time. They were too busy bringing up young kids, building businesses and taking care of her parents. After he left, it had been like a physical sting every time she heard through the shared-children grapevine that he'd made some grand gesture for Celeste. Not so much the flash car he bought her, or the honeymoon in St Lucia, but it was the flowers and the dinners and the way that he was so attentive to her, watched her when she entered a room, smiled when she paid attention to him.

A little bit like the way that Will looked at her now, she thought, a warm glow spreading through her. Two days in Paris. That was the ultimate romantic gesture. It gave her a thrill to think that this time tomorrow she'd be in France. It also gave her a slight panic, because she had to dig out her passport and pack, but she'd worry about that later.

Right now, she watched with amusement as Mitchell countered his daughter's cheek with some of his own. 'Thank you for the constructive feedback, darling. I'll be in touch if I need any more advice from an expert.'

The three of them – Mitchell and his daughters – were laughing now and Aggs' glow spread a little further. This was great to see. No matter what he'd done, he was a great dad, and he'd definitely done his best to be a good co-parent when they were growing up. Watching them all together now, she suddenly felt a massive pang of longing for her own father. It happened sometimes. Grief was a funny thing. Sometimes it came in waves, other times it came in stings that lasted a second but hurt deep. This was one of those moments and it sparked an irrepressible need to be somewhere else.

She glanced around. The café was quiet and Nasim and Sandra had it all under control. Skye would be hopeless, but Isla was still here. And, sod it, it was her birthday. If she wanted to have an hour or two to herself, she was absolutely entitled to do that. Hadn't she resolved to start living on her own terms and put her own needs first? Well, right now she had a need and she was going to do something about it.

'Listen, troops, I'm just nipping out for an hour.'

All three of them turned to stare at her as if she'd just announced she was going to get a Bakewell tart tattooed on her buttock.

Skye clearly wasn't thrilled with this announcement. 'You're what? Where?'

'I just want to go to the Botanic Gardens and say "hello" to your gran and grandad. I won't be long.'

Going to the Botanic Gardens was something she'd done every year on her birthday since she was a kid, first with both her mum and dad, then, after her dad died, she'd just go with her mum. This year, her first without Mum, she'd thought she might give it a miss for fear of disintegrating into a blubbering wreck in the middle of a public place. Now she realised she wasn't ready to change the tradition. Maybe she would never be ready.

Isla softened, as she always did at the mention of her grandparents and their special place. 'Aw, that's lovely, mum. Do you want me to come with you?'

The girls had lived with them and Aggs upstairs in this building for many years and they'd all adored each other. Mum and Dad had been the kind of grandparents every kid should have, the ones who picked them up from school, who took care of them when Aggs was working, who turned up at every show and sports event and sat there, proud as punch.

Aggs swallowed back the lump that was forming in her throat and told herself to breathe through it. She slapped on a smile. 'Thank you, sweetheart, but I'm fine. You two stay here and take care of the café for me. Try not to kill each other, and if blood is spilt there's bleach in the storeroom.'

'Can I give you a lift? Save you walking?' Mitchell asked, with a hint of urgency.

It was on the tip of her tongue to decline the offer, but she didn't want to seem churlish. Maybe he needed to talk some more? She felt bad ditching him, and besides, it was a twenty minute walk and if she hitched a ride, they'd be there in five. That would give her more time to get back and get a bit glammed up for dinner with the girls tonight.

'Erm, sure. That would be great, thanks. Give me two minutes.'

She ignored the pointed look that passed between Skye and Isla. She had no idea what it was about and that was probably a good thing.

Upstairs, she threw on a fine-knit cream cardi over her T-shirt and swapped her sandals for comfier trainers.

When she returned to the café, Mitchell and the girls were deep in conversation, but they broke off as soon as they saw her, guilty faces all round.

'What is going on with you lot?' she asked with amused suspicion.

'Nothing!' Skye protested. 'We're, eh, just talking about my finals.'

Aggs didn't believe a word of it, but she let it go. Whatever it was, if they wanted her to know, they'd tell her when they were ready.

'Good to go?' Mitchell asked.

'Sure am.'

It felt weird sitting in the car with him, new and strange, but at the same time it was like a flashback to a thousand other journeys. The ride home from their wedding, bringing the babies home from hospital, going to buy the girls their first school shoes, a dozen times they'd loaded up the car and taken off to the seaside on a summer's day...

'Thanks, Aggs, for listening back there. I can't tell you how grateful I am.'

'You don't need to,' she said honestly. 'I hope you sort it out. Ten years is a long time to throw away.' She wondered if he realised that applied to their marriage too.

He turned to her with a sad smile that told her he did. 'It is.'

Aggs shook off the inference, changed the subject, tried to get back on to more steady ground. 'So how are Skye's studies going?' That spurred a discussion that got them the rest of the way and as they turned onto Queen Margaret Drive, Aggs was almost sorry it was such a short distance. 'Just drop me anywhere,' she offered. 'I can jump out and let you get on.'

'There's a space,' Mitchell nodded to a rare gap in the parked cars just a few metres further along. He nipped in, accomplishing the kind of manoeuvre that Aggs knew would have taken her three attempts and a shout to a bystander to guide her in.

She unclipped her seat belt. 'Thanks, Mitch. Let me know how things go. I hope it works out for the best.' She didn't say what 'the best' was.

Just as she was about to put her hand on the door handle, he interrupted her.

'Look, feel free to say no, but would you mind...'

Oh, God, what now? He'd better not ask her to talk to Celeste because that was a step wayyyyyy too far.

'... er, if I came with you?'

First reaction, relief. Second, hesitation. She loved the peace of sitting on her mum and dad's memorial bench in the gardens and chatting to them on her own. But as she looked through the railings, she saw the lawns were packed with people, so it wasn't going to be a moment of serenity and reflection anyway. 'Sure. If you feel like it.'

This was turning out to be the most unpredictable birthday ever.

The gardens were heaving with tourists and locals, hundreds of them lying on the grass, loads of the men adhering to the law in Glasgow that decrees that as soon as it's over sixty degrees, you have to take your top off no matter your shape, size or whether you're wearing suncream. Aggs could already see a few red shoulders that were going to be agony tonight. There were kids playing, people walking dogs, elderly couples strolling along the paths. It was the very best of the city – sunshine, happy faces, and a beautiful setting.

Her mum and dad had brought her here all the time, not just on birthdays, and she'd done the same with the girls. Later, she'd brought Mum in her wheelchair, and they'd sit and watch the world go by, both of them wrapped in their memories.

After Mum had died, she'd arranged the memorial bench here, in Mum's favourite spot, and it was where Aggs would come when she needed to feel near to them, needed to talk to them and feel their presence. This was the first time she'd brought anyone but the girls.

As they got closer, she could see that a young guy and girl were already sitting on the bench, arms round each other, smooching like there was no one around to see them. Mum would be rolling her eyes right now, Aggs thought with a smile. Just as she was about to suggest turning back and leaving them to it, the couple got up and wandered off. Mum clearly deployed some divine intervention there.

Mitchell read the plaque on the back of the bench before he sat down.

IN MEMORY OF ALEX AND ELLA SANDERS, MUCH LOVED, NEVER FORGOTTEN, ALWAYS WITH US.

Aggs nudged him. 'Can you move along a bit there, because if my mum sends a bolt of lightning down in your direction, I don't want to get the ends of my hair scorched.' Ella had made no secret of her disgust with Mitchell when they split up. Other than when the girls were there and civility demanded it, her mum and dad never spoke to him again, refusing to grant him – or Celeste, for that matter – even a hint of forgiveness.

'Your dad once threatened to break my kneecaps, you know.'

Aggs gasped, stunned. 'He what? Nooooo! My dad didn't have a violent bone in his body.'

Mitchell gave her a rueful shrug. 'He did that day. I think it was the night after he found out about...' He shivered, didn't finish the sentence. 'I don't blame him. I'd have been the same if some guy did that to one of my girls.'

Aggs pulled her cardi round her, feeling a chill in spite of the warm day. 'It was a long time ago, Mitch. Bygones,' she said softly. 'And it wasn't all down to you. My choices were a factor too.'

'What I did wasn't your fault at all, Aggs,' he argued.

'I know that,' she said. No victim blaming here. He was the one who broke their vows and their family and that was all on him. And Celeste, of course. But she had to acknowledge that her own actions played a part too. 'I put you at the bottom of the pile. I was exhausted,' Aggs said, truthfully. 'Life was crushing me. I was too busy bringing up the girls, trying to look after Mum and Dad, and keep the café going too. You were working such long hours and I felt like I was doing it all on my own.'

Mitchell offered no argument. 'You were.'

She pondered that some more. 'I think it was the sleep deprivation that was the worst bit. I lived on four or five hours a night for so long that I stopped thinking, stopped feeling, just went into survival mode to get through the days and keep everything going. I wasn't much of a wife.'

'And I was a shit husband.'

'You were,' she said, nudging him playfully. 'You were great at the start, it just all went a bit downhill after the first few years.'

'I was exactly the same as you,' he conceded. 'Focused on other things. Trying to build the business. I got sucked into the other stuff too. Going out after work with clients, celebrating with the rest of the team when we won a case, commiserating when we lost, going to all those corporate functions. I became addicted to the challenge, to the money, to the need to make a success of it. Nothing else mattered. I think my ego was in charge for a long time.'

'I don't think it was just your ego that was running the show,' she said archly. 'Other parts of your anatomy were involved too.'

He had the grace to flush with mortification.

Aggs stared straight ahead, wondering if any of the other people enjoying the sunshine in the park were having the most brutally honest conversation they'd ever had, about one of the most traumatic events in their life?

Nothing that either of them said was contentious. They both remembered things the same way. Aggs felt another weight, one she hadn't even known was there, lift from her shoulders and she realised that this was a conversation that they should probably have had before now. They needed full closure to find real peace. This exchange was finally bringing resolution to an unfinished chapter. Releasing another tie to heartache and letting it drift off in the breeze. It was just a shame that it had taken Mitchell's life running aground to get here.

On the bench there was silence, but in her head she could hear her mum harrumphing, tutting, muttering. *'Ask him, Aggs. Ask the daft big bastard the question we always wanted the answer to. Go on.'*

Aggs fought against it. She'd gone without knowing for ten years, so what purpose did it serve now to drag it all back up? Bygones, she'd said, and she meant it.

'Agnetha Sanders, you ask him right now,' her mum demanded.

Aggs sighed. Whether it was her mum or her subconscious, there was nothing to lose by putting the question out there.

'If I ask you something, will you be completely honest?'

'Of course,' he said, like it was a ridiculous thing for her to say. Aggs chose not to point out that in their past, that wasn't a foregone conclusion.

'There's something I've always wanted to know.'

'What's that?'

'Go for it. Do it. Agnetha…'

Okay, Mum!

'Who made the first move? You or Celeste?'

18

Mitchell didn't answer immediately. The question had surprised him, and now he was waiting for the memories to untangle in his mind. Who made the first move? Maybe there wasn't a clear-cut answer to that.

Of course, there had been no ignoring the fact that Celeste was stunning. When Aggs had first introduced them, a couple of months after they began dating, he'd had to react fast to cover his astonishment. If he hadn't already known that Agnetha's best friend was a model, he'd have guessed. Not only was she breathtakingly beautiful, but she carried herself with a cool, almost aloof detachment that he found both standoffish and intriguing at the same time. She also had a trail of boyfriends that she seemed to tire of quickly, claiming they all bored her to tears. Mitchell suspected that keeping a woman like Celeste happy would be a challenge too big for any one man.

In the first few of years of their marriage they'd only seen Celeste a few times a year, when she'd come back to Glasgow. With two small kids, trips to London just didn't make sense. The girls wanted beaches and swimming pools, not busy city centre holidays.

It was at their fifth anniversary dinner in a local Indian restaurant that Celeste announced that she was moving back to Scotland permanently.

'You're not!' Aggs had screeched, before throwing herself across the table to hug her friend, narrowly avoiding her sleeves dipping in the korma. The irony was that Mitchell had been glad Celeste was coming home. It was obvious Aggs was struggling with two small kids, a busy café and her dad being ill, so maybe this would recharge her batteries. After a few years of building his business, they were starting to make a liveable salary, so they could afford a babysitter if Agnetha wanted to go out and have a bit of fun. Hadn't that been what had attracted him to her in the first place? Her sense of joy and her zest for life? Maybe Celeste would help her find that again.

She slotted right into the family. He'd come home from work and she'd be there. Christmas Day, she'd have a stocking next to theirs on the mantelpiece. If they had a rare night out on the town, Celeste would come too. She was a permanent fixture; the sister Aggs didn't have. She didn't pitch in to take the pressure off his wife by babysitting or lending a hand in the café, but she made her smile more and that was enough.

'I've decided to launch my own business,' Celeste had announced one night over a Chinese meal at their kitchen table. He'd had a long day at work and come home at 9 p.m. to find a chicken curry, fried rice and prawn crackers waiting for him. Aggs had looked like she was struggling to keep her eyes open, but Celeste was oozing enthusiasm. 'I'm getting too old to depend on modelling, so it's time to diversify.'

He hadn't been particularly interested, his mind still on the complexities of the case he'd been working on all day, but he didn't want to be rude. 'Great. What's the plan?'

Celeste went on a roll. 'Event management. Both corporate stuff and private parties. I'm going to use my contacts on the Glasgow social scene to get access to great venues...'

He knew that wasn't bullshit. Celeste had done a high profile Scottish lager campaign at the start of her career and used it to build a network of friends and acquaintances across the city. Even though she'd lived in London for years, she still seemed to know all the movers and shakers.

'... and I've got some pretty cool concepts that I came across when I was in London, so I just need to land my first client and get it off the ground.'

His curry was burning his mouth off, but he had managed to mumble his congratulations and make encouraging noises.

'Mitchell, can't you help?' Aggs had asked him, before crunching down on a prawn cracker.

He was distracted and didn't follow. 'What? How?'

'Well, couldn't you have some kind of event? Invite all your clients? Celeste could take care of it all for you.'

He was about to dismiss it out of hand, but he'd stopped himself. Actually, that wasn't the worst idea. If his fledgling firm was going to play on the bigger stage, they had to act like the bigger companies, the ones who had cash to throw about to make their clients feel valued.

Celeste had immediately seen how it would work for her too and ran with it. 'I'd make it fucking spectacular and I'd do it at cost, as long as I can network. That's all I ask.'

That's how it had started. She'd arranged a successful function for him and managed to get a couple of spin-off bookings from it. For the next few years, it was a mutually beneficial relationship. As she grew to be one of the hottest event planners in the city, she'd make sure he was on the guest list for anything that would raise his profile or allow him to get in front of people who could be advantageous for him. In return, he'd throw a couple of tax-deductible events a year and put in a good word with his clients if he thought they would benefit from her services. A perfect partnership. Even if it did mean he was either working late or out every night of the week.

When had it turned to something more? A couple of years later, at the Hilton Hotel in Glasgow.

Mitchell could recall most of the details, but some were a bit fuzzy thanks to the dozen or so bottles of wine his table had consumed at his firm's annual ball. Aggs was supposed to have been there, but she'd cried off because one of the kids had chickenpox. He wasn't pleased. Celeste had organised a couple of suites for him and his business partners as part of the deal, and now he was going to be going to bed on his own. What a waste. That's probably why he was still in the bar at 2 a.m., and happy that Celeste, this gorgeous goddess of a woman, had offered to keep him company.

Maybe what happened next was inevitable. Too much booze. Too little loyalty. A man with an ego that was out of control and who could only see the situation from his own perspective.

She'd unclipped the diamond drops that were hanging from her ears. Her slinky gold strapless gown had been turning heads all evening and at least half of the guys he worked with were in lust with her. 'What a brilliant night. We make a good team, Mr McMaster.'

He'd thrown back his shot of Drambuie way too fast. 'Yeah, we do.'

She'd taken a sip of her champagne. 'Are you okay?'

'Ah, fuck, I don't know.' He signalled to the bartender for another drink.

'Tell me,' she'd pressed, her beautiful eyes staring into his, her hand on his knee now. 'Is it Aggs? It doesn't take a genius to see that you two aren't exactly hitting it off at the moment. Look, you know I love her, but anything you say will stay between us, I promise.'

'I just think we...' He'd stopped for a second to formulate the words, distracted by the fact that her hand was now gently moving up and down his thigh as they spoke and... Shit, she was totally giving him a hard-on. '... We want different things.'

'I get that,' she said, still stroking. More stroking. This wasn't good. Strike that. What he meant was that it was too fucking good. 'To be honest with you, Mitch, much as I adore Aggs, I can see that she doesn't appreciate you. I think you need someone who will support you in what you're doing here, someone who is on your level. You're power-couple material, Mitch.'

He may have been drunk, but he could see the opportunity for a profitable merger when it was placed in front of him. Right at that moment, it made perfect sense. Celeste. Him. The unassailable fact that he was so turned on he couldn't think of anything he wanted to do more than unzip her gold dress.

She'd leaned in, put those perfect lips on his and it was a sealed deal. Done.

Of course, looking back now he'd have to question the morals of someone who would do that to her best friend, but back then, he'd slipped right into denial because if he questioned Celeste's actions, then he'd have to have taken a long, hard look at himself, and he should have been disgusted with what he saw. Oblivion and living in the crazy, sex fuelled moment was a far easier option to live with.

Who'd made the first move? Technically, it was Celeste, but he'd wanted it too. Equal culpability. The question was, which answer would hurt Aggs more?

He analysed the consequences, taking his current issues with Celeste out of the equation. Innocent until proven guilty and all that. When it came to their relationships, on the surface at least, Aggs was amicable with him, but she'd never forgiven Celeste and they had nothing more than a polite tolerance of each other. Perhaps it was time to nudge open that door, for both their sakes.

Maybe repairing their friendship even a little could bring some healing to both the women he'd loved.

The shrieks of a little kid playing footie with his dad on the grass in front of them brought him back to the moment. Aggs was still waiting for his answer.

'It was me. I'm so sorry.'

A pause. A long, excruciating silence, before Aggs raised her eyes and tilted her head back.

'You hear that, Mum? You were right.' She turned back to Mitchell, resigned but surprisingly calm. 'She always said it was you. Said you'd got above yourself and that you wanted Celeste because she matched with your new flash lifestyle. Like a Porsche for your penis, she said.'

'She said that?' He was stunned. Ella Sanders was not the kind of woman you'd expect to come out with something as... well... carnal.

'No, actually that might have been me. I said a lot of critical things about your penis back then. You're lucky it's still attached.'

A deep, uncontrollable roar of laughter erupted from somewhere deep inside him. It appeared to be contagious, because, the next thing, Aggs was howling too and people were turning to look at the two strange people doubled over in stitches on the bench.

'My mother is going to kill me for this,' she spluttered. 'If I get hit by a bus, you'll know it was Ella Sanders, dishing out retribution because I was talking to my traitorous ex-husband about his penis.' That set them off again, and all around them, other people were grinning now too.

God, he'd forgotten how much she could make him laugh.

It took him a while to calm down and get his breath back. 'You're some woman, Aggs, you know that?'

'I do,' she said, grinning, before taking his breath away with her next comment. 'Friends again?'

'I can't tell you how much I want that.' A flashback to a scene earlier in the day filled his head. 'Can I ask you something now?'

She scrunched up her nose in the way that he used to find absolutely irresistible when they were dating. 'Oh dear. Will it upset my mother?'

'No. Maybe. I'm just wondering, why now? Why are you prepared to forgive me now? Is it anything to do with the...' *Say it. Say it!* Problem was, he wasn't sure he wanted to hear the answer.

'With what?'

'With the guy? You know, the one from earlier?'

The wait for her answer seemed to go on forever and for some reason he felt a massive wave of relief when she said, 'No. It's more about me. My life. I'm having a... I don't know what to call it really. An epiphany? A midlife crisis? I feel like I lost myself there for a long time and now that Mum and Dad are gone, and the girls are adults, it's time to live my life for me again, to be a bit more like the person I was before. I liked her a lot. She was pretty good fun.'

'I liked her too,' Mitchell heard himself say.

It was true. No matter what happened or why, they'd had something great in the beginning and for a few years afterwards. And now, sitting here next to her, she was that bright, beautiful Aggs that he'd fallen in love with and he wanted to rewind all the shit that had happened.

Is this where they'd have ended up if they'd stayed together? Would they have weathered the storms and found their love for each other again, got to this stage in life and be reaping the rewards, hatching plans to make the most of the rest of their lives together? Did he take the wrong path? What was really bothering him about the prospect of losing Celeste? Was it because his ego couldn't take the rejection? Was it because fifty was careering towards him and he couldn't face starting all over again? Was it because he couldn't imagine life without someone on his arm? Or was it because he was truly still in love with his wife? Sitting there right now, he couldn't answer any of those questions. Which perhaps told him everything.

Aggs nudged her shoulder against his again. 'Good chat, Mitch,' she said, and he thought yet again how he didn't deserve this kindness. 'Slightly deranged, but good. Now I have to get back and get ready for my dinner with the girls. I'm wearing head to toe sequins. They're going to be mortified.'

'Yup, I'd pay money to see their faces,' he joked, clamping his jaw shut so he didn't let anything slip about the surprise party.

They wandered back to the car in companionable silence. Coming to see Aggs today had seemed like a ludicrous idea, but it was the best thing he could have done. How had he managed to fuck it up with such a special woman? What a complete fool he'd been.

They were back at the café in less than ten minutes. When he pulled up outside, she unclipped her seat belt. 'What's the plan then? Are you going to speak to Celeste or just keep commando-crawling round restaurants trying to catch her in the act?' She was teasing him, but doing it gently so he couldn't help but smile.

'I think I need to talk to her.'

'I think you do too. Good luck, Mitch.' She stretched over and gave him a kiss on the cheek. 'I hope you get the answers you want. Whatever they are.'

'Thanks, Aggs. For listening. And happy birthday.'

'You know what? It really is.'

With that, she was gone and Mitchell was left watching what might have been the best thing that ever happened to him walk back into a life that didn't include him.

As he slipped the gears into drive and pulled off, he realised that he couldn't wait to see her again at the party later that night.

But for now, it was time to go home and sort out his own life.

19

As soon as the lift doors closed, Aaron slipped his arm around Agnetha's waist. 'I can't believe you said yes.'

She kissed him slowly, sexily. 'I can't believe you asked me.'

'I can't believe I haven't vomited,' Celeste murmured behind them.

Agnetha immediately broke off from the embrace, suddenly self-conscious and worried they were being insensitive to Celeste. Zac had run out on her friend this morning and now she, Agnetha Sanders, was having the most wonderful, romantic day of her life.

However, that didn't stop the warm fuzzy rush that made her tummy flip again. They were doing this. They were actually doing it. The hotel manager had tracked them down after the proposal had caused a sensation at the pool and offered to arrange the whole thing for them. They were getting married tonight, at 7 p.m., at one of the wedding chapels in the hotel. At the pool earlier, Aaron had gone back on the microphone and invited everyone at the pool to join them, to uproarious cheers. The hotel had laid on a car to take them downtown to pick up a Nevada marriage licence at the Clark County Marriage License Bureau.

It had taken less than an hour until they were back and riding the lift up to their hotel floor.

The doors pinged open. 'Come to our room, Celeste, so we can decide what we're doing.'

Celeste wasn't exactly radiating love and joy, but hopefully she'd get used to the idea. Of course it was a shock. Agnetha was struggling to take it in herself, but that didn't mean that it wasn't right or that they were doing it for the wrong reasons.

When the fuss at the pool had subsided, and the two of them were alone again in the cabana, Aggs was still in a state of shock. 'Did that really happen?'

Aaron had kissed her neck. 'It happened.'

She'd needed more clarity. 'Wait a minute though. Why now? Why today. Why like that?' If anyone had asked her to guess how Aaron would propose, the last thing she'd expect was a public spectacle. Not that she was complaining about the outcome.

'Because I love you. Because I want you to be my wife. Because I want to spend the rest of my life with you. Because I don't want you to leave next week. And because now you'll be able to extend your visa because you've married an American citizen.'

That had stunned her into silence. He'd done it for a visa?

There was a split second of doubt. Would he have wanted this anyway? Was his hand being forced? Was this going to be a huge mistake?

Then she'd felt his arms go around her and all her doubts had disappeared. This incredible man was actually going to marry her so that they could be together. That might just be the most romantic thing she'd ever heard.

She was in, 100 per cent sold. Even if her best friend clearly wasn't.

A welcome blast of cool air hit them as they entered the room. Aggs dumped her beach bag on the bed, while Celeste immediately hit up the minibar, flipping the cap off a bottle of beer, then flopping down on the bucket chair by the window.

Aaron threw his arms out wide, laughing. 'Okay, future Mrs Ward, what's the plan?'

A jolt of reality hit Aggs when he said it. Shit. Mrs Ward. By the end of the day, she was going to be a whole other person. She ran that around in her mind for a minute and decided that she liked it. No, she *loved* it.

'Well, looks like I'm marrying you, otherwise all those people round the pool are going to be mighty disappointed.'

'So you're doing it for them?' Aaron teased, grabbing her and kissing her, making her purr with laughter.

'Nope, I'm doing it because I fricking love you, Aaron Ward.'

'I really am going to vomit,' Celeste muttered, staring out of the window.

The happy couple ignored her.

'Right, so what do we need to do then?' Aaron prompted again. 'I've got no idea on account of the fact that I've never asked someone to marry me before. Or had a wedding the same day. Jeez, everyone is gonna think we were wasted or high.'

Aggs sat down on the bed, trying to make her mind work. Okay, what first?

A shadow crossed her face, wiping her smile away.

Aaron spotted it immediately. 'What? What's up?'

'My parents,' she whispered, the words breaking as she said them. She'd been so carried away with the excitement and romance of it all (and a few pina coladas) that the logistical realities were only just hitting her. 'They won't be at my wedding.'

Over at the window, Celeste suddenly perked up. 'Oh shit. They'll kill you.'

Aggs bit her bottom lip, suddenly feeling nauseous as she thought it through. Would they be upset? Furious?

She closed her eyes, picturing her mum, her dad.

'You can't do this, Aggs,' Celeste went on. 'It would devastate them.'

Aggs blocked her out, trying to think. An image of her dad, on her twenty-first birthday, came into her head. He wasn't a man who was prone to emotion, so when he'd raised a toast at the party they'd thrown in the café, she'd held her breath. 'Agnetha, my love, you have made our lives wonderful for twenty-one years. Promise me that you'll always be you, that you'll make the most of every day of your life, and that you'll always follow your heart.'

Wasn't that what she was doing? Following her heart?

'Oh shit, babe, are you changing your mind? I mean, if it's a deal breaker I get it. I do. I just want you to be happy.' She could hear the panic in Aaron's voice, yet he was still putting her first.

Follow your heart, Aggs.

The solution came to her immediately.

'No, but I need you to do something for me. I'll marry you today, but as soon as we sort out the visa, will you come home with me and get married again there? I want my dad to walk me down the aisle and my mum to wear a big hat and...'

Celeste let out an audible groan.

'... and Celeste to be bloody happy for me,' Aggs added pointedly, grinning at her disgruntled pal.

Celeste ignored her and went back to staring out of the window.

'Yes!' Aaron visibly sagged with relief. 'Yes, yes, yes. I got you. We'll do it.'

Aggs climbed right back up on to cloud nine, everything clear to her now.

She checked her watch: 4.30 p.m.. 'Okay, so here's the plan. I'm going to grab my stuff and go to Celeste's room, and then we're going to go and find a shop and buy a dress. We've got two hours to find one. Oh, and a bridesmaid's dress for Celeste. A flipping huge meringue, so that for once she won't be sexier than me.'

Her attempt at appeasing her friend evoked no response, but Aggs shrugged it off. Celeste would get on board eventually, when she saw how right this was.

In the meantime, Aggs got up and wound her arms around Aaron's neck. 'And then I'll get ready with Celeste in her room and I'll meet you at the end of the aisle, Mr Ward. How does that sound?'

'Pretty fricking perfect,' he murmured, kissing her again. 'I'm gonna go get something to wear too. Unless it's okay for me to come like this?'

Aggs took in his cheeky grin, his pool T-shirt, his swim shorts. 'Works for me.'

'Right, that's it!' Celeste jumped up from the chair. 'Come on, Juliet. Put Romeo down and let's get going before I die of overexposure to all this fucking love stuff.'

Aggs kissed her fiancé again. Her fiancé! And in a few hours he'd be her husband. She still couldn't quite believe it. 'See you at seven o'clock?' she murmured, happiness oozing from every pore.

'See you at seven o'clock,' he repeated, their eyes locked, a promise passing between them. Every shred of doubt or worry about her parents' reaction was gone now. This was the man she was going to spend the rest of her life with and she knew, just felt deep in her soul, that this was right.

Unfortunately, her friend wasn't giving off the same vibe. Celeste tugged at the back of Aggs' T-shirt. 'Come on. Throw your stuff into your bag and let's go.'

Reluctantly, Aggs surrendered. She'd only brought stuff for a weekend, so it only took five minutes to pack it all. Aaron pulled on a fresh Tshirt and a changed his shorts, grabbed his wallet, and then walked down the corridor with them. At the lift, Aggs kissed him again as he left, before following a stomping Celeste along another branch of the hallway to her room.

Inside, it took less than a second for Celeste to make her feelings even clearer. 'What the hell was that about? Have you lost your mind?'

Aggs swallowed hard. She'd thought that Celeste's barbs back in the room were just her usual moans about PDAs and general cynicism about life, but now she could see that Celeste's reaction was so much more violent than she'd realised. 'Celeste, I know it's crazy...'

'It's fricking certifiable!'

'But please, please try to understand. I love him. This feels right. I need to do it and I want you to be happy for me.'

'So what, you're just going to move over here and be across an ocean from me?'

As soon as Celeste said it, Aggs got it immediately. Shit. Celeste's absolute worst nightmare was the feeling of being abandoned and now that's exactly what she thought Aggs was doing to her. No wonder she was losing it.

'Noooooo! I'm thinking you could move here, live with us, find a way to get a visa too. Celeste, they'd love you in LA and it's the best place on earth to get modelling work, maybe even acting, too. We'll work it out, I promise.' Aggs meant every word, but she could see that Celeste wasn't buying it.

Celeste threw down her bag and flopped onto the bed and Aggs knew better than to try to talk her round just yet. Give her time to calm down, let the temper subside, then she would make her see that this was a good thing.

'I just feel bad for your parents,' Celeste muttered.

Aggs knew that was only part of the story, but it gave her an idea. It was risky, but if it worked, it might at least get Celeste semi on board with this.

'I know, I do too,' Aggs admitted. 'But look, I'm going to phone them and tell them, and if they forbid it, I won't do it.'

Celeste pushed up on to her elbows.

'Seriously?'

'Absolutely.'

Aggs heart was thundering. *Come on, Mum and Dad, don't let me down.*

The phone at their flat above the café rang and rang. Aggs calculated the time. It would be about midnight there right now. Maybe they were already asleep.

Still ringing. Still ringing.

'Hello?'

Aggs immediately recognised the voice of Nancy, who worked the weekday morning shifts with her dad. Why would she be in her mum and dad's flat at this time of night? It didn't make sense.

'Nancy, it's Agnetha. Can I...'

'Oh, Agnetha, I... I... Oh my God. Your mum hoped you might call tonight. Made me stay here just in case.'

Aggs didn't get it. Nancy was practically hyperventilating and completely hysterical.

'Nancy, what is it? What's happened?' Aggs pleaded.

'It's your dad, Agnetha. We had a late function tonight – a birthday party for the councillor who... Oh, it doesn't matter. Anyway, he'd asked me to come in to help out and we'd just closed up, about nine o'clock, when he just collapsed right in front of me.'

Aggs buckled, bent double, as if she'd been punched in the gut.

'Nancy, where is he now? Where's my mum?'

In her panic, it took Nancy a moment to get the answers out.

'The ambulance rushed him to hospital and your mum went with him. She tried to phone you, but she said there was no answer at the last number she had for you. She'd already been calling it all day to wish you a happy birthday.'

A landslide of guilt almost consumed her. She hadn't called her parents on her birthday. With the time difference and all the drama, it had completely slipped her mind. And, of course, her mum couldn't reach her – the only number she had was for Aaron's apartment in LA. The landslide swallowed her whole, but still she could hear Nancy pleading.

'Oh, Agnetha, I don't know. I just don't know if he's... You need to get here, Agnetha. As soon as you can.'

Aggs dropped the phone.

Celeste, seeing that something was badly wrong, forgot her huff for a moment and jumped up. 'What is it?'

'I need to go,' Aggs blurted. 'It's my dad. He's collapsed.' She was panting between each breath, trying desperately not to scream. Her dad. Her wonderful, fabulous dad. *Please God, I'll do anything, just let him be okay. Let him be okay. Let him be okay.* Her brain went into repeat mode, no longer able to function.

Celeste picked up the phone. 'Nancy, it's Celeste. Tell Ella that we're on the way. We'll get back as soon as we can.' She hung up, and immediately threw her arms around Aggs. 'He'll be okay. He's got to be. Let's just worry about getting back.' She released her, and Aggs flew across the room and picked up her bag.

'A flight! I need to get a flight. There's a desk downstairs that arranges...' Her mind went blank, racing to keep up. 'Oh, fuck it, let's go.'

Bag over her shoulder, she ran out of the room, Celeste sprinting to keep up with her.

The lift felt like it took an hour to get to the ground floor, and they stormed out of it as soon as the doors opened.

At the travel desk, a smiley woman greeted them. 'How can I...?'

'My dad! I've just found out that my dad has been taken ill, and it's not good, and...' The tears were falling now.

Celeste stepped forward and cut to the chase. 'We need to get back to the UK now. Urgently. Can you help?'

The women's eyes widened. 'I usually only do excursions but...'

'Please help us,' Agnetha begged.

It was one of those situations where one human being feels another human being's pain and bursts into action. 'Hang on. My sister-in law works at the airport...'

She picked up the phone, dialled, explained the situation. Agnetha hopped from foot to foot, every second lasting a week.

'Okay. Okay, let me tell them that.' The guest services officer put her hand over the mouthpiece. 'There's one seat left on a flight to LA that leaves at 6.30 p.m.. If you can get to the airport in the next forty minutes, you'll just make it before they close the boarding. Then there's a flight to London leaving LAX two hours after you get there. She can book you on that too.'

One seat. Aggs didn't want to leave Celeste. She needed her friend with her, but her dad... she just had to get home to her dad.

'Yes! Please! I'll take it.'

'But...' Celeste began.

'Celeste, I have to! What if... what if...' She couldn't say it.

Celeste got it, knew what she was thinking. 'You're right. Let's go. Is your passport in that bag?'

Aggs tried to think, couldn't, so she ripped open the zip. It was there. Thank God. 'It's here.'

'Let's go! Thank you. Please book the tickets for Agnetha Sanders. Here's my credit card. Your receptionist took a copy of our passports when we checked in so all the details will be on there. Is that okay?'

The hotel employee nodded furiously. 'Yes! I'll make it happen. Go, go, go!'

The two of them dashed out of the hotel doors.

'I'm coming to the airport with you,' Celeste yelled, wrenching open the door of a waiting taxi before the uniformed doorman could even get near it.

The journey passed in a blur, Aggs willing the car to go faster, anxiety unbearable at every red light, every stop sign.

'Come on. Come on. Come on.' She said it over and over, willing them to get there.

They pulled up at departures with three minutes to spare, jumped out, Celeste throwing twenty dollars at the driver and not waiting for the change.

Still running, but... Fuck! A queue at the airline desk. She didn't have time. There was no way she was going to make it. Her legs went weak, she stumbled...

'Are you the girl from Caesars? My sister-in-law called...'

'Yes!' Aggs exclaimed to the suited check-in attendant who had appeared from a door behind the barriers.

'Okay, I got you. Come over here.' She beckoned her to a desk that was unopened, took her passport. 'Okay, Miss Sanders...' she said, reading the name as she input it into her computer.

That jarred something. Miss Sanders. Not Mrs Ward! She was bailing on her wedding and she hadn't even been able to explain why or kiss him goodbye.

'Celeste, can you go and find Aaron and explain what's happened? Tell him I'm so sorry. And please, please tell him... tell him I'll be back.'

'Don't worry, babe,' Celeste assured her. 'I'll make it all okay.'

The airline official handed back her passport, together with a boarding card. 'You're good to go. Through those doors there, through security, gate six.'

'Thank you. Thank you so much.' She grabbed Celeste. 'And thanks, Celeste. I love you.' She kissed her, then took off, running, Celeste's words ringing in her ears. 'I'll make it all okay,' she'd said.

20

HOPE

Update. I told him. He was lovely. Knows who my mum is. She's Scottish but they met in LA. Eeeeek! xx

Hope pressed send on yet another text sent while she was sitting on a loo, this time the one in Aaron's suite. This was becoming a habit today.

Maisie was straight back with a reply.

Wow. Was she an actress? I hope it's Tilda Swinton. I bloody love her.

No, not actress. Still finding stuff out. More later.

Can't stand this. I'm Netflix generation. Need everything in one binge.

Patience! Love you. Xx

Love you too. Just googled Tilda Swinton. You've got her chin. Xx

No one could make her laugh like Maisie.

Supressing a giggle, Hope texted her mum next.

All okay, Mum. Will call you soon to fill you in on everything. Love you. Xx

The reply came while she was washing her hands.

Love you too, sweetheart. xx

No matter who her biological mother was, Dora McTeer would always be her mum.

Back out in the lounge area of the suite, Aaron... nope, she still couldn't think of him as Dad... had just picked up the phone. 'I'm going to order more coffee. What can I get you?'

'Tea, please,' Hope replied, amused that he appeared to be pondering her request.

'Actually, I might join you on that. Time I started embracing my daughter's culture,' he said with a grin, before pressing a button and giving his order to room service.

Hope curled up on the sofa and watched him, fascinated by his mannerisms, his gestures, listening to his voice, and thinking she never wanted this day to end.

They'd left the restaurant half an hour ago, just after she'd asked him about how it ended with her mother. It was obviously tough for him to talk about, even all these years later. He'd hesitated. Squirmed a little. Then, at the moment he'd said, 'It's complicated,' the waiter had passed again, and asked them if they'd like anything else. That's when they'd realised they were the last people in the restaurant.

'Shall we just get the bill and have a break? Maybe a bit of fresh air?' she'd suggested, Aaron's visible relief telling her she'd made the right call. They'd been talking face to face for hours. Some heat on their skin and a Vitamin D boost would do them good.

Outside, they'd chatted about the weather (no, it wasn't always sunny like this), about Glasgow (yes, the architecture is stunning) and about her family (yes, her mum was supportive of her decision to find him) as they walked around the perimeter of the Blythswood Square gardens, passing the architecturally stunning Blythswood Square Hotel.

When they reached the Malmaison, Hope noticed the yellow Maserati that they'd almost rear-ended was gone. Presumably off to seek attention somewhere else. Enjoying the change of scenery, they'd cut into the centre of the park and sat on the grass for half an hour.

As they'd stretched out, Aaron had slowly shaken his head. 'I still can't believe I'm here. The closest I've come to Scotland was watching *Braveheart*.'

Hope had chuckled. 'We've moved on a bit since then. Although, I do insist that all new boyfriends wear blue face paint on a first date.'

That piqued Aaron's interest. 'Do you have a boyfriend now? Someone special?'

'I'm studying to be doctor and working thirty hours a week in a hospital,' Hope had deflected. 'There hasn't been time for romance since my first day of uni.' She didn't want to change the mood by revealing the other truth – it had been hard to strike up a relationship when she was hooked up to a chemo drip and focusing on staying alive.

'Tell me more about your boys,' she had prompted, moving the conversation back onto safe territory.

Straight away, he was off, telling her everything about these two great kids and Hope was glad they'd taken a break. His shoulders had lifted, he was smiling again, and she felt completely re-energised too.

'Can we take a photo?' she'd asked almost shyly.

'Yeah! Why haven't we done that already?'

'Probably because at least one of us has been in tears at all times today,' Hope had chirped.

He'd nodded, grinning bashfully. 'True. Man, it must be jet lag.'

'Sure, that's definitely what it is,' Hope had teased him as he bumped over to her on the lawn. 'It's well known that jet lag makes grown men cry.'

That's when he'd stuck his phone in the air and caught a snap of the two of them, heads together, laughing like someone had just told them the funniest joke ever. He'd airdropped it to Hope's phone. She'd thought about sending it on to Maisie but changed her mind, deciding that she just wanted to tuck her phone away and enjoy the moment.

They'd strolled back to the hotel when they were ready. 'Shall we just go and chill upstairs?' he'd asked, a welcome suggestion. At some point, Hope wanted to know the answer to her question about the end of his relationship with her mother, and going by his reaction earlier, it probably wasn't going to be something that he wanted to discuss in public. That was fine. They'd get there when he was ready.

The room service waiter left their teas on the coffee table, and Hope poured them both. 'How do you take it?'

Aaron shook his head. 'I've no idea. I never drink tea, only coffee. But your mum drank it all day long, and you drink it too, so I'm going with it. I'm a living-on-the-edge kinda guy.'

Hope found his self-deprecation amusing. 'Yep, you're so rock and roll. I feel like this is a major milestone in our relationship.' She went for milk, no sugar, the same way she took it, then watched as he took a sip.

'Not bad. I can live with it.'

'Yaaasssss! We're sucking you in to our ways,' Hope cheered.

This was the most bizarre day. One minute stressful, one minute sad, then funny, then loving, then easy, then hard... Now she was just hanging with her biological father in a hotel room. *Yep, that's him, lying on one side of the L-shaped sofa and I've got my knees pulled up under me, in my comfiest position, on the other side. No biggie.*

'She worked in a café.'

Hope was so deep into her incredulous train of thought that she had to rewind to make sense of it. 'Who did?'

'Your mum.'

Bugger. It should have been obvious.

She sat forward on the sofa, curiosity piqued. 'A café in Glasgow?'

His brow furrowed as he tried to nail down a memory. 'Yeah. Her parents owned it, I think.'

'Do you know what it was called?'

He rubbed his forehead as it creased in concentration. 'I don't think she ever said.'

Hope's spirits plummeted. 'Damn. There are thousands of cafés in Glasgow. And what are the chances of her still being there twenty-three years later? Pretty slim. I've just realised that I didn't ask you her surname.'

'Sanders. Agnetha Sanders.' He almost exhaled it, such was the sadness in the way he said it. Poor guy. Whatever had happened between him and her mum had obviously left scars.

Agnetha Sanders. Hope's right leg began to vibrate, the way it always did when she was getting anxious or excited about something. Agnetha Sanders.

Stay calm. Don't get carried away. Take it easy.

'Do you mind if I grab my iPad out of my bag and look it up?' It was blurted out in one big long urgent jumble of letters with no pauses in between.

He swung his legs off the sofa and sat forward. 'Let's do it.'

She was up, across the room and back in seconds. She sat next to him, fired up her iPad and went straight on to google.

Sanders. Café. Glasgow.

A hit.

'Holy crap!' she gasped.

Looking over her shoulder, Aaron was as shocked as she was. 'No way, it's there?'

'Yes, it's... Oh, no, hang on...' She stopped, her brain catching up with what her eyes were reading. The reference was in an article on West End Glasgow cafés of the past. *The past.* She read what it said.

The Sanders – 1955 – 2014. A family-owned business on Hyndland Road, passed down through the generations. Much loved through the decades for its speciality cakes and friendly atmosphere. Last owned by Alex Sanders (1945–2014).

'Yes! That was her dad's name. Alex.'

Hope let that sink in. 'So my... grandad... was this man, Alex Sanders?'

'I guess so.'

Wow. Another something to add to what she'd learned today.

'I wonder why it closed? Maybe there was no one else to pass it on to. Maybe my mum... I mean, do you think she could be... What if...?' She couldn't get it out, but the questions were screaming in her head. Was her mum dead? Had she missed her chance to meet her?

'Stop,' he said, realising exactly what she was thinking and putting his hand on hers to stop the spiral of where her head was going. 'There could be a hundred reasons that the place closed. Maybe it wasn't her thing. She was a trained pastry chef, so maybe she went on to do something else.'

'She was a trained pastry chef?' Another new fact. And how cool was that one.

Hope stared at the screen for a second, then had another go. Agnetha Sanders. A few hits, but most of them were abroad. There were a couple on Facebook though, so that was the obvious place to try next.

Beside her, she could hear Aaron's breathing getting quicker. 'Are you okay?'

'Yeah, great.' He shrugged casually. Hope knew a bluff when she saw it.

'I mean, are you okay with me doing this?'

'Honestly? My heart's thumping like a train and I could pass out at any minute, but I don't want you to stop.'

Hope gave him a cheeky wink. 'Jet lag again?'

He chuckled. 'Definitely gotta be jet lag.'

Back to the search. On to Facebook.

Agnetha Sanders.

Nothing in the UK.

Argh!

Next she tried just Agnetha and clicked 'People', then handed the iPad over to Aaron. 'Do you recognise her among that lot?'

He spent a few minutes scrolling through, Hope holding her

breath every time he clicked on a profile, waiting for a positive reaction. It didn't come.

'Nope. I know she'll have changed in twenty-odd years, but I don't think she's there.'

Hope groaned. 'Thing is, she'll be, what age...?'

'She was two years younger than me so she'll be forty-five.'

'Exactly. Forty-five – so I'm guessing she'll be married already so her name will be different and... What? Why are you staring at me like that? What did I say?'

'I'm an idiot. Damn, such an idiot. Why didn't I think...?'

'What?' The suspense was making her heartbeat race now.

'Today is the thirtieth, yes? It was an overnight flight so I didn't catch on, but today is the thirtieth of May.'

'Yes, but...'

'It's her birthday. Her forty-fifth birthday today,' he exclaimed, his excitement over this realisation making his eyes widen.

'No way!' Hope squealed as she threw her arms around him and hugged him, although she wasn't quite sure why. Because they had a lead? Because this would make Agnetha so much easier to find? Because there had to be something special in the fact that today, her biological mum's birthday, was the day that she met her biological father for the first time? That was just fate, laying it out there for them.

Right, what were their options? She knew there was a government records website, Scotland's People, that she could use. She'd seen that on a few of the many family search programmes she'd watched obsessively over the years. Probably start there.

She was about to click off Facebook when she had a thought.

She typed in;

Agnetha's birthday.

Nothing. It was always a long shot.

'What about forty-fifth birthday?' Aaron suggested.

Hope gave him a raised eyebrow of amusement.

'What? Is that a dumb idea? Look, I told you I don't do any of this stuff. If I wanna speak to someone, I call them up. I know – crazy, right?'

'It'll never catch on,' Hope deadpanned. Her fingers, however, were already at work.

Agnetha's 45th birthday.

If this worked she would...

One post. 'You have got to be kidding me.'

'What?' Aaron was gobsmacked. 'Did you get something?'

'I don't know, I...' She clicked on it, read it, then turned the screen so he had a full view of what it said.

To all friends, family and regular customers!

Tonight we're having a SURPRISE party to celebrate our lovely owner Agnetha's 45th birthday. If you love her, like her, or if she makes you a cup of tea more than once a week, you're very welcome! Cake supplied, but bring your own bottle!

7 p.m. The Ginger Sponge.

And, remember, it's a SURPRISE – anyone who spills the beans will be barred for life.

The two of them stared at the image, both dumbstruck. It was the same café that had been in the earlier article, the one that had closed down.

Hope was the first to find her voice. 'She changed the name of the café to The Ginger Sponge. And you're never going to believe this...'

Aaron slumped back on the sofa, put his hands behind his shaking head. 'Right now I'll believe anything.'

'I've been in there. I didn't recognise it earlier because it's been painted and has a different sign. I was in it once, meeting a friend for coffee.'

Hope forced her brain to flip through her memory bank. She couldn't pinpoint what day of the week it was, but she'd been served by a young girl and that was the only member of staff she could remember seeing. Definitely not anyone old enough to be her mother.

Hope scrolled up through the posts on the timeline. There were photos of the café, photos of the dishes they served, lots of them with a young woman in them, a pretty waitress with red hair. Could that be Agnetha's daughter? Were there more sisters or brothers out there? More scrolling... Stop.

A photo from a few weeks ago. It was from the 'Hyndland Kids and Coffee Club' and the café had been tagged in it. There was a group of women, all clutching children of various ages, and then another lady with a T-shirt that said 'The Ginger Sponge' across the front of it. Hope held her breath as she read the post.

Thank you to the fabulous Aggs at The Ginger Sponge for always making us so welcome. We love you! (And we love your cakes!)

Hope felt a little light-headed and she realised that she still wasn't breathing. She exhaled. Inhaled. Exhaled again. Then she held the iPad to out to Aaron again.

He leaned forward again, took it from her, stared at it for a few moments.

Hope could barely get the words out. 'Is that her?'

He stared for a few seconds more. Then finally, when she couldn't stand it a moment longer, he raised his eyes. 'That's her.'

There was a stunned silence, which Hope was the first one to break.

'So what will we do now?'

Aaron's grey eyes met hers. 'I guess before we do anything, I need to tell you what happened to us.'

6 P.M. – 8 P.M

21

AGNETHA

Aggs jumped out of the shower and chuckled as she caught her reflection in the mirror. She couldn't find a shower cap, so she'd shoved an Aldi bag on her head and twisted it around her hair to keep it dry. Somehow she didn't think it was a trend that would catch on. She grabbed one of her new, fluffy thick grey bath towels from her shiny chrome radiator and wrapped it around her body. The novelty of having her very own en suite after all these years would no doubt wear off eventually, but right now she was embracing the joy of it.

Humming to herself, she opened the door to her bedroom and...

'Aaaaargh! Jesus, what are you two doing here? You gave me a fright!'

Isla and Skye were both lying on her bed.

'We've come to help you get ready. And we've brought wine...' Skye held up a bottle of Prosecco.

'And we've brought music...' Isla wiggled her iPhone.

'And we've brought make-up because your make-up bag is like something that's been excavated from a time capsule,' Skye added, then gestured to Aggs' headwear. 'Do Aldi know you're endorsing their brand? I think Victoria Beckham wore the same thing last week.'

Aggs raised her chin and put her hand out, palm forward. 'If you two don't recognise fashion innovation when you see it, that's your problem.' She sat at the chair in front of her dressing table and slipped the Aldi bag off, still feigning aloofness. It was easy to do. She just channelled Celeste.

'What's that evil grin about then?' Isla asked suspiciously as she climbed off the bed.

Damn. She'd always been rubbish at hiding what she was thinking. 'Nothing,' she objected, with as much innocence as she could muster. 'Nothing at all.'

To Aggs' relief, Isla let the interrogation drop, more focused on getting the beautification session underway.

'Right, let's get started. What tunes do you want, madame?'

'Oooh, give us a bit of Shania.'

'Yaassss!' Amused by the choice, Isla turned to Skye. 'Want me to shoot you now?'

Skye rolled her eyes, disgusted. Isla and Aggs' love of country music was something that the older twin didn't share. She was definitely more of an indie rock listener. 'Please. Make it quick and aim for the ears,' Skye drolled. 'Tell you what, I'll go and get ready and you can get started on Mum. I'll swap with you as soon as I'm sorted.'

Aggs peered at her youngest. 'Get started with what?'

Isla pressed a button, 'Man, I Feel Like A Woman' blasted out, and then she danced over and stood behind her mum. 'We already said, we're helping you get ready, so just sit there, enjoy your wine and let the experts get to work.'

'God help me,' Aggs murmured, but her eyes were twinkling. This was bloody marvellous actually. She was forty-five. She had her girls. She had a lovely man who was about to whisk her off to Paris the following morning. That gave her a little jolt of anxiety, as she contemplated telling the girls and wondered if she should just get it over with and do it now.

No. She wanted to enjoy this moment for what it was – a fabulous, giggly interlude with her girls. She was being pampered and preened, and she was about to go out for a lovely dinner. Oh, and she didn't have a worry in the world, other than how to lose the half a stone that was stopping her from getting her skinny jeans on and the fact that she still had to pack for Paris and arrange cover in the café for Monday. Sod it, the new Aggs didn't care. She could go bootleg denim, she could get up an hour early in the morning and throw a few things in a cabin case, and Isla would be able to rustle up someone to help out on Monday. She had a few mates at uni who were always glad of the extra cash.

She did, however, have a quick work question. 'Are you sure Nasim and Sandra are fine with closing up on their own downstairs?'

Isla broke off from using a brush to apply Aggs' foundation, to practically shout over the sound of Shania. 'Absolutely! It's just the Menopausal Jogging Gang who are in...' she said, referring to a self-titled group of women who told their families they went out running every week, when they actually just strolled down to the café and drank tea and had a right old natter for a couple of hours. They usually came on a Saturday afternoon, but for some reason they'd asked Aggs if they could come later today. She was happy to accommodate them – even if it did mean keeping the café open a little bit later and an extra hour of wages for Nasim and Sandra. They'd promised they'd be out by seven, so Aggs could nip down and lock up on the way out to dinner.

Isla had been working away for a while when Aggs had a thought. 'Do not make me look like an explosion in a cosmetics factory, Isla,' she warned, her eyes closed now while Isla applied eyeshadow. 'I'm too old to wear too much make-up.'

'Mum! Gwen Stefani is older than you and she rocks a glam look.'

Aggs opened her eyes and looked up at her daughter. 'She also sleeps with Blake Shelton and I don't think I'll be doing that any time soon either.'

'Close your eyes!' Isla ordered, giggling. 'I'm nearly done.'

Aggs managed to blindly lift her glass to her lips. The wine was going down a treat.

'Okay, open them. Just the lips to do.'

Aggs did as she was told, loving every minute of this. She was desperate to look in the mirror, but Isla had draped a towel over it so she couldn't peek.

'Wine down,' Isla ordered, brandishing a lip pencil.

At that, Skye came through the door, closing it behind her. Aggs' newly mascara'd eyes took in the sight of her. 'Wow, you look gorgeous, darling! Even if there's a good chance you'll flash your knickers.' It was great to see Skye dressed up and not with her head stuck in a book. Maybe after her finals, she'd start going out more. Aggs didn't want her to get to forty-five and look back and see nothing but work. She wanted her girls to learn from her life, not copy it.

'They're nice knickers though, so I don't care,' her daughter retorted, swirling around in a body hugging pink dress that ended right below her bum.

'That's my girl,' Aggs chirped, loving Skye's attitude. Her daughters could wear what they wanted, when they wanted, and Aggs would cheer them on.

'You ready to swap?' Skye asked Isla.

Isla finished applying a last coat of lip gloss and stood back, surveying her work. 'Frigging gorgeous,' she decided, taking a bow. 'Right, your turn,' she told Skye. 'Don't mess up my masterpiece.'

Skye tutted and attempted a playful swipe, but Isla dodged it and dived out of the room. 'I'd never tell her, but she did a great job. You look fab, Mum.' Skye picked up a set of hair tongs that Aggs didn't recognise – one of them must have brought them – and a comb.

'Let's see if we can improve on Hair by Aldi,' she quipped, making Aggs choke on her bubbles.

By the time Isla reappeared, in a gorgeous emerald green halter neck jumpsuit, Skye was spraying hairspray and shaking Aggs' hair in at the roots, going back and forth like a consummate professional. Typical Skye. Always the perfectionist.

Isla tapped her watch. 'Right, Vidal Sassoon, let's get going. Table is booked for seven and it's five past already.'

Skye stood back, finally satisfied. 'Ready to see?'

Aggs felt ridiculously giddy. Must be the wine. 'As I'll ever be.'

With a dramatic flourish, Isla swept the towel away from the mirror. 'Ta da!'

Aggs froze. Couldn't move. Full system shutdown. She stared. Stared some more. Stared again. That wasn't her who was looking back, it was someone else, someone she vaguely remembered. A bit older for sure, but her eyes were bright, her cheeks were flushed and her hair was a fiery mane of glossy red waves.

'Nooooo, don't fill up, you'll wreck your eyeshadow!' Isla barked.

Aggs blinked away the droplets that had formed on her bottom lids. 'Girls, I can't believe what you've done. It's... it's...'

'Bloody gorgeous?' Skye offered.

'Bloody gorgeous!' Aggs blurted, their laughter even managing to drown out the final song on the Shania album. 'I love you two, I really do. And I'm so grateful that you're mine, you know that?'

The girls moved in for group hug. Isla kissed her on the cheek. 'We love you too, Mum.'

Aggs savoured the bliss of the moment. 'I just hope you're still saying that when you see my dress. Val made me buy it, I'm just warning you now. In fact, sit on the bed and close your eyes...'

Amused, they both did as they were told. Aggs pulled her new Spanx out of the drawer and wrestled her way into them.

'I've no idea what you're doing, but it sounds like you're either trying to change a duvet cover or you're jogging on the spot,' Skye said, sounding worried.

If only she knew. Changing a duvet cover would be easier.

Spanx on, Aggs took the dress from the wardrobe and slipped it over her newly sucked in shape. Off the shoulder, the top of the dress was covered in silver sequins down to the waist, where it became a black, figure hugging pencil skirt that finished just below her knees. Last week, when Aggs had tried it on during a shopping expedition with Val, she'd felt like a forties movie star.

'My God, Aggs, that clings in all the right places. If you don't get that, I'm shoplifting it and giving it to you for Christmas,' Val had joked, as they stood in the changing rooms of House of Fraser.

Aggs had been slightly nervous. She didn't do dresses. She didn't do legs. And she definitely didn't do expensive clothes. But she'd thrown caution to the wind that day. 'Okay, but only because I don't want you to have a criminal record,' she'd told Val, then rushed to the checkout before she changed her mind.

Now, she was glad that she had.

She stood in front of the girls and sucked in her stomach, just in case the Spanx were under pressure. 'Okay, you can look.'

Isla opened her eyes first. 'Oh my God, I'm the daughter of a disco ball!'

Aggs felt her confidence flop.

'And I fricking love glitter balls!' Isla added quickly. 'Mum, you are a goddess!'

'Really?' Aggs asked, needing a bit more reassurance. 'It's not too much, Skye?'

Skye got up and hugged her. 'Mum, it can never be too much. You're stunning.'

'Thanks, lovelies.'

'And if a plane needs to do an emergency landing on Hyndland Road, we can use you to guide them in.'

Aggs' cheeks were beginning to hurt with laughing, but she didn't care.

Okay, time for dinner. The truth was she'd have been just as chuffed with a takeaway on the couch as long as the girls were with her, but something different would be great too.

Isla finally flipped Shania off and they headed downstairs.

At the front of the three of them, Aggs listened for voices but couldn't hear anything. 'The Menopausal Jogging Club must have left. I'll just nip in and make sure Nasim and Sandra have locked up.'

She half expected a protest from one of the girls but none came. Now there was a birthday treat.

At the bottom of the stairs, she took a couple of steps in her gravity defying heels, then swung open the internal door to the café and...

'SURPRISE!!!!!!'

Aggs gasped. In front of her was a room full of beaming faces, streamers were flying, poppers were popping, hooters were hooting and there were balloons and tinsel everywhere.

Gobsmacked, Aggs turned back to see Isla and Skye clapping and cheering and everything suddenly made sense. The plans for dinner. The hair. The make-up. The very loud Shania. The strange booking by the jogging club – who were all, incidentally, over to her left, dressed in their finery and holding champagne flutes in the air.

Val and Yvie were right in front of her, Val in floods of happy tears, her first reaction to any emotion, happy or sad. Marge, Myra and the others from The Wednesday Club were there again too, for the second time today. But now they'd been joined by all her regulars and the friends she'd made as Isla and Skye grew up and she shared school runs and sleepovers. Face after familiar face. And as Isla pressed play on the café sound system and the opening bars of Abba's 'Dancing Queen' flooded the room, Aggs began to work her way round every person there, hugging them, kissing them, thanking them for coming, as they all congratulated her and wished her a happy birthday. It took half an hour just to get back to the girls.

'I can't believe you did this,' she told them, completely overwhelmed with gratitude and joy. 'It's everything.'

Skye was the first to kiss her, Isla next. 'You deserve it, Mum. We know what you've done for everyone. Now it's your turn.'

Her turn. Her time.

As she hugged the girls again, the thought took her mind back to a conversation earlier in the day. It was her turn. Tonight, she'd been planning to tell the girls about Will and drop the bombshell about her trip tomorrow.

She glanced searchingly around the room. Just like today at lunch time, before he'd finally wandered in, every other member of The Wednesday Club was there except him.

She tried to broach it casually. 'Girls, did you invite all of The Wednesday Club tonight too? I think there might be a couple missing.'

Isla was the first to answer. 'Mum, you're so bad at this!'

'At what?'

'At trying to pretend you don't have something going with Will,'

Isla drolled. 'Honestly, did you learn nothing about skilled subterfuge from our teenage years? Skye lied about shagging her study partner for years and I don't even want to break the news about Juan from the tapas restaurant up the road.'

Aggs was flabbergasted. Skye's study partner and Juan were a shock, but the major headline she gleaned from that was the comment about Will.

'How long have you known?' she asked them, not sure if she was more relieved or embarrassed. They knew – and they seemed happy about it. This was great.

'For weeks. Why do you think we disappear every time he's around? We spent over an hour camped out in the kitchen this afternoon so you could snog him after lunch. There's only so many games of "I Spy" that we can play in a small room.'

That set Aggs off. Tears of merriment and sides that – like her cheeks – were beginning to ache. Although, that might be the Spanx.

'He was invited, Mum, don't worry.'

At that, Val and Yvie joined the circle, passing out hugs and more flutes of champagne.

Aggs took the chance to peek around at the door. Will was invited. Everyone else was here already. So where was he?

22

MITCHELL

After dropping Aggs back off at the café, Mitchell drove straight home. It wasn't often that anything in his life surprised him, but this afternoon had definitely thrown in a couple of curveballs. Celeste's actions hadn't been a complete shock, but spending the last couple of hours with Aggs, finally putting their ghosts to rest, that had been unexpectedly wonderful.

Christ, what a fuck-up he'd made there. It would be easy to blame Celeste, but that was a cop out. He was the one who'd screwed around on his wife, and he wasn't going to try to shirk his culpability. That was all on him. The fact that Celeste had also betrayed her best friend was on her. Back in the beginning, he'd asked her once how she could have done that. 'Because I love you more than anyone else and you love me more than anyone else. This is our one life. I couldn't live it without you.'

He hadn't challenged her, because the truth was, that had been how he'd felt too. Or at least, how he'd thought he felt.

Would he do it again? For the hurt he'd caused Aggs and the girls, definitely not. But he wasn't going to whitewash the past either. He and Celeste had had some incredible years. They'd lived big, they'd partied, they'd had fabulous holidays and they'd built a beautiful home together. And that mattered to him. He was self-aware enough to know that he couldn't trade that for years with a wife who had had many bigger priorities than making sure that he achieved the career and lifestyle he'd always aspired to. He was also self-aware enough to know that he couldn't have done that without Celeste. The truth was, they were a formidable team who were greater than the sum of their parts.

He opened the door and listened for signs of life. There were none. She was still out then. He hadn't seen her car outside, but that wasn't unusual – she often put it in the garage at the back of the house if she wasn't going to be using it the next day.

He tossed his keys into the Wedgewood bowl that sat in the middle of the mirrored console table in the entrance hall. An aesthetic perfectionist, it drove her nuts when he did that, but hey... he wasn't exactly skipping through daisies today either. Childish, but right now, it felt like a small victory.

In the kitchen, he popped another antacid and made himself a coffee. The acid reflux wasn't a new thing. He'd suffered from it on and off for years and it always flared up in times of high stress. Too much coffee. Too much tension. Surely when your marriage was actually becoming detrimental to your health, it was time to call it a day? At this rate, he'd have an ulcer before he was fifty.

Mitchell pulled out a chair and took a seat at the marble kitchen table, a pile of Skye's books still lying open at the other end.

The question was, whether she was having an affair or not, did he want to stay with Celeste? Did he want to try to make it work and find their way back to a time when she didn't avoid him and he wasn't convinced that she was screwing someone else? He wasn't sure that he did. But, uncharacteristically, for someone who was usually so decisive and confident in his thoughts and actions, he wasn't sure that he didn't either.

What were the options? Divorce? God, the fallout from that would be massive. The disruption to their lives, the stress and there was no doubt that she'd take him for everything she could. The money wasn't what was bothering him right now though.

Was he really going to call it quits with Celeste without trying to sort things out? Would he look back, probably from the bar in some singles club filled with fifty-somethings who'd had midlife crisis divorces, and regret giving up so easily?

Of course, trying to get their marriage back on track was based on the optimistic possibility that she wasn't actually lying through her teeth to him every time she left the house. If she really was shagging notorious bachelor Derek Evans, they were done. No question. No going back.

There was a noise in the hall, the sound of the door opening, then heels on the tile floor. She'd be passing the bowl on the console table and gritting her teeth by now.

He wondered if she'd bypass the kitchen and go straight upstairs, but the heels got louder until she appeared in the doorway. He searched her reaction for some flicker of guilt or – worse – a sign that she'd seen him in the hotel today, but there was nothing obvious.

'Oh. Hi, darling. What are you doing sitting in here on your own?' Surprised, yes – suspicious, no. She was acting like there was nothing strange at all about the fact that she'd wandered in at... His eyes went to the kitchen clock... half past six on a Saturday evening, after going for what was supposed to be an introductory lunch with a new client. Had she even remembered that they were supposed to be over at the café for Aggs' surprise party at 7 o'clock? It took Celeste at least an hour to get ready to go anywhere, so that wasn't happening. He knew she'd deliberately come home late so that they didn't have to spend as much time at the party. In a way, he understood, because it wasn't her crowd. As long as they managed to pitch up at some point, they'd fulfil their promise to the girls to be there.

'Just waiting for you. How did the meeting go?' Easy does it. Nonchalance and non-confrontation.

'Really well. I definitely think we'll get the business.'

He stuck with casual interest. 'I don't doubt it for a second. Was it with anyone I'd know?'

She picked up mail from the worktop nearest the door and started to flick through it. That set off alarm bells. Classic subconscious diversionary tactic.

'It was actually with the chairman of a sports company. They own a soccer academy near Marbella and want to stage a launch to promote it in the UK. You know football isn't my thing, but this is a great chance to dip my toe in a new sector.'

She put the mail down and took her shoes off one by one, then slipped her jacket off and draped it on the back of the chair.

'Only thing is, darling, they want me to go over to Marbella next week to see their facilities and exactly what services they offer.'

The pulse in the side of Mitchell's jaw throbbed as he clenched his teeth together to stop himself reacting. *Do not show your hand. Do not give her reason to think you're doubting her. Bide your time... but don't quite let her off the hook with this.*

An idea came into his head and he forced a smile. 'You know, I don't have a lot on at work next week, so I could take a few days off and come with you. We used to have some great times over there.'

It was a lie. He had a case starting next week and there was no way he could take time off, but she didn't know that because it had been months since she'd shown any interest in his work. He'd only said it to get a reaction and there it was – a furrow, a line on her forehead between her eyebrows that even her Botox couldn't stop.

To her credit, she recovered quickly, came around to his side of the table, kissed him on the head on the way to the wine fridge, where she took out a bottle of rosé and poured a healthy measure into a glass the size of a small fishbowl.

'Darling, I'd love that, but I'm only going for a couple of days and there's a packed agenda – I won't have any time off at all. Let's wait and take a trip when we can devote some quality time to each other. I'll get my diary later and we can lock down dates. Right, I'm going up for a shower and a lie down. I'm exhausted.'

The perfect brush off, but he wasn't having it. 'Have you forgotten that we've got Aggs' party tonight? We're already late, so we'd better get a move on.'

Going to the party without Celeste would raise questions, especially with the girls, and he didn't want that kind of attention until he knew exactly where he stood and what he wanted to do with his future.

She screwed up the muscles in her face that hadn't been expensively frozen. She was definitely beginning to have a look of someone who was teetering on the edge of having too much work, but, of course, he wasn't going to tell her that. She'd never forgive him and, frankly, it was up to her. 'Urgh, do we really have to go?'

Irritation bristled. Here she went again. She didn't want to do something so she was trying to get out of it, even though he'd said it was important to him to be there. Christ, how had he managed to go from being married to the most selfless woman on earth, to the most selfish? And why was this bothering him more than ever? ·

'Yes. I don't want the girls wondering where you are.'

She rounded on him, eyes blazing. Once upon a time he'd found her meteoric temper sexy, but no longer. 'Why am I never the priority? Why does it matter more what they think than me?'

Mitchell couldn't believe what he was hearing. '*You're never the priority*? Are you kidding me? Do you have some kind of selective amnesia, Celeste?' His voice lowered, his words became clipped. Years of arguing in court had taught him that when you raised your voice it showed a lack of control, so he became more measured, more succinct when he was angry. 'I left my family for you. Wasn't that enough?'

'And you've never let me forget it,' she spat back.

There it was. The old argument she trotted out every time things got rough between them.

Again, Mitchell had two choices: rise to it or concede for now and keep everything as normal as possible until he chose the moment to change the situation on his terms. The logical side of his brain took over. His terms. And that meant defusing things now until he was ready.

It took a massive effort to soften his tone to something more conciliatory and loving. 'You know that's not true, Celeste. I chose you then and I still choose you now.'

Until a couple of months ago, that was absolutely true, but now it was a completely different state of play. She was lying. He was almost sure of it, but he needed proof. Not only would conclusive evidence convince him that he was right and it was over, but he also needed bargaining power if they were going to divorce.

His words extinguished the fire that was blazing in her eyes and he watched as her body language surrendered. 'Okay, let's just get it over with.'

Was she referring to the party or their marriage?

Mitchell thought back again to a couple of hours ago, to the way he felt when he was with Aggs, and wasn't sure what he wanted the answer to that question to be.

Had he made the wrong decision when he left Aggs ten years ago?

And was it too late to make it right?

23

Celeste watched the plane take off, just to be sure that it went and that Agnetha didn't come rushing back through. One seat. Why did it only have one seat left? She'd have gone with her in a heartbeat, although, it would wreck her plans to prepare for the call-back for the Next campaign, so it probably wasn't the end of the world.

Poor Alex. Celeste loved Agnetha's parents. They were the only people who had ever stepped up to care for her. Agnetha didn't know how lucky she was. Loving parents. Loving grandparents. Great life. Celeste had none of that. Her family had been a complete shitshow and even thinking about them now gave her a toxic taste in her mouth.

The temperature was beginning to drop pretty dramatically by the time she jumped in the taxi to get back to the hotel. Okay, she had to think about this. There was no ignoring the silver lining here – the fricking fiasco of a wedding couldn't go ahead now. They'd dodged a bullet there for sure.

Although... she heard Agnetha's parting shot in her head. *'Tell him... tell him I'll be back.'*

The reality was that this was just a temporary delay. No doubt

Aggs would be straight back over here as soon as her dad was well again, and the wedding would be right back on track. Where would that leave Celeste? Still in London. Still on her own. And missing a friend who was 4,000 miles away snuggled up with her new husband.

No. It wasn't happening, and it wasn't just for her sake. Alex and Ella would be devastated if Agnetha moved to LA, and Celeste would lose her link to them too. And what if it didn't work out? Aggs had fallen hard and fast in love before and it always blew itself out – it was just a matter of time before this did too, and by then she might have uprooted her whole life and be left up shit creek.

If it was going to be down to her to take care of everyone here, then that's what she was going to do. She just wasn't quite sure how she was going to manage to do it.

The doorman opened the cab door and she climbed out, not bothering to give him a tip. It wasn't as if she was going to need anything from him in the future – they were heading back to LA the next day.

In the lift, she ran through options for the speech she was going to have to give Aaron, contemplating the pitfalls and consequences of a dozen different ideas. He was the kind of chivalrous guy who would go bloody chasing after Aggs, so she had to make sure that wouldn't happen. At the same time, she had to find a way to make sure that if she was liberal with the truth, that it never got back to Aggs.

Think, Celeste. Think.

The doors pinged open and she checked her watch. Quarter to seven. Maybe he'd still be in his room getting ready. Okay, now or never.

Game face on, she half walked, half ran down the psychedelic-carpeted corridor to his room and banged on the door.

No answer.

She banged again.

Still no answer.

Bollocks. He must already be down at the wedding chapel. And, holy feck, he had invited everyone at the pool this afternoon to attend the wedding.

There was only one thing to do here and as she glanced down at her clothes she realised that she wasn't doing it in the vest and shorts that she'd thrown on over her bikini after they'd been at the pool today.

Taking off at a sprint, she ran to her room, threw her clothes off and pulled herself into a teeny thong, followed by a red stretchy bodycon minidress that was lying scrunched up in her case. She was glad she'd packed it because as soon as she pulled it on, the elasticated fabric lost all its creases and looked great. She shoved her feet into her matching scarlet shoes, then checked out her face and hair in the mirror. No time for make-up, but with her tan and the eyelash tint she'd just got last week, she could carry off just a quick slash of red lipstick. Hair. No time to do anything special. She sprayed some water through it, then combed it back off her face, letting it fall down her back. The total transformation took less than ten minutes. She grabbed the evening purse she'd used the night before, threw her cigarettes in it, sprayed some Chanel No 5 into the air and then walked through the mist on the way to the door.

She wasn't someone who ever got nervous, but the lift downstairs seemed to last way longer than it ever had before. Could she do this? Could she really go through with it? And would it work?

Celeste had been there when the manager had offered Aaron and Aggs the use of the Tuscana, which he'd told them was the middle sized of the hotel's three wedding chapels, so she followed the signs, eventually turning a corner to hear a buzz of conversation coming from an open set of double doors.

At the entrance, she stopped, wondering if her legs were going to hold her and get her through this. There were at least forty people in there, some of them still dressed in T-shirts and swimshorts, many of them looking like they'd had a few too many cocktails. One rather large gent appeared to be wedged in a rubber ring and there was an inflatable alligator propped up against the wall to the left. The back row on the right-hand side consisted of one long line of elderly women that Celeste had never seen before in her life. Perhaps gatecrashing weddings was all part of the tourist experience for Betty and Bunty from... she caught the wording on one of their T-shirts – Betty and Bunty and their chums from Missouri.

There was a moment of doubt as she wondered if she was in the wrong place, but then, at the end of the aisle, a figure stepped forward and turned to see if the change in volume in the room was due to the arrival of his bride.

Even when he saw that it was only Celeste, his expression didn't change, clearly waiting for Agnetha to walk in behind her bridesmaid. His eyebrows raised, his smile wide, Aaron had scrubbed up so well. He was wearing smart black trousers, with a beautifully cut white shirt, open at the neck, a self-tying bow tie left loose, and a tuxedo jacket that somehow managed to stretch across his wide shoulders, yet tapered in like Tom Ford had run it up on his kitchen table to Aaron's exact measurements. Celeste's first thought was that, ironically, the guy who had absolutely no interest in the LA movie industry other than the occasional trip to the cinema was standing there looking like the leading man in any great romcom.

Celeste's scarlet shoes refused to move as, for a split second, she wondered what it would feel like to have a guy like that waiting at the end of an aisle for her. Someone who'd chosen her. Who loved her so much he wanted to spend every day of the rest of his life with her. Someone who would promise, in front of a room full of people, that he would never leave her.

Walking down there towards him wasn't an option. It would be the ultimate catwalk, more important than any of the dozens she'd walked down in her career, but for once the thought of all those gazes on her was too much. Instead, she beckoned to Aaron to come towards her.

The shadow of a frown crossed his face as the energy in the room flipped from buoyed-up anticipation to confusion, with an overtone of foreboding.

As she watched him walk towards her, Celeste's resolve and the words she'd practised in her head failed her. It was all too risky. Too many things could go wrong. She'd promised Aggs that she would make it okay, and that's what she should do, but...

She'd lose her. She would lose her best friend to the other side of the Atlantic. Aggs' crazy idea about Celeste coming here too was just that – a crazy idea. She was realistic enough to know that she wouldn't get a visa to live here, and even if she did, she was just one pretty girl in a city awash with stunning faces. This wasn't where she belonged and Aggs didn't belong here either.

She took a few steps backwards out of the room, forcing Aaron to come just a little further and taking him out of the eyeline of the guests inside.

'Celeste, what's happening?' His eyes darted around the corridor. 'Where's my girl?'

This was it. Last chance to decide. *Make it all okay, Celeste.*

'Oh God, Aaron, I don't know how to tell you this, but...'

'What?'

'She left. She went home.'

Aaron's reaction was the polar opposite to the one she was expecting. He laughed, his gaze still searching, as if he was waiting for Agnetha to jump out and admit they were punking him. 'Yeah, sure. Course she did.'

Celeste felt everything inside her clench with tension. Again, she questioned herself – could she go through with her plan? The answer was that she had to.

'Aaron, I'm sorry, but it's not a joke. She left. She's gone home. She got the last seat on a flight out half an hour ago.'

He froze, searching her face for clues as to what was going on and finally letting the words sink in. Then there was an achingly slow, painful understanding of what she was saying. He took a step backwards, his hands on top of his head as if they were trying to stop his brain from exploding.

'But... but why?'

This was the moment. Now or never. Do what was best for her, for Aggs' parents, for Aggs too. She was saving her from herself. If she told him the truth, that the only reason she'd gone home was because her dad was sick, then he'd go racing over to be with her like a knight in shining armour. It had to be final. There had to be no going back. She hadn't quite worked out how to make that happen yet, but right now, her priority was making sure that he didn't jump on the first plane to the UK tomorrow morning.

'She called her parents and she found out that her dad was taken ill today...'

'Oh my God, is he okay? What happened to him?'

Thinking on her feet, she decided to minimise the panic and maximise Agnetha's doubt. It was the only way to stop him running after her.

'I don't think it's anything too serious...'

'Then why didn't she wait? I'd have gone with her; I'd have found a way to get us there.'

Celeste put her hand up to stop him speaking. 'Aaron, that's the thing. You see, Aggs is really close to her mum and dad, and I think... to be honest, I think it gave her a fright. It was a reality check. It made her realise that she could never leave them, that she could never come and live here. Her mum and dad needed her home and that was the only place she wanted to be. She didn't want to hurt you by dragging it out though, but she realised she'd lost her senses agreeing to get married this morning. She's gone home. The wedding is off. She changed her mind.'

'What? So I've just to let her go? Just forget I ever met her?'

'I know it's hard, but she asked me to tell you to leave her be, to let her go.'

He sagged against the wall, as if his legs wouldn't hold him up any longer.

'So that's it? I just have to wait? I can't contact her, can't go see her? We're just...' He couldn't say it. 'I can't believe she'd do this. I mean, I get that she'd want to go home to see her dad, but...'

Celeste felt a cold chill of remorse. It was all too obvious that she was breaking this guy's heart. But it was better that than Aggs' heart being broken down the line when this didn't work out.

'You know, I don't even have her phone number back home. How crazy is that? I was about to marry someone and I don't even know their phone number.'

'She asked me not to give it to you,' Celeste said dolefully. Christ, if this was an audition for chief bitch, the role would be hers. For the first time, she was thankful that they couldn't afford to use their mobile phones in the USA so they hadn't even brought them with them. 'I'm so sorry, Aaron. I really am. Look, let me go and get rid of that lot in there and then how about we grab a drink? You head to the bar and I'll meet you there in ten minutes.'

He didn't answer, so she took that as a yes.

The guests in the wedding chapel all turned to look at her expectantly when she appeared in the doorway again. She briefly made eye contact with Mr UCLA, and immediately averted her gaze. Tonight was complicated enough. She walked to the front of the aisle, and spoke to the celebrant, who had taken a seat, waiting for the happy couple to get a move on.

'I'm sorry, but I'm afraid there's been a change of plan and the wedding won't be going ahead. Would you please take care of, erm, notifying the guests?'

The consummate professional – he was well into his sixties, and Celeste guessed he'd probably seen everything in his job – the gentleman agreed without hesitation.

'Ladies and Gentlemen, I'm afraid...'

Celeste didn't hang about to hear his explanation. Instead, she practically sprinted back down the aisle and went straight to the bar.

Aaron was already there, sitting on a leather stool with a spirit glass in front of him. Celeste hid her surprise. He wasn't much of a drinker and she'd only ever seen him knock back a few beers. When she'd left her room, she wasn't sure she could go through with the plan that she'd come up with, but stage one had been a success. Tell him the wedding was off. Make sure he didn't go after Aggs.

Now she just had to go through with the second stage. And ironically, she knew the fact that he was already drinking was going to give her more of a chance of pulling it off.

'You've started without me,' she said, trying to ignore the genuine remorse that she was feeling. Drastic actions were necessary to protect the people she loved. And sometimes, the good guys like Aaron got hurt. That was just a sad fact of life.

What she was about to do was necessary to keep her friend and stop Aggs making a horrendous mistake. And right now, that was all that mattered.

Hope's chin felt like it was lying on the purple and grey carpet of the hotel suite.

'Wait, so...' She tried to take it in. 'She jilted you at the altar, and you never spoke to her again? Never saw her again after that? You just... let her go?'

Aaron was rubbing one hand across the top of his head and she wondered if that was another of his mannerisms, something he did when he was stressed or exasperated.

'I know it seems crazy now, but you gotta understand... it was a different time back then. There was no Facebook or social media. We didn't use internet the way we do now. Your mom's cell phone didn't even work in the USA. Shit, that all sounds like excuses...' He took a sip of his tea, then put the mug back on the table. 'The truth is, she left and I accepted it. It had been a one day proposal, a crazy gesture at the end of a whirlwind romance, and I guess I understood why she decided she couldn't leave her family back in Scotland. Her friend...'

'What was her name again?' Hope interrupted. He'd mentioned it in the telling of the story, but Hope had been so gobsmacked by the whole 'jilting at the altar' thing that she hadn't taken in a lot of the smaller details.

'Celeste. Her name was Celeste. She was so definite about Agnetha changing her mind and realising that I was a mistake, that... Christ, I was a fool, and I'm so, so sorry, but I let Agnetha go. Celeste returned to LA with me, packed up their stuff and left a few days later. I just licked my wounds and got on with my life. Thought about her every day for the longest time. I used to lie in bed in the morning and hope that I'd open my eyes and she'd be there. Or that there would be a knock on the door, and I'd find her there, back to say she still loved me, but it never happened. Couple of years later, I met my wife, moved on... I figured that Agnetha did too. Just wasn't meant to be.'

Hope put her hand out, palm upwards, on his knee and he immediately accepted the gesture, wrapping his fingers around hers. It was a story that was going to take her a while to digest, and she'd need to hear it a couple of times more, but there was something in there that touched her deep in her soul – her mum and dad had loved each other. Even if it was just for a short time, and they hadn't made it to the happy ever after, they'd loved each other for a while and there was something beautiful about that.

They sat in silence for a few moments, both of them lost in their thoughts, until the buzz of Hope's phone made them both jump.

IS IT TILDA???? Think you've got her ears too. Xx

Despite being in a shock fuelled daze, the corners of Hope's mouth lifted. 'It's my sister. She's asking if my mum is Tilda Swinton. That's one of her favourite actresses, so I can't help thinking I'm about to crush her dreams. I'll reply in a minute, because otherwise she'll spend the rest of the night texting for details. To be honest,

I've been texting her from toilets all day because I didn't want to interrupt our conversations.'

Aaron squeezed her hand. 'I like that she's looking out for you.'

'Me too.'

His eyes were glistening. 'And I'm sorry. I really am.'

'For what?'

'For not trying harder. That day... how it ended...' Hope couldn't bear the pain that she saw in every crevice of his face. 'It will always be my biggest regret. But what I don't understand is why she didn't tell me about you? I mean, she could have written, could have come back, even if she'd changed her mind about me – and I get that – but I would have wanted to know. I could have supported her, helped her.'

'Would you have respected her decision to have me adopted?'

That one winded him. 'I don't know for sure, but... I don't think I could have.'

'Then maybe that's your answer,' Hope said gently. 'Maybe, for whatever reason, it was the right thing to do for her, and she knew you wouldn't agree. Maybe that's why she never told you.'

He nodded dolefully. 'Maybe.'

Hope threw her arms around him and hugged him. 'Please don't feel bad. How could you have known?' She pulled back, seeing that this was shredding him and desperate to say something to console him. 'You know, I've spent my whole life wondering why I was adopted, but I learned to accept it and appreciate the outcome instead of driving myself crazy with "what ifs" and "whys". Right now, a part of me wants to rage because she stood you up, then didn't tell you about me, and abandoned us both, but the reality is that she must have had her reasons and we can't judge her without understanding what those were. I think we have to do this without tearing ourselves up about things that could have been done differently. I've had a great life, with a wonderful family who have loved me more than I could ever have asked. You need to forgive yourself, because there's really nothing to forgive. What happened in the past is done with. All that matters to me now is that we've found each other and that...' she paused, deciding to lighten the moment, '... and that you seem to be a pretty cool guy. For a dad. Even if you're only pretending to like the tea.'

It worked. A few years lifted from him. 'How'd you get so smart?'

'I take after my mother,' she quipped, taking the final sledge-hammer to the tension and getting them back on emotionally stable ground. This wasn't the time for the honest answer to his question. She knew that her strength and her ability to move forward through challenges came from her illness. Living with cancer so young had given her an extraordinary capacity to compartmentalise worry and anxiety, to put the tough stuff in a box and focus on making it through to the end result. It had made her stronger and developed the most dominant trait of her personality – it had showed her the power of hope. Her mum, Dora, had picked her name because she loved it. She had no idea how relevant it would be to her daughter's life.

'Don't forget to text your sister,' he prompted, making Hope jump.

'Crap! She'll already have called my mum...' she caught herself, '... my *other* mum, to say I must be missing and to notify authorities.'

Snatching up the phone, she typed a quick reply.

Aaron got up and headed to the bathroom and she heard the sound of a tap running. She guessed he was splashing water on his face. Poor guy must be exhausted. Sixteen hours of travel and then the most emotionally draining day ever. Maybe she should go and take this back up again tomorrow. In the meantime...

Not Tilda. Sorry. Her name is Agnetha

Fuuuuuuuuuuckkkkkkkkkkkk! The one from ABBA? That's why we saw
Mamma Mia six times!!!!! Your subconscious knew!!!!

Nope, not ABBA. She worked in a café

Oh. Bummer. But so many questions... X

Wanna see a pic of Aaron first?

Yaaassssss!

Hope sent the selfie they'd taken earlier in the gardens.

Oh. My. God. He's the spitting image of Tim McGraw!

Who?

TIM McGRAW!!! Legend! Ask yer new dad if he can take you back to
USA cos I've just disowned you

Hope quickly googled his name and saw that he was a country
superstar. That explained it. Country music had never been her
thing, but Maisie had donned a blonde wig to play Tammy Wynette
in a tribute show. 'Stand By Your Man' was now her first shower
song every morning and other country stuff blasted from her
speakers all day long.

Studying the images of Tim McGraw now though, Hope could
see that Maisie had a point. Same body shape. Same colouring.
Same jawline.

'My sister thinks you look like Tim McGraw,' she announced as he came back into the room, drying his face and rubbing his hair with a towel. She'd been right.

'Yeah, I get that a lot. Until I open my mouth. I sing like a jacked-up exhaust pipe. How about you?'

'I've been banned from karaoke because my singing is considered a form of torture.'

He sat back down on the sofa. 'Sorry about that. Definitely got that from me.'

Hope rolled her eyes, feigning disappointment, but his words took her mind elsewhere. What did she get from her mother? Did she look like her? It was hard to tell from the slightly fuzzy pic. Did she sound like her? Walk like her? Did she have the same heart, the same habits? Did they share more than just DNA? How crazy was it that she'd found her so quickly and it was all thanks to an unusual first name and her job in a café.

'You look deep in thought there,' Aaron's soft California accent was loaded with care.

'I was thinking about my mum and whether I'm like her.'

'You're smart and you're funny – she was both of those things.'

Hope wondered whether she should be honest about where her thoughts were going and then heard herself blurt it out. 'I need to meet her.'

A flinch from Aaron. That was completely understandable. This was someone who'd broken his heart and who had now brought him to the biggest shock of his life. It went without saying that there would be conflicted feelings, and fears and anxieties.

'I know you do. I'd like to come with you, but if it's something you'd rather do on your own I completely understand. You tell me how you want to play this. I'll do it any way you want.'

The answer came immediately. 'I'd like you to come with me, but only if you're sure. I know it won't be easy.' Hope was falling over her words, keen to give him a way out if it would be too tough.

'Honey, I haven't been here for you a single day of your life. I wanna change that now.'

A rush of gratitude led to another hug. 'Thank you.' She sat back, thinking how much more tired he looked now than when she'd met him this morning. The very last thing she wanted to do right now was leave, but she was very aware he'd gone more than twenty-four hours without sleep. 'Okay, let's work out a plan tomorrow. I'm thinking I should let you get some rest. You must be exhausted and...'

'Why tomorrow?'

That caught her off guard. Was it too soon? Did he need more time to psyche himself up for this? Again, that was understandable. She had to rein herself in, take this at a steadier pace.

He didn't wait for an answer. 'Why not tonight? Didn't that Facebook post say where she was gonna be?'

'Yes, but...' Hope suddenly felt her confidence go. 'We can't just march into her birthday party and do jazz hands and announce she's my mother. Her family will be there. Her friends. I'm probably a secret that she's kept from the day she had me. She has to process the fact that I've found her, and we have to be prepared for the possibility that she might want nothing to do with me. Not to mention you,' she added truthfully. 'And to be honest, that's pretty likely, given that she stipulated a closed adoption with no further contact. Pretty much suggests that she doesn't want to be traced.

Hope had had years to think this situation through and prepare for it, but she was aware that he'd only had a week and it was best to lay out her fears and the potential consequences. Just because their reunion had been as wonderful as she could ever have dreamt, didn't mean that it was going to be that way with her mother too. This had to be taken carefully. Thought through.

'You're right. I hear you. But I gotta be honest. There's no way

I'm sleeping tonight and I feel like I need to get out of this hotel room.'

Hope suppressed a cheer that he didn't want her to leave.

'How about we go see where she is? I've thought about it so many times over the years that I'd kinda like to see it for myself. We won't go in, because you're right, it takes time. Maybe we can grab some dinner while we're out.'

It made sense. Kind of. And Hope had to admit, curiosity was killing her too. A drive by, that's all. What harm could that do? But...

'Bugger, I've had a couple of glasses of wine. I can't drive.'

His surprise was obvious and made her chuckle.

'Scottish drink-driving laws. One glass of wine. We're strict about this stuff here.'

'Wow, okay. I kinda like that too,' he admitted. 'How about we take a cab?'

Hope nodded. That was a possibility, but... a much better idea came to her.

'You know you said you couldn't wait to meet my family?'

'Yeah.'

'Why don't we ask my sister to join us for dinner? I'm sure she'd be happy to drive...'

Two birds with one stone. And it would stop her having to spend way too much time texting in toilets.

'Great idea.'

Hope picked up her phone.

Hey, wanna join us for dinner and be our designated driver? xx

HELL YEAH!!!! Tell Tim McGraw I'm on my way!

8 P.M. – 10 P.M

'Are you enjoying yourself, Mum?' Isla shouted over the strains of Aretha Franklin's 'Respect'. All the tables in the café had been shoved against the walls to form a makeshift dance floor in the centre and Aggs had been swinging her Spanx for the last hour.

The café was absolutely packed, with people in every corner, sitting on every surface, mingling out in the corridor and even behind the counter. It had spilled over to the tables and chairs that had been placed outside too, so there was a mini street party going on out there.

Aggs wrapped her arms around Isla's shoulders. 'I'm having the time of my life, sweetheart. I can't thank you and your sister enough for this.'

'You're welcome, Mum. I'm glad you're enjoying it. We were a bit worried because we know you hate surprises.'

Aggs kissed her on the cheek. 'This is perfect, though. In my favourite place, with everyone I love, so I'll let you off.' Everyone she loved, but not quite – Will still wasn't there.

Before Isla could answer, Aggs saw her daughter's gaze dart to the door and realised there was a new arrival. Her heart began to race. Was he here? Had Will made it?

'Oh, oh, incoming. Enemy advancing. Take cover and evasive action,' Isla parroted in her best army voice.

Aggs' spirits sank. Not Will then. In fact, she knew exactly who it was before she even looked. Yep, it could only be...

'Hello, Isla. Happy birthday, Aggs.'

Aggs turned round and came eye to eye with Celeste, immediately adopting the special face she'd developed just for dealing with her former best friend. On the outside it was smiling and perfectly civil, but on the inside it was shooting invisible laser darts that could set Celeste's hair extensions on fire, explode her face fillers and pierce her silicone boob implants. Of course Celeste and Mitchell would be here. The girls would have invited them because for the last ten years she'd made a gargantuan effort – and yes, it was bloody hard – to act like she and Celeste were perfectly chummy for the girls' sake. Although, frankly, she was surprised Celeste hadn't tried to get out of it. Both women knew that under the surface, there was no love lost there.

Aggs took the small gift bag that Celeste was holding out to her. It would be something ridiculously expensive, that they both knew Aggs wouldn't use. Jo Malone perfume perhaps. Or maybe a voucher for an extortionate spa, the kind of place where everyone did colon cleanses and ritual chanting, and left Aggs desperate to smuggle in a bottle of wine and a six-pack of pickled onion crisps.

It went without saying, too, that Celeste would absolutely be looking down her nose job (oh yes, it was a different one and Aggs had the old photos to prove it) at this party. For Celeste's fortieth, Mitchell had thrown an exclusive soiree at an eye wateringly expensive private club in the city, for three hundred of Celeste's closest friends. Unfortunately, Aggs hadn't made it due to a bout of completely fabricated norovirus. Afterwards, Skye let it slip that her dress was Armani, the catering cost more than Aggs made in a year, and Celeste planned almost every detail herself, then acted surprised when Mitchell delivered her to the room full of illustrious guests. Agh, what a load of nonsense.

However, as always, Aggs reminded herself that keeping things civil wasn't for her own benefit. Inside, she'd be lying if she didn't admit that she despised Celeste because she'd hurt her kids, her parents, and of course, Aggs too. In many ways, her betrayal was worse than Mitchell's because she was considered a sister, the person who would always have her back no matter what. And although they'd apportioned more blame to Mitchell because he'd broken up the family, her parents had never forgiven Celeste, refusing to speak to her again for the rest of their lives. Agnetha had been more pragmatic. This woman was her daughters' stepmother whether she liked it or not (and she didn't), so they'd maintained a polite front and she wasn't going to be the one to break it now. Unless, of course, Mitchell was right about Celeste having an affair, in which case she'd probably put up bunting and hire a brass band to celebrate the cow being out of their lives.

Speaking of which... Mitchell moved in and hugged her, and for a second she felt something inside her give a weird burst of recognition. He was wearing Lagerfeld, the aftershave he wore every day when they were together, and it set off a chain reaction in her senses. God, she'd loved this man. Truly loved him. And yet Celeste had to pick him. Or rather, as he'd confirmed earlier, he'd picked her. He'd made the first move. He was the one who'd made the promise to Aggs and he'd broken it. She just wished it hadn't been with her best friend. Many times she'd wondered if Celeste hadn't been there, would it have been someone else? Would a man with the drive and lifestyle aspirations of her ex-husband ever have been happy with a wife who cared for her ill parents, brought up their kids, worked in a café and took no interest whatsoever in the life of glamour and success that he was determined to live? She doubted it very much. And it gave her no pleasure now to see that some of his choices were putting him on a crash course to unhappiness and divorce at this stage in life. There was still love there – they'd created two wonderful kids together – and she wanted to see him happy. Although, it was slightly worrying that the Lagerfeld had stirred something that was making her feel a little flustered and warm. Maybe it was time to confer with the Menopausal Jogging Club on the best way to control hot flushes.

'Happy birthday, Aggs. And thanks for today,' he whispered in her ear, the background noise making sure that it didn't reach Celeste. He hadn't told her that they'd met up today, then. Made sense.

'You okay?' she asked.

'Not sure yet,' he murmured. He obviously hadn't confronted Celeste either. That figured. If she was up to no good, it was a sure bet that she was being sneaky about it, and Mitchell needed to have facts and proof before he challenged her. This was a woman who had continued to act as if she was Aggs' best friend for a solid two years after she began sleeping with her husband. She could hold masterclasses in subterfuge and duplicity.

Mitchell's confession to the affair was a day that would live with Aggs until the end of time, but even back then, Celeste had been absolutely unapologetic.

Aggs shrugged off the memory. Now wasn't the time for melancholy. It was a time for dancing and celebrating and being absolutely bloody ecstatic that, after some hellish tough years, she was getting a new start. No drama. No surprises. No looking back. Just happiness and adventure going forward.

The tune changed to Dolly Parton's '9 to 5' and the next thing she felt was her hand being grabbed and a playful tug as Val and Yvie rescued her from the clutches of her past life. They whisked her on to the dancing area and sang the first verse of the song at the top of their lungs, hands swinging in the air.

Only when it was done, did Val lean towards her, gesturing over to the unhappy couple, who were now standing as close to the door as possible without being outside. Aggs knew Celeste would make a rapid escape just as soon as she could. And, of course, there was no way they would mingle with anyone. Mitchell could be very personable and charming, and he'd enjoy meeting some of her friends, but Celeste would only speak to someone if there was something in it for her.

'Is that him and her? The ex-dick and the trollop?' Val asked.

'It is indeed,' Aggs confirmed, shaking her shoulders now as the opening bars of 'Wannabe' by the Spice Girls changed the tempo. There was a blast from the past. She remembered dancing with Celeste to this in a nightclub in Vegas and... The sound of a metal door crashing to the ground shut that memory down before it was fully formed. Vegas was yet another excruciating wound that she had no intention of reopening.

She saw that Val was still eyeing Celeste, while murmuring from the side of her mouth. 'You know that I'll always provide an alibi. Just saying. You were with me and we were watching *Strictly*. So as long as you make it a Saturday night between seven and eight, you'll be sorted.'

Aggs chortled as she danced, not an easy combination for someone who hadn't been near a nightclub or a disco in twenty years and was well out of practice.

She hoped to change that with Will. They'd talked about having a night out on the town, maybe dinner and a club, as soon as their relationship was out in the open. Well, tonight was going to be the night that everyone learned about them, so she should probably get shopping for shoes that didn't give her blisters when she danced.

She glanced over at the door. Still no sign of him. Argh, she felt like a fifteen year old at the school disco, waiting for the boy she had a crush on to show up. Only, when Aggs was fifteen, she was usually standing outside the toilets, keeping guard while Celeste was inside with the captain of the school football team.

'Looking for someone special there, Aggs?' Yvie asked with a wink. 'You can't stop looking at that door.'

Aggs felt herself blush. Bloody hell, what was this tonight? She was definitely regressing to her fifteen year old self.

Yvie put her out of her misery. 'He'll be here, don't worry. He said at lunch today that he was definitely coming. He's probably just taking ages to wrap your pressie.'

Aggs threw up her arms. 'You two know as well? Dear God, are there no secrets in this world?'

Val threw her arm around her. 'We're delighted for the both of you. You deserve some happiness, you really do. Although, we've not told Myra yet. I think you could be in for some competition.' They all turned to see Myra, who was over near the window, slow dancing with Bernard, an eighty-four years young former soldier who came in every afternoon for soup and a ham sandwich, with 'none of that mayonnaise muck'.

Laughing, Aggs took Val's free hand, then Yvie's too. 'Thank you, both. I wouldn't be anywhere near ready to start living again if it wasn't for you two,' she said honestly, expressing her gratitude to them for the second time that day. It was the least she could do. After her mum died, she'd been on the floor. They were two of the people who'd lifted her back up and she'd always be grateful that they had her back.

Right on cue, the music changed and Val got an evil twinkle in her eye. 'A wee one I asked the DJ to play,' she quipped and Aggs spluttered with hilarity.

'Before He Cheats' by Carrie Underwood bounced off every wall. Val threw a pointed glance and a knowing smile in Mitchell and Celeste's direction, and their stony expressions made it clear that they both got the message.

Trying and failing to hide her amusement, Aggs followed Val and Yvie off the dance area and they shuffled over to their drinks, left on a nearby table.

'I bloody love you two,' she giggled.

'Understandable. We've got great dance moves.' Yvie joked.

Val responded with a hug. 'We love you too, pet. And don't worry, he'll be here.'

Aggs shrugged. 'I'm not so sure. The thing is, his ex-wife texted him before he left today. He agreed to go and see her this afternoon and I haven't heard from him since.'

She couldn't miss the glance that went between Val and Yvie.

'You two would be rubbish in a spy situation!' Aggs teased, before giving a rueful shrug. 'It's fine. Really it is. If it works out with us, then great, because he's the loveliest guy I've met in a long time, and if it doesn't... well, I've been through so much worse. It's just a blip.' The words were coming out of her mouth, but she wasn't sure if she was trying to convince them or herself, even if her fingers were crossed the whole time she was saying it.

Yvie and Val were unceremoniously bumped out of the way as Marge barged in, arms outstretched. 'Right, ma sweetcheeks, it's almost ten o'clock and we haven't been out to two parties in one day since the seventies. We've had a lovely time, but I'm getting Myra out of here before she pulls something. Either a muscle, or that bloke with the walking stick,' she informed them.

'Oh, Marge, I'm so glad you came,' Aggs told her truthfully, giving her a grateful squeeze. 'Come on, I want to say goodbye to Myra too and I'll see you out.'

It took another fifteen minutes to actually get outside, given that neither Myra nor Marge could walk past anyone without either introducing themselves to strangers, or giving a full rundown of that week's medical ailments to anyone with whom they had a passing acquaintance.

When they finally got outside, Aggs hugged them tight. 'You two are good for the soul, do you know that? Thank you so much for today. I've loved it.'

'Och, you deserve it, cookie. You take care of yourself and our Will.'

Really? Was there anyone here who didn't actually know that she was seeing Will? Had there been an announcement on the news? A viral Twitter feed? Maybe a billboard somewhere?

'Aye, still can't believe he picked you instead of me,' Myra sighed, eyes twinkling with mischief. 'I think you only swung it because of the cakes. And maybe the thirty year age difference, but cougars are all the rage these days.' With that and a hoot of amusement, they climbed into Marge's Reliant Robin and off they went.

Aggs waved until they were out of the street and then stopped, took a breath, looked upwards and smiled.

Thanks, Mum. Thanks, Dad. Today has been amazing and I'm okay. I really am. I hope you two are dancing up there too.

She meant every word. They weren't here with her right now, but look at the love that had surrounded her all day. All she needed to make it completely perfect was Will to arrive and they could tell the girls all about tomorrow's trip to Paris. She was pretty sure now that they'd be thrilled for her.

Just as she was turning to head back inside, she stopped in her tracks as she spotted a car coming slowly down the street. Her spirits soared. Hopefully, that was Will. There was nothing that she wanted more right at that moment than to finish off one of the best nights of her life with somebody special by her side.

The fact that Celeste was itching to leave the party was, perversely, making Mitchell want to stay longer. And, yes, he realised that was petty, but having reached a low point of sneaking around a restaurant trying to spy on his wife, a bit of pettiness was far from the bottom of today's barrel. By the time they'd finally got here it was well after eight, and he had no intention of bailing out after an hour. Besides, he was actually glad to be somewhere that was a welcome break from the clusterfuck at home.

He'd prised Celeste away from her chosen spot next to the exit, and now they were at the serving counter, in the throng of the action. The music was great, the food was sensational – Isla had apparently been secretly slaving away for days, working on curries, lasagnes, pots of chilli and, of course, all of the café's exquisite cakes were there for dessert.

It was the atmosphere that he was enjoying the most, though, despite one or two obvious digs from Agnetha's friends. He was man enough to take the message in the Carrie Underwood song on the chin and see the funny side. Her pals were just sticking up for Aggs, and the fact that she was obviously so well liked didn't surprise him at all. Watching her now, she radiated happiness and, yep, she was looking absolutely gorgeous too. Not Celeste-type gorgeous, with the fillers and the expensive grooming schedule. But the type of natural beauty that radiated out of someone who was happy in her own skin and surrounded by love. The whole room was just one big party of fun, joy and warmth. Even if it was decidedly frosty in their corner right now.

'Hey, old man,' Isla chirped, stretching up on to her tiptoes to hug him. On the other side of him, he felt Celeste bristle. Of his two daughters, Isla was definitely the biggest challenge where her stepmother was concerned. Since Skye had come to live with them, she'd had a pleasant, even friendly, relationship with Celeste, but Isla didn't follow suit. In fact, it was almost as if the older Isla got and the more she grasped Celeste's role in the trajectory of their lives, the more disdain she had for her. He sometimes wondered if there was a bit of misplaced guilt there too, because when she was a kid, Isla had seen more than she should have, and that's what had inadvertently pressed the button on the nuclear explosion that had decimated his first marriage.

It was not long after Alex Sanders' second stroke, and Aggs was spending all her time over at her parents', taking care of her dad in the evenings, helping her mum to feed him, to bathe him, to get him in and out of bed, while working in the café during the day to sustain their income at the same time. On the evenings that Mitchell was working late, Celeste had offered to help with the girls. Aggs was so grateful for the support that she didn't even question Celeste's motives. They fell into a routine. Aggs would work at the café all day, then pick the girls up from school and take them home for dinner and baths. Celeste would then come over and put them to bed, while Aggs went back to stay with her parents, to help her dad if he woke during the night and give her mum the chance to get a solid sleep.

When Mitchell came home from work, usually around 9 p.m., he'd have a glass of wine with Celeste and they'd talk for a while. They'd been seeing each other for a couple of years, but in his house, there was an invisible line that he didn't go over. Somehow, his mind could deal with having incredible sex with Celeste at her place or in any one of many hotels in the city, but in the home he shared with his family? Absolutely not. He avoided any physical contact at all. But, of course, Celeste had to push it, to prove to herself that she could always have her way. One night, he'd got home a little early, around 8 p.m., and let himself in the front door. In the kitchen, Celeste was pouring a glass of red wine.

'Kids in bed?' he'd asked her, and she'd smiled that gorgeous, teasing, fucking irresistible smile of hers.

'They are,' she'd murmured, before taking a sip of wine and then walking towards him. When she'd kissed him, the taste of the red wine transferring to his mouth was suddenly the sexiest turn-on. On any other night, he would have stopped her, reminded her where they were, but not that night. He was tired, he was horny, and he wanted her. Without thinking, he'd dropped his jacket, picked her up and before his brain caught up with the action, she was sitting on the edge of the kitchen table and he was standing between her legs and they were kissing and it was hot and their hands were everywhere and she was biting his tongue and...

'Daddy, why are you kissing Aunt Celeste?' It was one of the most devastating moments of his life. His nine year old daughter was standing in the doorway watching them, a frown on her beautiful face. Until the day he died, he would always be grateful that they were still fully clothed. What a fucking fool he'd been though.

'Isla, get back to bed,' Celeste had snapped, but his daughter didn't move.

Instead, she'd stood there, eyes blazing at the woman whom

she'd called 'aunt' since she could speak. 'You said you were going to bring me up some water.'

Months later, when they'd moved out of the eye of the storm, he'd wondered if Celeste had deliberately set him up, knowing that Isla would come down for her drink, determined to force his hand. When they'd talked about being together, he'd always stalled her, said the kids were too young, it wasn't the right time, they couldn't hurt Aggs like that when she already had so much on her plate. 'And what about me?' his mistress would argue. 'Don't I matter? I'm going to lose just as much as you, but I'm prepared to do it so we can be together. I love Aggs, but I love you more. Nothing is more important to me than us. Nothing at all. Why don't you feel the same?' She'd goad him and he'd delay and then she'd goad him some more, but, to his eternal shame, he'd never once considered giving Celeste up. He couldn't. She was like a drug, an addiction, and he couldn't get enough of her.

That night Isla came downstairs, perhaps Celeste orchestrated it, maybe she didn't. There would never be any way to prove it, but it forced him to act. He couldn't bring himself to tell his nine year old daughter not to share what she saw with her mother, but at the same time, he couldn't walk on eggshells until she did.

The following night, he and Celeste were waiting at the same kitchen table for Aggs to come home. She'd been with her parents for thirty-six hours, two day shifts in the café, then a night shift with her dad, and when she came in she was visibly exhausted, her eyes almost disappearing into the dark circles around them.

As soon as she saw their expressions, she'd reacted. 'What's happened, are the girls okay?' she'd asked urgently.

'They're fine,' Mitchell had told her hastily, then watched, feeling like the biggest bastard on earth as she visibly sagged with relief.

'Oh, thank God. I don't think I could cope with anything else today. Or this week. Or this year.' She caught on to the fact that the atmosphere in the room was still sombre. 'What am I missing?' she'd asked warily.

'Sit down, Aggs,' Mitchell had said, voice breaking, dreading this with every fibre of his being. How could he hurt her like this? But how could he not?

'No. I don't need to sit down.' Her eyes had darted from one to the other. 'What is it? You're freaking me out. Has my mum called while I was on my way home? Is it my dad? Has he...'

'Aggs, we're seeing each other,' Mitchell had blurted. Celeste had stared down at the table in front of her, making no eye contact. 'Celeste and me. We've been... we've been... together.'

Aggs hadn't responded for so long that he wasn't sure she'd actually caught what he'd said. Eventually, she'd spoken. 'Is this some kind of twisted wind up?' The hope in her voice almost broke him.

'Aggs, I'm sorry, but we really are in a relationship. I'm so sorry. I...' he couldn't say any more because he was shamed to silence by the visceral pain that made Aggs reel like she'd been punched in the face.

'You're... you're... no. This has to be a joke. Celeste? Celeste, tell me!'

No reply.

Aggs was shaking her head now, hanging on to the worktop for support, gasping for breath as she spoke. 'No. You wouldn't. You wouldn't do that.'

Mitchell couldn't take it any longer. The clichés had poured out of him. 'I'm so sorry, Aggs. We didn't mean to hurt you, it just happened and...'

'Stop.' Her whisper was deafening.

He'd expected her to scream, to shout, to call them every name, and they would deserve every single word of it, but she'd shocked him by simply reaching for her keys, then picking her bag up off the worktop beside her.

'I'll be back in two hours,' she'd said, deadly calm. Her gaze went to Mitchell first. 'You have your stuff packed and be ready to leave.' Then to Celeste, 'And you... we were family,' she'd said, with visible disgust, making the point that it was past tense. 'I just hope he's worth it.'

With that, his wife had walked out of the door, head held high.

For months, they didn't communicate unless it was absolutely essential. Aggs sold the house, moved in with her parents full time, and they'd both helped her to bring up the girls. Over the next couple of years, Mitchell and Aggs had patched over the cracks where the kids were concerned, with Aggs – and Mitchell would forever marvel at her strength and magnanimity – never, as far as he knew, saying anything negative to the twins about Mitchell or Celeste.

At the same time, Celeste was determined that the girls would accept her as a stepmother, so she took them shopping, treated them to manicures, to pedicures, to weekend trips and nights out at the theatre. Isla was a tough nut to crack though. She went along with it all, until she was around fourteen and old enough to choose where to spend her weekends. After that, she refused to go on the stepmother/stepdaughter bonding sessions. Or 'blatant bribery' as she so articulately, and accurately, called it.

Mitchell didn't force the issue. As long as things were civil at family gatherings, and as long as Isla was happy to spend time with him alone every week, he could live with it. Now, neither Isla nor Celeste even bothered to make an effort with each other.

'How are you doing, sweetheart? You managed to pull it off then?' Mitchell gestured around the room at the party, which was now in full swing.

'Yeah, where were you?' Isla punched him playfully on the arm.

'You were supposed to be here at seven. Mum's face was a picture, you should have seen it!' She rounded off the sentence with a pointed glare at Celeste.

Of course, she knew it would be her stepmother's fault. Mitchell was a stickler for punctuality, whereas Celeste always preferred to be fashionably late. Unless it involved Aggs, that was. In the case of his ex-wife, Celeste pushed 'fashionably' late to a borderline rude 'way too bloody late'.

'Sorry, sweetheart, just one of those things. Time got away from us.' Even as he was saying it, he could hear how lame it sounded.

Isla nudged him, full of mischief. 'You should have brought the new sports car then – you might have got here quicker.'

Celeste's eyes narrowed on Isla's, while Mitchell rewound what she'd said in his head. 'The new sports car?' he parroted questioningly.

Isla shrugged, as she directed her answer at Celeste. 'Yeah, the yellow one. Saw you climbing out of it at the yoga studio the other morning when I was opening up here. I assumed you'd been out for a test drive. Bit early, right enough. Must have been before eight. What day was that? Tuesday?' Isla clasped her hand to her mouth dramatically, eyes popping as she took in Celeste's face. 'Oh no, have I spoiled a surprise? Were you buying it for Dad?'

Mitchell couldn't even look at his wife. Tuesday morning. He'd been in London preparing a client brief on the Monday. He'd stayed overnight. Sounded like Celeste had had a sleepover too. How stupid to get dropped in the same street as Aggs' café. But then, Celeste wouldn't have been able to resist the offer of a lift in a car like that. And she was way too arrogant to think she'd get caught.

Every doubt, every worry, every feeling of mistrust that Mitchell had felt in the last couple of months rose up, took control, and blew all restraint out of the window.

'A yellow sports car like the one Derek Evans owns by any

chance? A Maserati, if I'm not mistaken?' he asked Celeste, then watched as the muscles in her neck tightened so much, he could see every throb and sinew.

He should stop now, but he couldn't. He was on a roll.

'The same Derek Evans who is a director of a soccer academy just outside Marbella?'

Her face was truly like thunder now, but still she stayed silent.

As always, the angrier he was, the calmer he seemed on the outside. He sounded almost nonchalant as he added, 'Did you honestly think I wouldn't check? That's what happens when you take so long to get ready. Although, no wonder you needed a long bath, as I'm guessing that was also the same Derek Evans that you spent the day with in the Malmaison today.'

That was it – that was the moment that Celeste gave up the pretence. And when Celeste was in the wrong, she attacked and then bolted. He could write the playbook.

'You what? Had me followed? You've been spying on me? You sad fuck. You know what, Mitchell? Sod it. Stay here. Stay with your family. They've always been yours, never mine. I'm done, Mitch. Just done with the whole bloody lot of you.'

With that, his wife answered several of the questions he'd been asking himself all day.

Was she having an affair? Yes, she was.

Was their marriage over? Yes, it was.

Was she leaving him? Right now, as she started heading for the door, he'd say that was definitely the case.

No matter what, he wasn't going to let her go and find a taxi on her own. If they were finally being honest, they may as well go home together, hash the whole bloody lot out and get it over with.

'Sorry, Dad,' Isla whispered, and he could see that she was completely stunned over what had just happened. 'I was just messing with her. I genuinely thought there was an innocent explanation.'

Mitchell could see that she was being truthful. He gave her a kiss on the cheek. 'Don't be, honey, it wasn't your fault. It's been a long time coming.'

He glanced around quickly to see if he could spot Aggs, but there was no sign of her.

'Tell your mum I said goodbye. I'll call you tomorrow, love.'

Thankfully, Celeste wasn't getting very far, because she was having to excuse herself to get through groups of people all the way to the door. Following in her wake, he caught up with her just as she pulled the door open and stepped outside to see...

Ah, there was Aggs. She was standing leaning against the window, smiling as she watched a car approach from the other direction.

Maybe it was a taxi. If so, they could jump in, go home and get this whole fiasco sorted out. Time for truth. Time for decisions.

Celeste spun to the left, ignoring her former friend, clearly not interested in goodbyes. For a second, he was torn between saying goodbye and catching up with Celeste.

Aggs had now stepped forward towards the car that was slowing down as it approached her. From where he was standing, he couldn't see who was in the vehicle, but it must be someone coming to join the party.

As he turned to follow his wife, he was struck by the thought that unlike all those years ago, this time he didn't want to leave Aggs.

Maybe it wasn't too late to change his mind.

27

AGNETHA AND CELESTE – 1997

The plane had barely touched down in LA when Aggs had felt the first wave of nausea. She made it to the loos inside the terminal just in time to lose her stomach contents, then she slid down the side panel of the cubicle, crouching at the bottom, her head on her knees, her arms around her shins. God, she felt awful. It must have been something she ate at the pool. Or maybe just the anxiety about her dad. How could he have collapsed? Her dad was a big strong man, way over six feet and broad as his pizza oven. Sure, he had high blood pressure, but he took pills for that and he was fine. He was indestructible. A force of nature. The kind of man who protected everyone else. How could something awful have happened to him?

She kept telling herself that Nancy must have it wrong. Maybe he'd just slipped. Or fainted. Maybe Nancy was making it all sound so much more dramatic than it really was.

Pushing up off the floor, she went out to the basins, washed her hands and gargled with the mouthwash she always kept in the bottom of her backpack. For a moment, she thought she was going to be sick again, but she held on to the white porcelain of the sink until it passed.

Now, half an hour or so later, she'd made her way to terminal two for her flight to London, and she was sitting in a café with a cup of tea that was making her nauseous just looking at it. The prospect of food made her want to heave again, so she'd given the trays of pizzas and the rows of burgers a miss. A glance at her watch told her it was just after eight o'clock. Sixty minutes ago she should have walked down the aisle. If she squeezed her eyes tight shut, she could imagine Aaron's face when Celeste told him what had happened. He'd be gutted, but he would understand. He was a good man, Aaron Ward. She just prayed that Celeste had got to him before he went to the chapel, because the thought of him standing at the end of an aisle, waiting for a bride that wasn't going to show made her stomach lurch again.

Do not throw up here. Do not throw up.

She had to get a grip on this. She'd read somewhere that airlines didn't let you travel if you were being physically sick.

Too restless to sit any longer, she pushed the cup of cold tea away and picked up her backpack. In the shopping area, she searched for a pharmacy and finally spotted one a hundred yards or so down the terminal. Walking slowly, afraid any sudden movement would make her retch, she eventually made it to the counter. 'Anti-nausea pills please.'

'Airsickness?' the brusque man in the white coat asked her.

If she admitted she thought she had some kind of bug, would she get offloaded from the flight? She couldn't risk that. She had to get home to her dad. 'Erm, yes, I think so.'

'Any chance you could be pregnant?'

'No,' she blurted automatically. Of course there wasn't. She and Aaron had been careful and had used condoms every time. Well, almost every time. There had been one brief slip up but that was it. Nothing, really.

The pharmacist slid over a box of pills and she took it gratefully, handing over ten dollars in return.

'Could you give me all the change in quarters please?'

She'd spotted a bank of phone booths just outside the shop and headed there with her handful of silver. Before she picked up the receiver, she popped a couple of the pills in her mouth, then washed them down with some water. Steadying herself, she inhaled, then exhaled, praying that the pills would stay down. They did.

A rummage in her bag located a matchbook she'd taken from Caesars as a memento of the trip. Aggs popped four quarters into the slot, then dialled the number that was on the matches. It was answered after one ring by a very polite receptionist who announced the name of the hotel in a sing-song voice.

Aggs forced the words out through a watery mouth. Urgh, these pills had better work soon. 'Room 306, please.'

'Can I ask the name of the guest you'd like to contact please?'

'Ward. Aaron Ward.'

The receptionist appeared to approve of her answer. 'Certainly, madam. Please hold on and I'll connect you.'

The line went dead and for a second Aggs thought she'd been cut off, then she heard the ringtone. Closing her eyes, she could see the room they'd spent the last two glorious nights in.

More rings. *Please be there.*

More rings. Still no answer.

Damn. Where was he? Probably in the bar, or maybe he'd found a way to follow her and right now he was on his way back to LA. Maybe he'd hired a car. Maybe a seat had become available on a later flight. Maybe Zac had worked his magic and pulled some strings to hitch a lift for his friend on yet another celebrity jet. Wishful thinking, she knew, but she was desperate.

'I'm sorry, madam, there's no answer from Mr Ward's room. Would you like to leave a message?'

She thought about it, but she wanted to speak to him in person. It was the least he deserved. Maybe Celeste would be in her room and Aaron might be there too. 'Can you try Room 332 then please?'

'Certainly. Can I have the name for that room too?'

It was booked under Zac's name, but Aggs' mind went blank. What was Zac's surname? Crap. Shit. Bugger. She couldn't remember. It was... it was... She remembered Celeste teasing him about the fact that it sounded like a porn star's alias. 'Stone! Zac Stone.'

'Just putting you through now, madam.'

Ringing. More ringing.

Come on, Celeste. Come on.

More ringing. Damn it!

She hung up, a little too violently, and a couple of passing travellers swerved to give her a wider berth.

Maybe they'd both checked out. No, the receptionist wouldn't have put her through if that was the case. Maybe they were in a bar somewhere. She didn't blame them.

A thought struck her. If she'd stayed in Vegas, the wedding ceremony would be over by now and that's exactly what she should be doing – drinking champagne in the bar with her new husband and her best friend. She briefly thought about calling his cell phone, but he'd left it in LA so that he didn't get bothered with work calls and, besides, she didn't know the number off by heart. It was written on a Post-it on the front of the fridge back in the LA apartment and she'd only used it a couple of times. Damn, why hadn't she taken a note of it?

How could today have turned out like this? One of the best days of her life to one of the worst. How did that happen? And when were these pills going to kick in and take away this nausea?

She checked her watch again – half an hour until boarding for the eleven hour flight to Heathrow. She couldn't wait that long to find out how her dad was doing. She calculated the time difference again. It would be around four o'clock in the morning. Could she phone home now? She thought about it for a moment. If her mum answered, that meant that her dad had got home from hospital too, because there was no way that her mum would leave him there alone if it was serious. And if the panic was over, then of course her mum wouldn't mind Aggs calling, even at this time of night. When they were younger and Celeste still lived with them, her mum had been the one who always told them to call when they were leaving a nightclub. At 3 a.m., Ella would show up, a jacket thrown on over her pyjamas, happy to pick them up because it meant they got home safe.

Aggs flipped back to the deliberation about whether or not to call. Best-case scenario, her mum answered and it was all a false alarm – in which case, she was turning around, getting on the next flight back to Vegas and marrying Aaron Ward. And if the phone rang out... She clenched her eyes shut, scared of where that option would take her. It would mean that they were still in hospital and that Nancy hadn't overreacted at all.

Aggs pumped the phone box with at least five dollars' worth of quarters, hoping beyond hope that she'd use them all to hear her mum's voice telling her that her dad was fine. It would be the best five dollars she ever spent.

With shaking fingers, she dialled the country code and then the number. Just like the hotel rooms, it rang, but it was a different tone, a more familiar one.

It rang again. And again. Aggs felt the sickness welling in her throat once more. She was about to hang up when...

'Hello?' The voice was groggy, but, oh, the relief.

'Mum, it's Agnetha. Oh, Mum, I was so worried. I'm at the airp—'

'Agnetha, it's Nancy.' Aggs' world crashed. 'Your mum asked me to stay here overnight, pet, in case you called back. She knew you'd be sick with worry.'

Her mum and dad were still at the hospital. This wasn't good. She closed her eyes, willing herself to stay upright. When she opened them again, she could see the digits counting down on her cash. Two dollars spent already. She fired the rest of her quarters into the slot.

'Nancy, how is my dad? Is there any news?'

She heard a sob catch in Nancy's throat. 'I'm going to be honest with you, pet, because your mum told me to. He's had a stroke. They've got him in intensive care and they've stabilised him. They've said that he's not out of the woods, but they're hopeful they got him in time. They said the next twelve hours are critical. I've never been more scared in my life, Agnetha, it was awful. Your poor dad. He's such a good man.'

Aggs rested her head against the cold steel of the booth, trying not to cry. She loved Nancy, but the woman could talk for weeks about her feelings if she was given any encouragement. Aggs tried to concentrate on what she needed to know before the quarters expired. 'Did my mum ask you to tell me anything else, Nancy?'

'Just that he's in the best place and that you've not to fret. I told her you said you were coming home.'

'I am, Nancy.'

The bing-bong of an announcement from the speakers above her made her pause, as she heard the words London and Heathrow.

'Nancy, that's my flight, so I have to go. Please tell my mum that I'm flying from Los Angeles to Heathrow, and then I'll get another flight up to Glasgow. I'll be there tomorrow afternoon and I'll come straight to the hospital. Shit, what hospital is he in?'

'Glasgow Central Hospital.'

'Okay, I'll get a taxi straight there. You try to get some sleep now and, Nancy, thank you. It was good of you to stay.'

'I wouldn't be anywhere else, pet. You just get home as soon as you can. I'll tell your mum everything you've said, don't you worry.'

Beep beep beep. The digital display went to zero as her money ran out.

Aggs replaced the receiver and checked the departures board. Her flight was in final boarding now, gate 10.

She took off, running, her stomach churning with every step, but she didn't care. She had to make that flight. It was going to take her at least fourteen hours to get to the hospital, and that was only if she could get a quick connecting flight from London to Glasgow. Nancy had said that the next twelve hours were crucial.

Hang on, Dad, I'm coming. Please hang on until I get there.

She made it with minutes to spare, took deep breaths in through her nose and out through her mouth as the plane took off until the buildings on the ground were too small for her to see.

As the clouds enveloped her, she thought about Aaron and her sore heart chipped a little more.

Goodbye my love, she said silently. *I'll be back as soon as I can.*

28

Hope swung open the hotel room door. 'Did you come by helicopter?' she asked her sister, genuinely fearful about how fast
Maisie must have driven to get there so quickly. Her sister was a
mass of wild hair and typically eccentric clothes.

'Red lights are for losers,' Maisie joked. At least, Hope assumed
she was joking. With Maisie, you never knew. God, she was so
happy that she was here. Saying goodbye to her this morning
already seemed like a lifetime ago.

As Maisie passed her, Hope took in her outfit. 'Helena Bonham
Carter or Cyndi Lauper?'

'Helena. Too much?'

'You're never too much. Aaron is going to love you.' Hope was
careful not to throw the 'D' word out there to Maisie just yet. Baby
steps. Their adoptive dad had meant the world to them and she
didn't want Maisie to feel that Hope was replacing him without a
second thought. This was all so much to take in. It would be understandable if Maisie was overwhelmed, especially when Hope hadn't
had time to process it all herself yet.

A few steps past the wardrobe on one side, and a bathroom on the other, and they were in the sitting room of the suite. Aaron was already on his feet and Hope felt a surge of... what was it? Pride? Joy? She wasn't sure, but it was wonderful to see her biological father hug her adoptive sister, even if her sister then promptly burst into tears.

Hope nipped into the bathroom and retrieved some loo roll. Maisie took it with an apologetic shrug and blew her nose noisily.

'I'm so sorry,' Maisie laughed through the sobs. 'I'm the dramatic one. You're lucky you got Hope and not me. I'd be doing Insta updates every five minutes and dragging a fly-on-the-wall documentary team behind me.'

It was one of Maisie's most endearing traits – she babbled uncontrollably when she was nervous, often complete nonsense. She once met Kate Winslet and was thrown into such a flap that she asked her where she'd bought her shoes and offered to show Kate her appendix scar.

'No need to apologise,' Aaron said, kindness oozing from his words. 'There's been a lot of that in here today.'

'Jet lag,' Hope told him and they both smiled. Their first father/daughter in-joke. Maisie was too busy drying her eyes to wonder what they were on about. 'Why don't we go and grab something to eat and we can fill you in on everything over dinner?' Hope suggested, keen now to get going. It suddenly felt a bit overwhelming again, and she needed neutral territory and a distraction to decompress for an hour or so. And there was no greater distraction than her sister.

They opted for one of their favourite Indian restaurants, just off Charing Cross and next to the beautiful Mitchell Library. They were shown to a table straight away, and a large plate of poppadoms magically appeared in front of them. The waiter took their drinks order and left them with menus.

Now that Maisie was sitting directly across from Aaron, Hope wondered how long her sister would be able to keep it in.

'Has anyone ever told you that you look like Tim McGraw?' Maisie blurted. Approximately one and a half seconds was the answer to Hope's question.

Aaron had the grace to act like the question was unexpected and Hope decided not to point out that she'd already shared Maisie's text with him. 'Yeah, once or twice,' he told her, his square jaw cracked by a grin.

It was the perfect icebreaker.

Over the next hour, both of them piping into the conversation, they brought Maisie up to speed with the main points of discovery so far.

Maisie swooned when he described his romance with Hope's mum, blinked back tears when Aaron revealed he'd been jilted at the altar, and listened with astonishment as they recounted how they'd tracked down Agnetha.

'And she's definitely not the one from Abba?'

'Definitely not,' Hope confirmed, then watched as Maisie tried to act as if she wasn't gutted by this news. A bit of teasing was in order. 'I know it's disappointing, but try to focus on the brilliance of the fact that I found her so quickly, instead of mourning your loss of backstage passes if Abba ever get back together.'

Maisie played along. 'It's just such a blow. I know all the words to "Fernando".'

To his credit, Aaron totally clicked with her sister's sense of humour. He was genuinely interested in hearing Maisie's story too. 'You've never tried to track down your biological parents?' he asked gently, while Maisie shredded a peshwari naan.

'I haven't. I guess I think...' she paused, trying to articulate her feelings. 'I think that if they wanted to meet me, they'd come looking. What if I find them and they want nothing to do with me? Or they're people that I have nothing in common with except genetics? I don't want to set myself up for a whole lot of hurt.'

Aaron listened to her carefully. 'I completely understand that. Although, maybe there could be a reason that they haven't sought you out. Maybe not all the facts are out there.'

It was obvious that he was alluding to his own situation and Maisie saw that immediately.

'Why do you think Hope's mum never told you she was pregnant?'

'I honestly have no idea. I just wish with everything I have that she'd shared what was happening so that I could have been there for her.'

The intensity of the conversation was too much for Maisie, who broke into a grin. 'Can I just check – you didn't have a fling with a dark-haired beauty who looks like me approximately two years and two months before you met Hope's mother?' she asked hopefully.

Hope let her forehead fall on to the table, narrowly missing a bowl of vegetable pakora. 'I can't believe you just said that.'

'What?' Maisie feigned huffiness. 'Can't believe you don't want to share Tim McGraw. It's like the Christmas with one skateboard between us all over again.'

Aaron was laughing hard now, the colour restored to his face by food, laughter, and the easy banter that had flowed between them all since they sat down.

By the time they left the restaurant and climbed back into Maisie's ancient old Mini, Hope could see that they liked each other and was surprised by how important that had suddenly become to her. Another connection in her new family. It felt good.

She climbed into the back, letting Aaron take the front passenger seat, so he could chat easily to Maisie. She didn't want him to feel out of it in the back.

'Okay, are we doing this?' Maisie asked, hands on the steering wheel.

In the front seat, Aaron turned and Hope could see the doubt on his face. This had to be every bit as terrifying for him as it was for her. This was the woman who'd jilted him at the altar, left him, borne his child and told him nothing about it. It would be perfectly understandable if he had reservations about going anywhere near her.

'I'm good, if you are,' he replied with a certainty that Hope wasn't feeling.

Woman up, she told herself. *You've got this. It's just a drive-by.* 'Yep, let's do it.'

'Eeeek!' Maisie couldn't contain her excitement. This was the kind of drama that she usually only found on stage or in scripts. 'Can I get clarity on the plan, though? You know, as the official badass getaway driver. In the movies, it's always the driver that gets killed or arrested. Just thought I'd mention that.'

Hope could see Aaron grinning again. He must be wondering what the hell he'd got himself into. A week ago, he was just a normal guy, living in LA, going about his life. Now he was in Glasgow, and he'd acquired a daughter and a getaway driver who was channelling Helena Bonham Carter. If he got the first flight back to LAX tomorrow morning, Hope wouldn't blame him at all.

Hope put the address into her phone and put it on speaker, and Maisie took off, following the directions as barked out by the automated voice on her maps app. Hope knew where the café was, but using the satnav made it easier for her sister. Plus, it gave her time to think. Was she ready for this? Was she prepared to be this close to the woman who'd given birth to her?

All they were going to do tonight was drive past the café, see what was happening, get a feel for how it all looked. It wasn't as if they were going to gatecrash the party and announce their arrival.

That would be crazy. There were too many risks, too many pitfalls that could blow the whole relationship before they'd even given it a chance.

No, just a look. That was all. Then they'd go back to the hotel and work out a plan to contact Agnetha and then meet her when she was prepared for them. That was if she agreed to a meeting. There was every possibility that she wouldn't. Hope was going to cross that bridge when they came to it.

She stared out the window for a while, watching Glasgow go by, before her eyes flicked to the satnav. Five more minutes. They were on Woodlands Road now, a street that she'd travelled more times than she could count, but that suddenly seemed daunting now that every turn of the tyres was taking her closer to the woman she'd wondered about her whole life.

'You okay there?' she asked Aaron.

'Just taking in the view,' he said, staring out of the window at the Victorian terraces that lined each side of the street. Even at this time of night, it was still daylight. In the winter, the city was plunged into darkness by three o'clock in the afternoon, but the reward was that summer evenings stayed light until after eleven.

There was a brief stop at a traffic light, then they carried on to Highburgh Road, then on to the gentle curve of Hyndland Road.

Hope checked the satnav screen. Two minutes to the destination.

'We're almost there. It's just up here on the right hand side,' she said, wondering if they could hear her over the noise of the steel band that was suddenly playing in her chest.

Aaron leaned forward, so that he could get a better view out of the front windscreen.

'That's it, there,' Hope pointed ahead, through the gap between the two front seats, 'The one with the tables and chairs outside.'

They were about eighty metres away now. Seventy. Sixty.

'Slow down a bit, Maisie.'

Her sister's knuckles were white on the wheel. 'Oh my God, this is nerve-wracking. I may be the first getaway driver ever to pee my pants. I'm just putting that out there.'

'Thank you and noted,' Hope deadpanned, but her attention was immediately grabbed elsewhere. Eyes trained on the bright frontage of The Ginger Sponge, about fifty metres ahead now, she gasped as she saw a man and woman exit the door. The woman turned and began to walk in the opposite direction, but the man... Hang on, there was another woman there too. She was leaning against the front window of the café, as if she was waiting for something or someone, and now she was watching their car as it approached her.

Forty metres. She had red hair that fell in curls past her shoulders.

Thirty metres. She was wearing a dress that was silver on the top and black on the bottom. Now she'd stepped forward on the pavement and was watching them, smiling, as if she was expecting someone.

Twenty metres. She was staring right at them and Maisie was so entranced that she had taken her foot off the accelerator and they were slowing down with every second that passed.

'Oh my God,' Aaron whispered. 'That's her. That's Agnetha.'

The woman's expression suddenly turned from a smile to puzzlement.

Five metres. The woman's gaze went to the driver of the vehicle, then the passenger. Her eyes locked on Aaron's face and her hand flew to her mouth.

Before Hope could panic, or faint, or yell at Maisie to keep going, the car rolled to a stop right in front of her mother.

10 P.M. – MIDNIGHT

29

Aggs froze, the synapses of her brain shutting down, no longer able to send signals to any part of her, except her heart, which was somehow continuing to beat.

It had been over twenty years since she'd seen his face, yet even now, there was no mistaking it. But it couldn't be him. Not here. Not now.

The passenger door of the car opened and he climbed out, stood just a few feet in front of her. A million times she'd pictured this moment, wondered how they would react, and now she knew – the two of them would slip into some other world, where time would stand still and they would stare at each other for what felt like a lifetime. And while the world stopped turning, inside her body she'd feel an explosion of every emotion she'd ever shared with this man: love, excitement, happiness, sadness, devastation, and a punch of loss and regret so painful that it felt like a physical blow.

'Aaron?' she whispered.

He didn't reply and it seemed like his words were failing him, until slowly, like a black and white movie playing at the wrong speed, she saw the smile she'd played back in her memory so many times and listened to the voice she'd only heard in that twilight time between waking and sleeping. 'Good to see you, Agnetha.'

A pause while she waited for her reactions to catch up and then, in an instant, colour flooded her vision again and suddenly his arms flew open as she moved towards him and then she was cocooned in a place that felt so familiar she could have been there only a moment ago.

They hugged for too long and not long enough. It felt right and it felt wrong. She wanted to run and she wanted to stay there forever. To cheer with joy and to sob with sorrow.

Aggs was first to break the spell. 'I think I need to sit down before my legs give way.' She took a few steps back to one of the tables outside the café, glad that the gang who'd been sitting there earlier had now moved inside. 'Please...' she gestured to an empty chair next to her, then watched as he walked towards it. He still moved in exactly the same way as before. Even if she hadn't seen his face, she would have known it was him. Her voice was hoarse as she spoke. 'Is this... real?'

'Definitely real.' That smile. The line of his jaw. Age had barely touched him. 'I can't believe we found you. I have so many questions, so many things I need to say, but first, I need you to meet someone.'

Aggs' gaze followed his, as he turned to the two women in the car and beckoned them to join them.

They opened the doors and, straight away, Aggs guessed that they were in their early twenties. The driver with the ebony hair bounded towards them and Aggs immediately fell in love with her look, a kaleidoscope of styles that were definitely a throwback to some vintage time. The other girl's hesitation was obvious, as she slowly climbed out of the back.

'Aggs, this is Maisie.'

The dark-haired girl's hand shot out, and Aggs shook it, not quite able to decide what questions she wanted to ask first. Was this his family? Was he here touring Scotland, as he used to say he wanted to do, and he'd just decided to look her up? And where the hell had he been for the last twenty years?

As always, Aggs found a way to calm her racing mind and focus on the moment. There would be time. They'd get to that.

'Pleased to meet you, Maisie,' Aggs greeted her.

'You too,' Maisie said, as she reclined into one of the other free seats at the table.

The other young woman reached them, and Aaron stood up, took her hand. 'And this is Hope.'

Aggs gasped. The resemblance was unmistakable. The same eyes. The same colouring. This could only be...

'Hope is my daughter.' His voice was loaded with emotion, but Aggs didn't think to wonder why, too busy focusing on taking this in and holding it together. Aaron Ward. The love of her life. Even a ten year marriage to Mitchell hadn't erased the memory of the pain she'd felt after she came back from America, leaving him behind. The truth was that she'd loved Mitchell, but even in their best moments, he didn't have all her heart, because a tiny part of it had broken off the day she left Vegas. The love she'd felt for Aaron had never been matched.

'I could see that immediately. You look so alike. It's lovely to meet you.'

His daughter. Oh God, his daughter. Aggs slipped her shaking hands under the table, truly hoping that they didn't realise the effect that the introduction was having on her. His daughter...

Hope responded with a smile that was almost nervous.

Must be shy, Aggs thought, as Aaron pulled the last chair at the table out for his girl, then sat down again. Aggs noticed Hope slipping her hand into his, and it warmed her heart. She used to think he'd make a great dad. Given the loving way he was treating Hope, it seemed she was right.

'I'm so sorry to ambush you like this,' Aaron began. 'We didn't plan it. We just managed to track you down today and we thought we'd drive by to see if we had the right place. We were going to call you first, or get a message to you...'

Trying to relax, Aggs let out a throaty chuckle. 'The shock has probably aged me a few years, but I'm so, so glad you're here. I can't believe it though. It all seems so surreal. Are you on holiday? Travelling?'

'No, I'm...' As he paused, it was obvious to Aggs that he was struggling with the words.

She sensed something else too. A confusion. A feeling that there was a weight, an anxiety there. Something he didn't quite know how to say. Was he still upset at their break-up? Did he still bear some kind of a grudge? If so, that was totally unreasonable, because he'd been to blame too. And why did her gaze keep returning, as if being pulled by an invisible force, to the young woman at his side? The grey eyed girl who had just nodded her encouragement to him and whose stare now felt like it was burning a hole through to Aggs' soul?

'Agnetha,' he began again, 'I'm just going to unload all this and I'm sorry if it doesn't come out right...'

'That's okay,' she tried to reassure him.

'I arrived in Scotland this morning and that's when I met Hope for the first time.'

What? That didn't make sense. That couldn't be right. Had she misunderstood him?

Hope spoke her first words since she'd got out of the car. 'I did a DNA test. That's how I tracked him down.'

The accent. Aaron's revelation that he just met his daughter. That's when the penny dropped. 'Wait a minute... you're Scottish?

I'm sorry, I assumed you were American. I don't understand.' None of this was adding up at all.

'Yes, I'm Scottish,' Hope confirmed. 'I grew up in Glasgow.'

Aggs realised that she must be wearing exactly the same confused expression that everyone else at the table seemed to have too.

'I feel like I'm missing something and I don't know what it is. Help me out here, Aaron.'

Even in the dimming light, Aggs could see that the colour was draining from his face.

'Aggs, I...' he began, but Hope cut him off.

'I've got this,' she told him gently, before taking the lead. 'I know this must be a massive shock for you and I understand that you might have blocked out a lot of what happened for whatever reason. Please believe me when I say that I'm not judging you for that.'

Hope took a deep breath, and Aggs desperately wanted to ask more questions, but she was too perplexed, and she didn't want to interrupt something that Hope was obviously finding extremely emotional to say.

'I was born on the twentieth of March 1998, in a hospital in Edinburgh and adopted by a couple from Glasgow. I've had a lovely life, with great parents, and a fabulous sister...'

'That bit is definitely true.' The woman Aaron had introduced as Maisie threw that in, making Hope and Aaron smile.

Aggs didn't have the same reaction, too busy trying to grasp all the fragments of the story.

Hope carried on, 'But I have a health condition and that's why I decided to track down my biological parents.'

Aggs was now desperately trying to do the calculations. Nine months before... Oh God. Oh God. In some outlandish way, this was starting to make sense and she couldn't believe she was only realising it now.

'As I said, I found Aaron through my DNA test and we met this morning and he told me all about your time together. And how... it ended.'

Wow. That hit Aggs straight in the solar plexus. How it ended? How she had come home to look after her sick father? How he'd refused to take her calls afterwards? How she'd waited every single day for months for him to appear on her doorstep and he never came?

'And I'm so sorry that we're hijacking your night like this – I know the timing is terrible, but I needed to find my mother and Aaron agreed to help me, so here we are. As I said, I'm not judging you for putting me up for adoption and I promise I don't want to disrupt your life or spill your secrets, but I just needed to know who you were. If you don't want a relationship with me, I promise you I will accept that. And so will Aaron.'

Aggs could see that Hope was watching her with glistening eyes full of the most extraordinary combination of bravery and fear and Aggs wanted to wrap her arms around her and protect her with every single fibre of her being from what was about to happen, but she couldn't.

Supressing every negative feeling she was suddenly experiencing towards Aaron – anger, betrayal, disbelief – Aggs focussed on what mattered most right here and now. She leaned forward and offered her hand to the young woman.

With only a split second of hesitation, Hope took it, a single tear running down her face.

'Hope, I am so, so sorry...' She choked, devastated to be dealing another blow to someone who had obviously been through so much already. This was something this poor girl was going to have to process. And it's something that Aaron should have prepared her for. The story had been laid out in front of her – everything but the final chapter that revealed secrets, explained twists, and came with a sledgehammer shock. '... and I can't tell you how much I would love to tell you what you want to hear, but I didn't give birth in 1998, and I've never put a child up for adoption. I'm not your mother.'

For a moment, Aggs thought Hope was going to argue back, to challenge what she was saying, but she didn't say a word, just turned her gaze to the father, her voice so low it was almost a whisper.

'Aaron? I don't understand. If Agnetha isn't my mother, then who is?'

30

MITCHELL

Mitchell almost bumped into the back of Celeste when she stopped suddenly in the street and turned to see who had just got out of the car in front of the café.

'Is that a taxi?' she spat, peering back the forty metres or so to where Aggs was standing, before answering her own question. 'Nope, it's a shitty little car. Look, Mitch, stop fucking following me. I'm perfectly capable of getting home on my own. Go back in there to your perfect bloody family and their tuna fucking vol-au-vents.'

Mitchell wasn't going to point out that he hadn't seen a vol-au-vent all night. Seemed pretty irrelevant on the scale of tonight's events so far. What a day. He really needed for it to be over.

'I'm not going anywhere except home with you, Celeste. We need to talk and we need to...' His words trailed off as he saw that Celeste wasn't listening. Instead, she was staring over his shoulder, watching the man who had just got out of the car and stepped onto the pavement in front of Aggs. In almost twenty years of knowing her, and ten years of marriage, Mitchell had never seen his wife speechless. Until now. Nothing. Not a word. Just an astonished, horrified expression. 'Celeste?'

Her answer was to grab his hand with more force than he knew she possessed and pull him into the doorway of the gift shop they were now standing outside.

'Celeste, what the hell...?'

Now that they were out of sight of anyone else in the street, she finally answered him. 'It's... it's... complicated.'

'What is?' Mitchell was beginning to wonder if she'd slipped something into her drink.

'The guy. Back there. With Aggs.'

Mitchell peered back out into the street, and yes, the man was still there. He and Aggs were sitting at a table now and appeared to be in deep discussion, completely oblivious to the rest of the world.

Mitchell ducked back in. 'Yeah, he's still there. Who is he?'

'That's... that's Aaron.'

Mitchell flicked back through the floppy disk of his mind. Aaron. The only person of that name Aggs had ever mentioned was an ex-boyfriend, a guy in the USA that she'd had a relationship with. She'd never shared all the details, and to be honest, Mitchell hadn't wanted to know. What she'd done before they met was irrelevant to him.

There was the sound of a car door opening and closing, and then another one doing the same.

'Did Aggs get into the car with him? Have they left?'

This was the most irrational he'd ever seen his wife. Why would she think that Aggs would leave her own party? That would be ridiculous.

Mitchell peered around the corner again. 'No. Two girls are sitting with them now. About the same age as Isla and Skye, maybe? It's hard to tell.'

Celeste lurched. For a moment he thought she was going to faint and he prepared to catch her, but instead, she stepped out of the doorway. She watched what was going on for a few seconds, then stepped back in, put both hands against the slate tile of the entranceway and fought to control her breathing.

'Celeste,' he tried again, getting seriously worried now. 'Is this a panic attack? Do I need to call an ambulance?'

Her head was shaking violently and he watched, dumbstruck, as she tried to regulate her gasps for breath. All thoughts of that muppet, Derek Evans, and his wife's affair were gone now as he tried to deal with what was going on here. One crisis at a time was all he could handle.

'The girl...' That was all Celeste said and it came out as a strangled cry.

'What about her?'

'Mitch, it can't be, it can't be her...'

'It can't be who?'

She began to mumble, almost to herself now. 'Give me a minute, let me think. Let me think.'

For thirty or forty seconds, she paced back and forward in the tiny space, Mitchell letting her work out whatever she was doing, completely at a loss as to what he should say. Eventually, she stopped, and as if some silent decision had been made, she took a breath, pulled back her shoulders and transformed back into Celeste again.

'Fuck it,' she hissed, before stepping out of the doorway.

There was a couple walking some kind of large wolfhound along the street in front of them, shielding their view, but there was no mistaking where Celeste was headed. She strutted back towards the table where the four people sat, Mitchell following just behind, still trying to figure out what the hell was going on.

Aggs and her visitors were so deep in conversation that they didn't even notice their arrival until they were almost next to them. Only then did Mitchell hear snippets of the conversation.

'... and I've never put a child up for adoption. I'm not your mother,' Aggs was saying. What the hell?

One of the young women – he could see now that she definitely was in her early twenties – was speaking to the guy now. 'Aaron? I don't understand. If Agnetha isn't my mother, then who is?'

'I think I know the answer to that,' he heard Celeste say.

Shock turned the guy's head around so fast Mitchell was fairly sure he'd be left with whiplash.

'Celeste?'

Mitchell heard the American accent. Yep, definitely must be the bloke that Aggs had dated before they met.

He made eye contact with his ex-wife and saw that this wasn't some kind of happy reunion. She looked aghast. Stunned. Shocked. And when she spoke, her voice had an exhausted resignation to it.

'You two had better pull up a couple of chairs.'

Mitchell grabbed two seats from the other table and swung them round.

Just at that, a group of about eight or ten women emerged from the café. 'Aggs, we're off now,' one chirped. 'Thank you so much,' another said, slightly slurred. 'Best Menopausal Jogging Club meeting we've had for ages!'

Aggs aside, everyone who was seated stayed that way, saying nothing, while each of the women, oblivious to the solemn atmosphere, hugged Aggs in turn. They then tottered off down the street, one of them bursting into the chorus of Wet Wet Wet's 'Angel Eyes', which the others then joined in with.

'This is the craziest night of my life,' the darker-haired of the two girls at the table couldn't hide her astonishment.

Mitchell was getting exasperated. What the hell was going on and why was no one explaining this to him?

As if she could read his mind, Aggs spoke up first. 'Celeste, this is Hope. And this is Maisie, her sister. Hope was adopted when she was a baby and only found out recently that she's Aaron's daughter.'

Mitchell was confused. What did any of this have to do with Celeste?

Aggs continued with the introductions. 'Hope, this is Celeste. We used to be friends. Best friends, actually. We grew up together and Celeste was part of our family.'

Celeste's eyes blazed, but surprisingly she said nothing.

'Celeste was with me in Los Angeles and then in Las Vegas when I was seeing your dad. She was dating his friend, Zac. On the night I left, I'm guessing the dynamics of those relationships changed.' Her meaning was unmistakable.

'I'm so sorry,' the American bloke was saying now. Mitchell wasn't sure if that was directed at Aggs or Hope, but it was the young woman who reacted first.

'Wait a minute,' she blurted, staring at Celeste now. 'So, *you're* my mother?'

Whaaaaaat? No. Couldn't be. Mitchell's heart was hammering, but even as he searched his wife's reaction for answers, he could see that Hope had called it right. Their eyes were different. The colouring too. But there was something in the shape of her face, in the way she raised her chin, that Mitchell knew, without a doubt, this was Celeste's child.

'Why didn't you ever tell me?' he blurted, realising that Celeste still hadn't spoken.

'Mitchell,' Aggs reprimanded him softly, and he immediately saw why. His questions didn't get priority here. That went to the girl he now knew was his... what? Jesus, he had a stepdaughter.

Finally, Celeste spoke, 'Yes, I think I am.'

Aggs' head fell into her hands, but to her credit she said nothing.

'Christ, Celeste, how did that happen?' Aaron pleaded, before

Mitchell had a chance to jump in with a similar question. All these years and she'd never once mentioned having a child.

Celeste's eyes flared, challenging him. 'Do you want me to draw you a diagram?'

This time, Mitchell stepped in, before tempers got even more frayed. He was a lawyer. De-escalating situations, getting to the root of issues, and establishing the background to complex problems were his speciality areas and he could see that they were all needed now. 'Aaron, I'm Mitchell. I'm Celeste's husband. And I'm actually Aggs' ex-husband too.'

'Woah!' cried Maisie. 'You have got to be kidding me. Let me get this straight. You were married to Agnetha, and now you're married to her friend.' That was addressed to Mitchell. Then she flipped her attention to Aaron. 'And you dated Agnetha, but then... then... made Hope with her friend.' Her gaze went to Aggs next. 'You really need to get new friends.'

'Already done,' Aggs said quietly, and Mitchell tried not to squirm with the embarrassment of complete strangers no doubt concluding that he was a complete prick. Thankfully the heat was elsewhere, so he stayed quiet.

'I need you to tell me what happened,' Hope was asking her father now, 'because I honestly don't understand all this. It's too much...'

Aaron sighed, and Mitchell watched him slump. If this was a witness, Mitchell would pull him from the stand right now because the guy looked as if he was one tough question away from breaking.

'I need to be honest, Aggs,' Aaron said to her. 'But before I say this, I want you to know I'm sorry.'

Aggs nodded, and despite how much this must be killing her, she gave a resigned sigh. 'Go right ahead.'

Celeste had dipped her head and had her hand over her eyes now, as if she couldn't stand to watch the truth unfolding. That was out of character for his wife. Her standard MO was to pull her shoulders back and remain defiant in the face of adversity. Whatever was coming next had to be seriously messed up if it was defeating her.

Aaron was still holding his daughter's hand. 'It's just as I told you earlier, Hope. Agnetha and I were supposed to get married in Vegas, but she didn't show up. She changed her mind.'

'You mean, Aggs didn't show up, as in jilted you at the altar?' Mitchell heard his own voice asking that question, and it came from a place of complete disbelief. That wasn't Aggs' style. Absolutely no way. If she'd done that, he'd have heard about it. This American bloke was either mistaken or lying or... The thought was derailed by the sound of Celeste wincing, just as Aggs spoke up, clearly agitated.

'I didn't change my mind. I got a phone call to say my dad was seriously ill and had been rushed to hospital. Turns out he'd had a stroke. Anyway, I had to get home straight away. Celeste knew that and she...' Aggs stopped, staring at Celeste, at the truth that was written all over his wife's beautifully twisted face. 'You didn't tell him that, did you? You lied. You let him think I'd run out on him?'

'What does it matter now?' Celeste muttered.

'Christ on a bike.' That came from Maisie.

Aggs jumped right in there. 'It matters, Celeste!'

The sharpness of Agnetha's tone ignited a flare in his wife and she immediately switched back to her usual form, going on the defensive, flipping it around and turning it into an attack. 'I did you a favour. You could never have lived there. You couldn't have stayed away from your mum and dad and this...' she gestured to the café behind them. 'You were about to make the biggest mistake of your life and I saw that and I saved you from it.'

'You lied to me.' That came from Aaron. And it wasn't a question.

'I didn't see you complaining,' Celeste bit back.

He shook his head. 'You know that's not true, Celeste.' That's when, like a slow motion bomb exploding in an action movie, Mitchell could see all too clearly what was coming. Fuck. But before he could ask the question and confirm his fears, he was interrupted.

'What about me?' Hope cut their conversation off. 'Was I the biggest mistake of your life?' she challenged Celeste, who didn't answer, so she pressed on. 'I need to know what happened. All of it. And I need to know why.'

She wasn't the only one, Mitchell thought, but he, and everyone else, left Hope's question hanging, all of them staring at one woman.

The silence was excruciating, but Hope didn't back down, just kept her gaze fixed on her mother until eventually Celeste began to speak.

31

Celeste had lost count of how many shots the extremely attractive bartender had served up to them in the last few hours. He'd already told her that he got off at 2 a.m., but even if she'd been interested – which she absolutely wasn't – he was wasting his time on two counts. First, it was only 11 p.m., but already her head was spinning and there was no way she could carry on drinking for much longer. And secondly, she had other, far more important things on her mind than a one night stand with a crazy-gorgeous barman.

'I think I'm drunk,' she whistled.

Beside her, Aaron raised his refilled shot glass, clinked it against hers and they knocked them back in practised synchronicity. 'Only way to be.'

She'd thought he was already tipsy when she'd first reached the bar, but he was on a whole other level of wasted now. Three solid hours of shots and heartbreak. This was the kind of stuff they wrote country songs about.

The catalyst for his over-consumption of tequila had come just after she'd joined him, when he'd asked mournfully, 'Do you honestly believe she won't come back?'

'She won't, Aaron. I'm sorry. You need to accept it.'

Of course, that wasn't true. As cynical as Celeste was, she could see that Agnetha had been hopelessly in love with this man. It wouldn't surprise her in the least if she was straight back over here as soon as her dad was feeling better. That's why she had to carry this through.

Either the tequila was turning her stomach, or it was a grip of dread over how she'd played this. If Aggs spoke to Aaron, then she'd find out that Celeste hadn't been entirely truthful. And where would that leave their friendship? She'd never forgive her. No, Celeste had to make sure that Aaron would never speak to Aggs again. Once again, she reminded herself that it was for her friend's own good. This wasn't the life for her. Aggs should be living with Celeste in London, having a great time and travelling the world, not tying herself down at the age of twenty-three.

Celeste had run through a stack of possible scenarios in her head. She could have told Aaron that Aggs was going back to an ex. She could have said that Aggs had realised he was just a holiday fling. But both those strategies came with the real possibility that Aaron would fly to Scotland to try to win her back.

As for the other side of it... She had to find a way to make sure that when Aggs landed in Scotland and called Aaron, that he wouldn't take the call. It would be tough for Aggs to let him go, but Celeste would help that along. She'd convince her that the best thing for her was to forget she'd ever met him. It was the only way. But handling Aggs' reaction to it all was a problem for later. Right now, she had to make sure there was no going back for Aaron.

'Do you think she'll come back to me?' Aaron was asking her again now, three hours into their tequila session.

For Christ's sake, that was at least the third time tonight. Her answer wasn't going to change.

'Two more shots, Blaize,' she shouted to the barman. 'And no, Aaron. You need to forget her.'

'How can I forget her? Don't you get it? I love her.'

Jesus, this was going to go on all night. He'd morphed from a young, sexy, cool guy into a fairly pathetic, heartbroken drunk who kept repeating himself and who was getting more morose with every passing minute. It wasn't a good look on him.

Two more shots and half an hour later, he was swaying and in danger of falling off his stool. Celeste had always prided herself on her ability to drink any man under the table, but she recognised that she was dangerously close to her limit. Time to call this a day. Sorrows drowned. Time to close this down permanently.

'Look, why don't we call it a night, huh? We can go upstairs, put the TV on.'

'Will she be there?' he asked, completely senselessly.

Oh, for fuck's sake. He was the worst drunk and this was the worst drunken night ever.

'No, she won't be there, Aaron. She's gone. She'll be halfway across the Atlantic by now. Come on. Let's go.'

'Nope, not going. Tequila.'

Behind the bar, Blaize had overheard the conversation and seemed to be in agreement. 'I think the lady is right, buddy. I can't serve you any more drinks. You're already way over our limit.'

'Thank you,' Celeste mouthed to him, and he replied with a surreptitious wink.

'Tell you what, there's a bottle of tequila up in the minibar. How about we go and finish that?'

Bingo. That got his attention. He lurched off the bar stool and she caught him before he fell.

'I'm okay, I'm okay,' he insisted, in that wasted way that absolutely confirmed he was anything but okay.

'I know you are, tiger. Let's just keep it moving. Don't worry, I've got you.'

Now that she had him on his feet, she made an executive decision. He had to walk this off a bit, sober up just enough so that she wasn't worried he'd vomit in his sleep and choke to death. There were many things her conscience could live with, but she drew the line there.

Arm through his, she coaxed him to take a detour round the hotel, out on to the pool deck for some fresh air, eventually reaching the room about half an hour later, by which time, he was once again capable of coherent speech. He'd also gone almost an hour without asking if Aggs was going to come bloody back. Another win.

In his room, the first thing she did was check the phone for a red flashing light that would indicate a message. There wasn't one. Excellent. Aggs would be on the plane from LA to Heathrow right now, so she was safe for the next ten hours or so. Relieved, she poured Aaron a glass of water, while he sat on the edge of the bed and pulled off his shoes, then unbuttoned his shirt.

As Celeste slid the curtains closed, she felt her eyes drawn to the curve of his shoulders, and the perfectly parallel ridges of his abs. For the second time today, she mused that Zac had been the perfect personality for her – in all honesty, Aaron would have bored her to death. But when it came to the physical side of the attraction equation, Aaron had exactly the kind of body that turned her on – tall, fit, athletic and muscular. From the neck down, he could be the body twin of Mr UCLA from the pool hook-up earlier. A flashback to that interlude combined with the tequila to give her a shiver of excitement.

Aaron drank the water, then stood up and unbuttoned his trousers, shoving them down, then kicking them off. There was nothing provocative there. They'd lived in the same apartment for weeks, so they were used to seeing each other in their underwear. It was no big deal. Yet, there were definitely parts of her anatomy that were suddenly declaring interest.

The bed springs creaked as Aaron flopped back onto the mattress.

'This isn't how I imagined spending my wedding night,' he mumbled, his eyes heavy.

'I'm sorry, Aaron. I really am. You deserve better. I do too. Zac totally did a number on me.'

'Fuck, yeah,' he muttered. 'Guess we both got blown off today. Sucks to be us, huh?'

That was the moment. Right there. After years of working behind bars, Celeste could see that he was in that space between drunk enough to lose his inhibitions and too drunk to do anything about it.

It was now or it was never. She made her choice.

'Do you mind if I sleep here tonight? I really don't want to walk back to my room on my own.'

Come on, baby. Come on. Say the right thing.

'Sure,' he shrugged, eyes even heavier now.

Celeste slipped down the straps of her bodycon dress and then shrugged her way out of it. She left just her tiny red thong on, then walked towards the bed, her high heels making tiny indentations on the carpet.

Aaron had rolled on to his side now, and as his eyes flicked open, he saw her in all her almost naked glory. 'Celeste...?' he murmured. There was a question in there that she didn't answer with words.

Kicking her shoes off, she slid on to the bed, then reached over and flicked off the light, plunging the room into darkness.

He didn't move and, for a second, Celeste didn't know whether to admire him or feel offended. The number of rejections she'd received in her life while naked amounted to exactly zero.

Just to stack the odds, she gently ran her finger along the side of his face, then across his lips. Next, she trailed her nails down his chest with the lightest touch, eliciting a barely audible but reassuring gasp.

'Don't you think we deserve to feel good just for a little while today?' she asked him, her lips touching his shoulder now.

'Celeste, we can't,' he slurred. 'Zac... Aggs...'

Oh, for crap's sake. Even now, jilted at the fricking altar, drunk, and lying in bed with a naked woman who couldn't give him more signals that she wanted to have sex with him if she wrote it on a neon sign and flashed it at him, he was still being decent. But that was the point, wasn't it? If they had sex, she knew that tomorrow he'd be so racked with guilt that there would be no going back for him and Aggs. She was counting on it.

Still he didn't move. The tipping point – had she misjudged it? Was he about to reject her? Or worse, had he fallen asleep while she was in mid-seduction?

'She's gone, Aaron, but I'm here. And I don't want to feel like it sucks to be us anymore. I want to make you feel good again. We deserve that.'

All hope was almost lost and she was about to retreat and chalk it up to a bad idea that she'd have to permanently erase from her memory, when she felt his hand move towards her, cup her neck, and his lips touch hers. Without breaking their kiss, she pressed against him, her hands kneading his back.

'Condom,' he whispered, but she hushed him.

'I'm on the pill.' That wasn't strictly true. But she didn't have a condom with her and she wasn't letting anything halt proceedings here in case he changed his mind. Stuff it. It would be fine. 'Don't worry.'

Those were the last words she said until it was over, a drunken shag that was fully executed, yet left them both barely satisfied. When it was done, they both lay on their backs in the darkness, until she heard his breathing change as he slipped into sleep.

Closing her eyes, she was almost asleep when she heard the sound of one mumbled word.

'Agnetha.'

Hope had the strongest feeling that reality had just slapped her right across the face. The elation, the excitement, the absolute joy of meeting the man who'd provided half of her DNA had been shoved to one side to allow room for the mind-boggling shocker of finding a mother who was absolutely nothing like the one she'd hoped for.

There it was, laid out in front of her. She was the product of an illicit coupling between a drunk guy, in mourning for the girl he thought had jilted him at the altar, and a woman with a twisted agenda.

Well, hello, Mum and Dad. Don't you just love playing happy families?

'So what happened next? You just all went back to your own lives and never contacted each other again?' Maisie was unable to hide the fact that she was absolutely riveted by all of this. Hope was grateful. Her sister was taking the pressure off her by asking all the questions that Hope wanted to but couldn't quite articulate right now because she was still in a state of – as Maisie would put it – complete shockfuckery.

Agnetha was the first to reply. 'It took me a couple of days to call because I went down with an almighty dose of food poisoning on the way home. I nearly ended up in the same hospital as my poor dad. But as soon as I was well enough, I called you. Loads of times,' she said, staring at Aaron. 'You never picked up. Then your number went dead and now I understand why.' Hope thought he looked like he wanted to crawl under the nearest rock.

'I couldn't face speaking to you,' he admitted. 'I was devastated that you'd run out on me, but I was far more disgusted by what I'd done. I knew I'd blown it. I changed my number. Thought it was the best thing for both of us. I couldn't face Zac either. A couple of weeks after we got back, he moved to New York to look after some actress full time and I let our relationship fritter away. I've no idea where he is now either. Damn, I've been such a coward and such a dick. I'm so sorry, Aggs. I know that means nothing now, but I really am.'

Hope felt a wave of sympathy as Agnetha put both hands to her face and tried to rub away the weariness that was there now. She seemed like a nice lady. A decent person. Hope was trying desperately not to make judgements, but she couldn't deny an overwhelming feeling that this would all be so much simpler if it had turned out the way they'd anticipated and Agnetha was her mum.

Just as that thought formed in Hope's mind, Agnetha let out a sigh that was loaded with decision. 'You know what?' she said, her hands going to the arms of her chair, ready to push herself up. 'I think you all have a lot to talk about, so I'm going to go back and join my party and leave you to it. You're very welcome to stay here for as long as you need. You're also very welcome to come inside if you're chilly. There's plenty of food and booze, and God knows, we could probably do with a drink. So I'll leave you for now. And Hope...' As Hope met her gaze, Agnetha's voice softened. 'I think you're very brave and it was so lovely to meet you. I... I wish things had worked out differently.' Agnetha's sad smile told Hope that she meant every word. 'Please don't leave without saying goodbye.'

'I won't. Thank you. And I'm sorry again for gatecrashing your party.'

'Please don't be,' Agnetha said, leaning over and squeezing her hand.

As Agnetha stood up, Celeste's husband got up too. She had to remind herself that he was also Agnetha's ex-husband. This whole set-up was both incestuous and confusing – she still couldn't believe that her mother had relationships with two men who had been involved with Agnetha first. What was that about?

'I think I'll join you for that drink,' he said to Agnetha, and Hope noticed that he couldn't even look at Celeste. No wonder. That must have been a tough story to listen to. Celeste hadn't gone into intimate details about the night Hope was conceived, but they got the general gist of it and no guy wanted to hear that his wife had sex with his ex-wife's first love out of some sense of twisted jealousy. And Hope guessed that he wouldn't be happy about Celeste keeping her child a secret from him either. God, what a mess.

Aaron watched Agnetha go. The fury had left his eyes now and Hope saw the pain in his face as he spoke to her mother. Her mother. Celeste. It was going to take her a while to get her head round that.

'Why didn't you tell me, Celeste? I would have helped you. Supported you. We could have done it all differently.'

Hope pulled her denim jacket around her, feeling suddenly cold. Aaron saw this and immediately took off his jacket and put it around her shoulders.

It gave Celeste... her mother... time to think about her answer. 'So you could rescue me and we could make a go of it? Don't be ridiculous.'

Wow, this woman definitely had edges. Maisie's eyes were on stalks.

Celeste exhaled and dialled it back a notch, alternating her eye contact but mainly focusing on Hope. That was understandable. It was obvious there were a whole lot of complicated emotions flying around between Celeste and Aaron. 'After I left LA, I came back to London and just went back to my life. I didn't know that I was pregnant, didn't realise until I was over four months gone. My cycle had never been regular so I hadn't thought anything of it.' She broke off there and spoke directly to Aaron. 'I genuinely was on the pill, but I'd run out the week before because we'd extended our stay for so long.'

Hope was darkly fascinated by Celeste's reactions. If the woman was embarrassed talking about such sensitive things, she definitely wasn't showing it. She seemed almost brusque. Business-like.

'Look, I know it seems like I was reckless with you but I didn't think for a minute I could get pregnant so soon, I thought the pill would still be protecting me. I didn't deliberately set out to get pregnant with your baby. I know that's no consolation here, but I just wanted that to be clear.'

Aaron didn't reply, so Celeste went on, her gaze now veering between Hope and the far distance, where her memories seemed to reside. 'I'd landed a big job, an advertising campaign, and it was at the fittings that I realised I'd gained a bit of weight and then... Well, that was that. Job gone. I did a test and... well, I was devastated. I'm sorry, Hope.'

'That's okay,' Hope replied, and then wondered why she was trying to console her. She should feel angry, furious, beyond hurt to hear that, yet instead she felt almost removed, like she was watching a movie and she wasn't one of the leading roles.

'Anyway... Christ, this gets worse and worse... The truth is, I wasn't sure whose baby it was. It could have been Zac's. Or yours,' she was back with Aaron again. 'Or one or two others from when I got back to London...'

Maisie turned to meet Hope's eyes with a flabbergasted look that Hope immediately translated as, *Holy shit, your mum was a bit of a slapper.*

'And I was too late to...' She didn't finish, but she didn't have to – Hope knew exactly what she was going to say. She was too late to terminate the pregnancy.

Wow. That was a sobering thought. Hope only existed because her mother ran out of contraceptive pills and then didn't realise her periods had stopped. And slept with her best friend's boyfriend, and several other potential daddy candidates...

Something else occurred to Hope. 'You said you lived in London? But I was born in Edinburgh, and adopted by a family in Glasgow.'

Celeste let out a bitter laugh. 'Pure coincidence. I was working with an adoption agency in London, whose clients were all over the country. When they told me the parents who were going to adopt the baby were from Glasgow, I was initially apprehensive, but then I realised it didn't matter. I'd stipulated a closed adoption. I didn't want to give birth in London, where I might meet someone I knew, and I had the same problem with Glasgow, so I went to Edinburgh. Had you there. Handed you over. And then... please don't think I'm a callous bitch, but I went back to living my life. I stayed down south for a few more years, before eventually coming home to Glasgow permanently.'

'Did you think about keeping me?' Hope's throat tightened as she asked that.

Maisie heard it and reached over and took her hand.

Celeste shook her head. 'I'm sorry, Hope...' That was the first time she'd used her name and it sounded strange. Her mother. Calling her by her name. If she'd thought this morning that this would happen today, she'd have been elated and yet now it just felt... wrong. In Hope's mind, she saw her own mum, Dora, heard her calling her down for dinner, or in from the garden, and she recognised the affection in her mum's voice. She had a sudden longing to be in her mum's arms, to be telling her all about this, while feeling the protection and love Dora had given her unconditionally every day of her life. '... But I just didn't have the capability to do that. I had no support system. My parents weren't in the picture, I had to work to earn a living... The only people I had were Aggs and her parents, and they were dealing with her dad's illness.'

'Which made it all the more surprising that you screwed Agnetha over,' Aaron said. His words were harsh, but his tone was one of pure defeat and Hope felt her heart go out to him too. He'd made a mistake. A huge one. But he'd paid for that by missing twenty years of her life and she knew he'd beat himself up about that until the end of time.

Celeste took the hit. 'You're right. But in my mind I saw it differently. Back then, I thought that keeping Aggs and you apart meant that she wouldn't leave me. Flawed thinking, especially given how it all worked out.'

Hope cut into their exchange, unable to hold back the question that was burning a hole in her mind. 'Did you ever think about me?' She wasn't sure she wanted to hear the answer. Celeste wasn't exactly coming over as Mother Earth here.

'Sometimes. But I knew that you'd gone to a good family and that you'd have a great life. Trust me, I'd have been a terrible mother. It's something I never learned to do.'

Surprisingly, Hope felt a tug of sympathy. Had Celeste had a tough childhood? She made it sound like happy family life was a concept she wasn't familiar with back then.

Well, she was about to find out if there was any chance that Celeste's theory that she'd be a terrible mum was on point.

'I think there are a couple of things you should know,' Hope began, surprisingly sanguine in the face of the potential for a life threatening rejection. She went on to tell Celeste the same story she'd shared with Aaron earlier. Her cancer as a teenager. The recurrence a couple of years ago. The risk that it could come back. The need for stem cells if it did.

When she finished, Celeste was silent for a moment before seeking clarification. 'Let me make sure I understand. You want me to get tested to see if I'm a match?'

'Yes.'

Hope didn't know Celeste well enough to decipher if the shadow that crossed her face was horror or concern. 'Can I think about it?'

Aaron's eyes widened, clearly shocked. 'Celeste!' he blurted.

Hope cut him off. 'Of course you can,' she answered calmly, aware that there was no other reply she could give. So Celeste hadn't automatically and instinctively agreed to help her. Her biological mother would have to contemplate whether or not to step up if she was needed to save her daughter's life. Of course, that reluctance was always a possibility, but in her childhood dreams, her mum would scoop her up, shower her with love and do anything for her. But there was no scooping. No love. Nothing.

As she was digesting that, Hope's attention was diverted to a car that had just pulled up and parked behind Maisie's Mini. A man climbed out of the driver's seat, and a heartbeat later, the café door slammed open.

'Will, you big darling! Where the hell have you been? It's bloody midnight!'

Even given the tension of the moment, it was impossible not to smile at the gregarious welcome from a woman with a blonde bob and bright blue eyeshadow who was now standing in the doorway with her arms outstretched.

'I'm going to come here every weekend from now on,' Maisie said quietly but with wonder. 'It's like an alternate universe of drama and excitement just revolves around this café.'

Hope ignored her, too busy listening to the new arrival's response. 'Sorry, Val, I got held up. It's a long story.' He nodded a friendly acknowledgment as he passed their table.

'Well, hurry up because your girl has been on pins and needles all night. I think she thought you were standing her up...'

The burst of joy lifted Hope's spirits a little. By the sound of it, at least someone was going to get a happy ending tonight.

'... and you can't do that to our Aggs on her birthday!'

This was obviously Agnetha's boyfriend, then.

Hope saw two very distinct reactions. First of all, Celeste's head whipped round, suddenly having a need to see the new arrival. And, at the other side of the table, Aaron's eyes narrowed as he watched the man with undisguised interest and maybe something else. Sadness? Regret?

As the guy went inside, Hope watched as Aaron's shoulders slumped just a little more.

MIDNIGHT – 8 A.M

'Dad, do you know that Cruella is still sitting at a table outside? I was going to go out and do a nosy, but she gave me the death stare.' Isla danced into the café kitchen and plonked another stack of dirty dishes down on the worktop.

Aggs, elbow deep in soapy water, glanced over at Mitchell, who continued to scrape leftover food off a platter, straight into the bin. She wished she had a camera. Over twenty years she'd known him, and this was the first time he'd ended up in a kitchen, helping her clear up at the end of a party.

Mitchell gave a casual shrug. 'I know, sweetheart, but probably best to just leave them to it.'

'Who is she talking to anyway? I don't think I recognise them.'

Aggs jumped in to help out. 'An old friend we knew a million years ago. I'll tell you all about it later.'

'Any more dishes out there, darling?' Mitchell asked, before Isla could attempt to dig for more information. He was trying to play it cool, but Aggs could hear the tension in his words. Understandable. It had been quite a night.

'I'll go and check. Dad, can I ask you something?'

'Anything, love.' Aggs saw him brace himself for something deeply personal or painful. 'Hypothetically speaking... Killing a twin because she's sitting on her arse and refusing to help clear the buffet table – twenty to life or could I get a reduced sentence by pleading extreme provocation?'

'Definitely extreme provocation.'

Isla seemed satisfied. 'Excellent. If you hear screams, just ignore them.'

As Isla sashayed back out to continue the clear-up, Aggs saw Mitchell's forced cheeriness dissolve into a weary sigh.

'You okay there, Mr McMaster?'

He put the empty platter down next to Isla's discarded pile of plates and thought about that for a second or two. 'Is it weird that I am?'

'Yep,' she teased, realising it felt good to laugh with him. Weirdly, she actually felt some sympathy for him. It couldn't be easy to learn that his wife had always been an immoral, manipulative cow on the same day as he discovered she was cheating on him too.

But then, she wasn't exactly in a position to judge him on his perception skills. She hadn't known that her best friend had had a baby and put it up for adoption. She'd been clueless for over twenty years as to why Aaron had ghosted her. And she'd had no idea those two things were connected, or what she'd have done if she'd been aware of the truth. Seeing Aaron tonight had been bittersweet. It was both incredible and devastating, exciting yet confusing. He'd betrayed her, just like Mitchell. Sure, Aaron had been a fool and made a drunken mistake, while Mitchell had known exactly what he was getting in to, had plenty of time to retreat and choose to stay faithful, but had opted not to. Were they both on the same level of treachery?

Mitchell opened the drinks fridge and took out a beer, then

came and stood next to her, leaning against the worktop. A memory flashed into Aggs' mind. The two of them, in exactly the same positions so many times before, back in the early days when he would come in from work and hang out with her while she cleared up, telling her all about his day. They'd been good once. Sometimes it was easy to forget that.

Mitchell took a swig of the beer, then folded his arms, tucking the bottle in at his elbow. 'I think it's clarified in my mind what I need to do. What I should have done a long time ago, if I'm honest. The problem with me and Celeste isn't that she's having an affair... The problem is that we should never have got together in the first place. I was such a fucking idiot.'

Aggs chose not to argue that point.

'I'm sorry, Aggs. I really am. I wish I could go back and do it all differently.'

'But you can't,' she said, with a sad shrug of her shoulders. In truth, she wished the same thing. Although, if she'd gone back to Aaron, she wouldn't have Isla and Skye and they made all the pain and struggles worth it.

He held her gaze. 'Can't we? It doesn't have to be too late for us. Couldn't we try?'

Aggs felt a jolt of surprise as she realised what he was asking. *Could they try again?*

'Look who I found out wandering the streets!' Val's gregarious bellow cut through the moment, as she burst into the kitchen, her beaming grin leading the way.

Aggs and Mitchell jumped, snapped out of the loaded question that was still hanging between them. *Could they try again?*

Val made a gesture like a game show hostess pointing to the star prize as she stepped to the side to allow Will to come in behind her. 'I found this one!' she exclaimed proudly.

Will. He was here. He'd made it.

'Hey, you,' he greeted her.

She had no time to respond before Val threw her arms wide and then wrapped her in a hug. 'Right, my love, I'm off. Are you sure you won't let me stay and clear up?'

'I'm sure, Val. Thank you so much for everything. This has been the most unforgettable day.' That was definitely true.

Just at that, Yvie came barrelling in, somehow managing to balance a tray of empty glasses in one hand and a black bin bag in the other. 'Those years as a waitress while I was at college weren't wasted,' she quipped, expertly placing the tray down on the table, then putting the bin bag over by the back door. 'That's everything pretty much sorted out there. There are still a couple of stragglers finishing their drinks, but I don't think they'll be much longer. Did you say that we're off now, Val?'

'I did. Aggs threatened to hold on to my ankles so I wouldn't go.'

Chuckling, Aggs whipped off her Marigolds and hugged Yvie goodbye. 'You're fab, do you know that?' she told her friend, feeling a rush of love.

'Right back at you, honey,' Yvie replied, matching her squeeze.

'Christ, it's like one of those American talk shows in here, where they all hug at the end. I'm getting out before I start weeping and baring my soul.'

'Is there a soul in there, Val?' Yvie asked, eyes twinkling with cheek.

Val raised one eyebrow. 'Aye, but I mostly keep it doused with vodka, so it doesn't give me too much trouble.'

Aggs was still laughing as they enveloped her again, this time in a three way hug, before giving her a flurry of kisses and then disappearing out of the door.

There was a strange and slightly awkward silence as the three people remaining in the room recalibrated to the new situation.

Will looked at Mitchell. Mitchell looked at Will. Aggs looked at both of them and felt her toes curling inside her sparkly shoes.

Mitchell was the first to break. 'Right, well, I'll... go and see what the girls are up to.'

Aggs threw him a smile of gratitude, an echo of a thought still playing in the background of her mind. *Could they try again?*

Will gave Mitchell a nod as he passed on his way out of the door.

'You look like you could do with a drink. Beer?' Aggs asked.

'Coffee?' Will countered.

'No problem,' Aggs said, taking two cups from the cupboard beside her and filling them from the half-full pot that was already brewed on the coffee machine. She put them on the small table at the side of the room where she and Isla would sit and chat during their breaks.

Pulling out a chair, Aggs watched Will as he followed suit, taking the seat across from her. It didn't take deep insight or keen perception to see that this was a very different man from the one who'd been here this afternoon. The body language. The aura. The exhaustion in his eyes. He was a stranger to the guy who'd kissed her. No relation to the bloke who had excitedly presented her with a trip to Paris and gushed about what a great time they were going to have.

'Go on,' she coaxed softly, eliminating all small talk from the conversation. She'd been through enough to recognise sadness and right now it was oozing from every pore of Will's skin.

He wrapped his hands around the cup, taking comfort from the heat as he stared into the black liquid. 'Carol wants to try again.'

Aggs closed her eyes, took it in, felt the weight of his feelings as if transferred to her by his words, realising that she'd known since the minute he walked in the door. And she also knew that there was no choice when it came to what he should do.

'And you want that too?' she asked gently, no trace of judgement.

'I don't know,' he answered honestly. 'When we split up, we were broken.' His emotions threatened to spill over, so he paused, took a breath, steadied himself. 'I understood. Really, I did. We were both drowning in grief over Barney, and we couldn't keep each other afloat any more. We were pulling each other down and we had to let go.'

Aggs reached over and put her hand on his, her sad smile encouraging him to go on. He had to work this through for himself and all she could do was listen while he did that.

'I wasn't looking for anyone, but then I met you...' He raised his eyes and she saw pools of unshed tears. '... and started to feel something like happiness again. I don't expect that to happen, but it did. That was real.'

Aggs' voice was barely louder than a whisper. 'I know.' It was true and she understood because she'd been through a similar journey after she'd left Aaron, after Mitchell cheated, after her dad died, after her mum passed away too. The grief, the feeling that nothing would ever bring joy again, and then the very slow and gradual shedding of the scales of pain, until there was still enough protection there to keep her together, but the shell was soft enough to let new love in.

'But now...' he stopped, unable to force out what she knew he'd come to say.

Her natural instinct to comfort him kicked in. He was a good man. It was killing her to see him struggling through the turmoil. Hadn't they both had enough of that? 'Will, it's fine, I promise.'

It was as if her kindness gave him the courage to go on, to make the decision.

'I have to go back. I owe it to Carol and I owe it to Barney. We will always be the parents whose son died, but now, maybe we can be together and remember what we had – our beautiful boy for twenty-one years of his life.'

Aggs had two hands on top of his now. 'I think you can,' she told him. 'And I think it's the right thing to do.'

'You do?'

Her smile came naturally, no need to force it because she was being completely honest. 'I do.'

'Thank you,' he told her, with quiet but palpable relief.

'For what?'

'For being a friend.'

'Always,' she told him, meaning it. Will would always be part of her recovery and she'd always be grateful that he was in her life.

As he got up to leave, his hand trailed along hers. 'You're a special lady, Aggs. See you at The Wednesday Club?'

'Yup, I'll see you there.'

As soon as he was gone, Aggs sat back in her chair, winded, sore, but unbroken. Their friendship would survive this and she knew they would continue to support each other. No hard feelings. And the Paris trip? Maybe she could take the girls. They deserved that and more for everything they'd done for her today.

She was so deep in thought that she didn't even hear the footsteps until the words came.

'Can I talk to you?'

The hairs on the back of Aggs' neck bristled as she raised her head. Could she really do this?

'Sure, Celeste,' she said wearily. 'Take a seat.'

'Dad, I don't want to scare you, but Celeste just went into the back kitchen to talk to Mum,' Skye told him as he came back into the café from the gents. His first reaction was to glance outside, where he saw that Aaron was still sitting with Hope and Maisie, but Celeste's seat was empty. Shit.

'Skye, do me a favour.'

'Is there money in it for me?' she quipped. 'A free holiday? Shoes?'

He felt a wave of gratitude for his daughters' quick mouths. Even in times like this, they could lift his spirits. He kissed her on the cheek. 'Nope, just my undying love.'

'I'd rather have shoes.'

His chuckle made her grin too.

'Okay, Pops, what do you need?'

'Can you go outside and ask those people to come in and maybe get them a drink and offer them some food?'

'Sure thing.' She was peering out curiously now. 'Who are they? Isla said the guy is an old friend of Mum's, but I thought I heard an American accent?'

Mitchell wanted to explain, but just thinking about Celeste being in the back kitchen with Aggs made him want to reach for the Gaviscon. 'She met him when she was in LA. Before we were married.'

Skye's eyes widened. 'A romance?' She peered out at Aaron again. 'Go Mum. I can definitely see the attraction. He must have been gorgeous when he was younger.'

Mitchell shook his head. 'I'm going to pretend I didn't hear that. Can you just go? Go...' he shooed her towards the door.

Skye seemed to think this was hilarious. 'Okay, keep your pants on. And if you're not out of there in ten minutes,' she gestured to the kitchen, 'I'll call in a crime scene team.'

As he approached the kitchen door, Mitchell wondered if he was already too late as there were no sounds at all coming from inside. No voices. No movements. Although, maybe a good sign, no screams.

It was a relief when he saw Aggs acknowledge his arrival with a raise of her eyebrows. He knew that look. It was the same one she gave when the kids were small and she wanted him to jump in with some co-parental support.

'Are you two okay? Want me to leave or stay?' he asked, not sure which answer he'd prefer.

Of course, it was Celeste who replied. His wife always had to be in control. 'You may as well stay. Save me repeating everything twice.'

He saw a flicker of relief from Aggs. Stay, it was then.

His beer from earlier was still lying on the kitchen worktop by the sink, so he picked it up and resumed the position he'd been in when he'd been talking to Aggs. It was there, just a few feet from both women, that a couple of observations struck him. Will wasn't here, and he hadn't seen him out in the café, so he must have left. And closer to home, Celeste spent a fortune maintaining that beautiful face with an exhaustive routine of freezers, fillers, facials, lasers, chemicals and cosmetics that cost the same as a meal for two in a Michelin star restaurant. There was no doubt that with her glossy hair and exquisitely curved cheekbones, she was still stunning, but...

His contemplation moved to Aggs. What was remarkable was that somehow, despite none of the treatments that Celeste swore by, Aggs actually looked younger, and had changed so little from the gorgeous twenty-four year old with the wild flame red hair that he'd fallen in love with.

'Did I miss anything?' he asked, to a head shake from Celeste.

'No.' He watched as she turned back to Aggs, and for once, he thought he saw a flicker of self-doubt on her face. 'You must hate me right now,' his current wife said calmly to his ex-wife.

Watching the palpable discomfort between them, it seemed unfathomable that they had once been as close as sisters. He took full responsibility for his part in destroying that relationship.

Aggs was almost nonchalant as she answered, 'Hating you isn't worth the energy it takes, Celeste.'

He felt like applauding Aggs for being the epitome of dignity and class.

Celeste took the hit and stayed upright. 'Ouch. Deserved though,' she conceded.

'What do you need to tell me, Celeste?' Aggs urged her to get to the point, but there was no malice in her voice and Mitchell admired her reasoned calmness. Once upon a time, he remembered thinking that Celeste was absolutely a class act. Now he saw that it had been Aggs who was the more impressive one all along. What a dick he'd been to miss that, so swayed by the surface stuff to see what was going on underneath. The reality was that Aggs was worth a million Celeste's.

'The thing with Aaron... I want you to know that it wasn't

planned. It doesn't make a difference now, I see that. I know you think I'm a heartless bitch...' she gave a bitter laugh. 'And you're not wrong, but back then, I wasn't trying to hurt you.'

'So why? Why do it?'

Celeste winced. 'Because I didn't want to lose you, didn't want you to go and live in LA. You and your mum and dad were all I had, and I wanted to hang on to you. If you'd married Aaron, I'd have lost you and I wasn't ready for that.'

Mitchell waited for Aggs to ask the obvious question and she was already there. 'But even if I accept that, Celeste, what you did later makes no sense. If you slept with Aaron because you didn't want to lose me, why did you have an affair with my husband? You had to know that would kill our relationship completely. Why take him too?'

The shame was acute, and Mitchell was sure he could feel his bollocks slightly retreat inside him when she said it. Much as he wanted to escape the discomfort, he knew he deserved this.

'Because by then everything was different. When I was pregnant, I lost the biggest break of my career and by the time I'd had the baby...'

Mitchell noticed that she wasn't calling Hope by her name. Obviously Celeste was associating the young woman out there with what had to have been a traumatic time in her life. Or was he being too kind? Was Celeste's lack of connection more down to the fact that she'd never felt anything for her child at all?

'How did I miss you being pregnant?' Aggs interjected.

'Because I stayed down in London for the latter months and you were up here looking after your dad. Anyway, when I went back to work, I'd discovered I'd missed the boat. I was twenty-five by then, and the jobs were drying up. Career over before it had really begun and that twisted my mind, made me furious and bitter. And, somehow, I blamed you.'

This was all news to Mitchell, and he was hanging on every word, watching as Aggs took it all in too but gave no reaction.

'When I moved back to Glasgow, I had nothing. No job. No money. No relationship. I wasn't even thirty and I was washed up. And there was you, with the parents who loved you, and the two perfect children, and the house and the hotshot lawyer husband... you had everything.'

'Except a life,' Aggs countered. 'All I did was work and take care of everyone. I was exhausted.'

Celeste put her hands up in acceptance. 'I get that now. But back then, I was so wrapped up with jealousy and ambition and rage over what I'd lost. All I saw was that I had nothing and you had everything that I didn't have, yet I didn't think you appreciated it. You didn't have time for Mitch, or for me... I'd wrecked my life trying to keep you and it had been for nothing. So I cut my losses. I saw a way to get a man I'd fallen in love with, to get a family, a home, status... everything I wanted and if it cost me a friendship with someone who didn't have time for me anyway, well, it was a price worth paying.'

Aggs smiled sadly. 'So you took it.'

'So I took it,' Celeste parroted. 'I felt I deserved it.'

Aggs blinked, as if realising something and he knew instantly what it was. Celeste's words had caught out a small fib he'd told earlier. 'Tell me something, Celeste – who made the first move?' Aggs asked the same question she'd put to him that afternoon in the Botanic Gardens.

'I did,' Celeste answered truthfully. Damn it. He'd taken the blame for that to try to help the relationship between the two women. Not that it mattered now. Whatever happened from here on in, that bridge was fairly certainly incinerated.

Aggs threw him a knowing glance, while Celeste put both hands on the table, as if she was trying to find steady ground to balance her. 'Aggs, I'm sorry. I don't expect you to forgive me, but I just wanted you to know I'm sorry.'

It had been ten years in coming, but now she'd said it there was a stunned silence until Celeste broke it with another whammy.

'And, Mitch, you know I owe you an apology too.'

They both knew why. Derek Evans.

'Why are you saying all this now, Celeste?' Mitchell asked, with a gut feeling that he already knew the answer.

The resignation was in every word that his wife uttered. 'Because today pretty much proved that secrets come back to bite you on the arse. And because, this feels like a turning point, you see that, don't you, Mitch?'

'We're done,' he said, a confirmation, not a threat.

'We are,' Celeste said. 'We should probably have been done a while ago, but I think we were so defensive over what we did, so arrogant about what we thought we deserved, that we were determined to prove a point and make it last.'

He hadn't thought about it like that, but he knew there was something in what she was saying.

'Anyway, I'm going to go. I'll move my stuff out over the next few days.'

Mitchell checked himself for signs of pain, but there were none. This morning he'd woken up fearing that his marriage was over. Now the reality of that was like an incredible pressure being lifted off him.

'What about Hope?' Aggs asked.

Celeste got up, obviously having said everything she came to say. 'I don't know,' she answered honestly. 'Motherhood clearly isn't my strong point, but I owe it to her to try and I will.'

'Good luck with that,' Aggs said with all sincerity. 'For Hope's sake, I hope it works out.'

'Me too. Happy birthday, Aggs.' It was her parting shot, and for a few seconds after she'd gone, Aggs and Mitchell just stared at the door.

'I couldn't be more shocked if George Clooney walked in here naked right now,' Aggs admitted, giving Mitchell a mental picture he could probably live without. 'I didn't think she understood the concept of apologies. First time I've ever heard her say sorry.'

Mitchell walked over and took the chair Celeste had just vacated, turning it around and sitting on it backwards, so that he didn't have to squeeze his legs under the table. 'It was definitely a first.'

'And she made the first move,' Aggs said softly. 'Why did you take the blame?'

'Because either way, it was my fault. I let you down. And I didn't want it to look like I was shirking the responsibility for that.'

He reached over and put down his beer, then took a breath, unable to resist the need to continue the conversation that they'd hinted at earlier. It made so much sense now. Them, the girls, all together. He was ready to cut back on his work, to make changes, to get rid of this bloody indigestion by changing his lifestyle and his priorities. He and Aggs could make it work now. He was sure of it. He just had to make the case for it, to convince her, to make her see how great it could be. 'Aggs, what we were talking about earlier – I've been thinking that we could...'

'Don't.' Aggs stopped him. There was no vehemence there, no anger, just more of the same calm resolve that she'd shown Celeste. 'Mitchell, I loved you and that will always be there. You're a fantastic father – if I'm honest, I don't know that you'd have been so close to the girls if we hadn't split up and you didn't have to prioritise making time to see them. Our daughters adore you, and I'm so glad that you're in their lives and in mine too. I hope that you always will be.'

It was like watching the face of a judge right before she delivered a verdict, and being horribly sure that her demeanour suggested you were going to lose, but hoping beyond hope that you were wrong and about to snatch a seismic victory.

'But there's no going back for us. It's time for me to go and find a new life, and I want one that comes on my terms, not one that's based on the person I used to be. I'm sorry, Mitchell.'

He considered arguing, but he knew it would be pointless. Time to retreat, perhaps to come back another day, perhaps not.

'Friends?' he asked, putting his hand out.

She took it, squeezed. 'Friends. But, Mitch...'

'What?'

'Don't ever think about sleeping with any of my pals ever again. If you try it on with Val, she'll kick your head in.'

'Point taken,' he surrendered, hands in the air. Friends. Friends who made each other laugh. For now, he'd take it.

In the pause, the sound of chatter from the café drifted through.

'Are Aaron and the girls still here?' she asked, surprised, but he could also sense something else in her reaction. She was pleased.

'Yeah. I asked Skye to look after them and make them something to eat.'

'Good God, what's wrong with you? Those poor people have been through enough without being subjected to Skye's cooking skills.'

She was laughing as she rose, and Mitchell realised now that he'd known since the moment he saw Aggs speaking to Aaron on the pavement that there was unfinished business there.

'Come on,' she said, holding her hand out. 'Let's go and see what's happening.'

35

Aaron heard the banging sound first, then the pain seared across from one temple to another, as if his head was in a vice that was being tightened by an invisible force.

What the hell...? Where was he?

His eyes adjusted to the darkness and he realised he was in the hotel room. Relief. But it was only temporary, until the pain shot through his skull again.

Shit, what had he drank? And had someone beaten him up with a baseball bat on the way home? Actually, how had he even got here?

As he tried to wade through the fog, each step coming with another punch to the head, he heard the unmistakable sound of breathing next to him. Aggs was there. He relaxed a little. She was there. His girl was with him and everything was going to be okay. He tried to push back the fear that felt like it was suffocating him, just as some of the mist cleared and...

Fuck, no.

Rewind.

Image after image was playing back now, like watching a movie on fast forward. Aggs had left. He'd gone to the bar. Celeste was with him. They'd got hammered. She'd come back to the room. The dress. The thong. She'd climbed in beside him and...

He lurched from the bed and made it to the bathroom just in time to vomit his guts into the toilet. When there was nothing left but the sour, foetid taste of alcohol and regret, he slid back on to the bathroom floor, his head against the cool tiles of the wall.

What the hell had he done?

Unfortunately, the answer to that question was now playing in excruciating frame by frame detail in his mind. He threw up again, thought about standing, then decided that his legs wouldn't hold him yet.

Celeste. He'd had sex with Celeste. And he could blame the booze, or his sorrow over Aggs leaving, or a million other reasons he could probably come up with if his brain cells hadn't been eviscerated by tequila, but he didn't stand for all that excuses shit when Zac came home moaning about one of the many drunken hook-ups he'd had in the last few years, so he couldn't cut himself any slack either.

His body, his dick, his decision, his mistake.

Now his skin felt like it was burning on the inside but shivering on the outside and his brain was melting like candle wax too close to a flame.

When he was sure he could move without retching again, he pulled himself up using the basin for support and came face to face with a reflection he didn't recognise.

A cheating douchebag. That's what he was looking at. And what he'd have to look at every day from now on.

The stab of self-loathing felt like it had drawn blood.

He splashed water on his face time and time again, then used his cupped hand to lift cold water to his mouth and drank from his palm.

Still a cheating douchebag.

No amount of water was going to wash that away.

Regardless, he switched the shower on and stepped into it, desperate to wash away all traces of what he'd done.

He stood under the water jets, maybe for a minute, maybe for an hour, yet still he didn't feel clean.

He'd blown it.

Yes, Aggs had left him, but before he'd slept with Celeste he could have gone after her. He could have jumped on the next flight to the UK and found his way to her. He could have shown her that he was serious, proved that they could find a way to make it work. He couldn't go now. How could she possibly believe him?

A few hours ago, there was a chance, but now that was gone and all that was left in its place was shame and disgust.

He dried off, wrapped a towel around his waist and went back into the bedroom. Before he even got to the bed, he knew Celeste was awake.

She flicked on the light and he saw that she was up and dressed, pulling on her shoes. 'I'm going back to my room,' she told him, as if this was a casual conversation and they'd just had coffee and maybe watched a bit of TV.

'Celeste, I'm sorry...'

'For what? Aaron, we were consenting adults. We had sex. End of story.'

End of story. Christ, she was either a heartless piece of work, or like him, she'd made a massive mistake that she was already regretting. He wasn't sure he wanted to know which shoe fitted.

'But here's the thing... you can't tell Aggs. It goes without saying. That's the deal. You don't tell her, I don't tell her. Do we understand each other?'

What option did he have? Aggs was gone, she'd made her decision. If he went after her, her couldn't live with lying, but he couldn't live with the truth either.

Celeste picked up her bag. 'I'm going to try to change my flight back to London and catch an earlier one, so hopefully I won't be around the apartment for too much longer.'

He nodded, barely taking in her words. She crossed the room and left to the sound of a soft rub of wood against carpet as the door closed behind her.

Aaron opened the curtains, desperate for light to permeate the darkness. As the sun came up, it brought with it a whole load of devastating realities.

He knew for sure that he'd just made an irrevocable mistake, one that he'd regret until the end of time.

And he knew, with absolute certainty, that he'd destroyed every chance of spending the rest of his life with the woman he loved.

'Did you call Mum?' Maisie asked Hope, as she came back into the café from the corridor.

'I did. She said to tell you she loves you and that you'd better not be acting dramatic.'

Maisie's first reaction was outraged indignation, then she realised Hope was joking and the two of them dissolved into giggles. For once, Maisie had been the calmest, most reserved aspect of a day that had been packed with more drama than they could ever have anticipated.

'Hope, lift up your glass,' Isla chirped, thrusting a bottle of wine towards her from the other side of the table.

Hope obliged, happy to accept the refill and enjoying the company. Aggs' daughters were lovely. Skye had invited them in and popped open a bottle of wine, while Isla had conjured up a tray of gorgeous mini-wraps and sushi.

There had only been one awkward moment and that was when they'd first come inside. Celeste and Mitchell were, according to Skye, in the back kitchen chatting to Aggs, so that left the five of them – Isla and Skye, Maisie and Hope, and Aaron – sitting round a table, everyone else from the party long gone.

Introductions had been made, and drinks had just been poured when Isla had leaned into the table, puzzled after hearing Hope's accent. 'Hang on. I know you're a friend from years ago,' she'd said to Aaron, before swinging her question round to Hope and Maisie. 'But how do you two know Cruella?'

'Cruella?' Aaron had clearly been puzzled.

'Sorry, force of habit. I meant Celeste.'

Cruella? Isla clearly wasn't a fan then.

Maisie had slowly turned to Hope, eyes wide, an unmistakable smile playing on her lips, as if to say, *On you go then, you do the honours.*

'She's... erm... she's my mother. My biological mother, I mean. I was adopted,' Hope had said, with a shrug of fait accompli.

Isla had frozen, staring at Hope's face. 'Shit, you're not kidding, are you?'

'Nope.'

'But I thought...' Skye had rounded on Aaron. 'I thought you were an old boyfriend of my mum's?'

Aaron had visibly squirmed and Hope had thought about rescuing him, then decided against it. The truth was the truth and there was no point trying to gloss over it.

'I was, but... it's complicated,' he'd admitted, clearly mortified, stuttering over his words. 'I had a very brief...' He'd struggled to find the term. '... *encounter* with Celeste too.'

Stunned, Isla had dropped the bottle on the table, thankfully managing to keep it upright. 'Holy shit, that woman must have a vagina like a Venus flytrap.'

Aaron had flushed bright red, while Maisie's gaze had shot to the floor, but Hope could see her sister's shoulders were shaking.

'If you've finished discussing my vagina...' Celeste's voice had rung out loud and clear behind Isla, who'd clenched her eyes tight shut, nose wrinkled, caught in the act. 'Then I'm going to go home. It's been a long day,' she'd said. 'Hope, can I speak to you before I go?'

'Of course.' Face flushed and ignoring the curious glances from around the table, Hope had got up and walked to the door with her.

There, Celeste had fished into her handbag and given Hope a small rectangle of glossy cardboard. Yes, her mother really had just given her a business card. 'Will you call me tomorrow?' Celeste had asked.

Hope had nodded, grateful that while Celeste definitely wasn't warm and bubbly, there seemed to be at least a chance that they could try to build some kind of relationship. 'I will.'

That had seemed to please Celeste. 'And just so you know, the medical tests you spoke about earlier...' When they were sitting outside, Hope had explained more about her condition and the potential need for donor cells in the future. '... I'll give you anything you need.'

'Thank you. Maybe we could start with a friendship?' Hope had offered.

For a moment, she'd thought Celeste was going to come in for a hug, but instead, Hope saw her surreptitiously brush away one solitary tear. 'Yes. Let's start with that then. I'd like that very much.'

Then she was gone, and Hope had returned to the table, just as Skye had punched her sister's arm. 'Venus flytrap?!! Honest to God, you need to tape up that mouth.'

Isla had responded by letting her head fall on the table.

'This is like looking in a mirror,' Maisie had laughed. 'Aaron, do you want to run now? Flee the scene while you can still save yourself?'

Aaron had grinned and it had actually reached his eyes, the first real smile Hope had seen since Celeste had appeared and the truth had emerged. 'I think I'll take my chances.'

All tension had dissolved then, and that's when Hope had gone to call her mum. She'd only given her an edited version of the story. Tomorrow she'd go round to her mum's house, drink tea, and sit at her kitchen table until all the details were out. Or better still...

'Aaron, would you come with me tomorrow to meet my mum? My other mum.'

He lifted her hand and kissed the back of it. 'I'd love to.'

'You know, I've just realised something,' Skye announced. 'If you're Celeste's daughter,' she nodded to Hope. 'And your Hope's sister,' that was to Maisie. 'And Celeste is married to our dad, then, technically speaking, that makes the four of us almost-kinda-maybe sisters. Wow. I have three sisters. And I already like you two better than Isla,' she joked, with a wink to her twin.

Hope loved that thought, but before she could reply, Agnetha and Mitchell emerged from the back kitchen. Agnetha joined them at the table, while Mitchell said his goodbyes, kissing both his daughters and then hugging Maisie and Hope in turn.

'I'm guessing we'll be seeing a lot more of each other,' he said to Hope, and she could see that didn't faze him at all. Her biological mother's husband seemed to be a decent guy. Yet, she got a feeling that they weren't very happy together. Perhaps she'd misjudged that. She hoped so.

Agnetha pulled out a chair between Isla and Skye and Hope watched as Aaron followed his old girlfriend's every move with obvious affection.

'So, Mum,' Isla said, pouring wine into an empty glass and handing it over. 'What do you want to do for your birthday next year? Any more long-lost boyfriends we can track down for you?'

Agnetha shook her head, blushing furiously, but her laughter was infectious. 'Any chance of a nice quiet day with a cup of tea and a good book?'

'Talking about boyfriends,' Skye interjected. 'What happened to Will. Has he gone?'

Just as Agnetha's blush was beginning to fade, it flared right back up again. 'Erm, Will and I have decided that we're going to go back to being just good friends,' she said, and Hope caught the way her gaze flicked to Aaron for a split second before she pulled it back again.

Isla and Skye's eyebrows raised in synchronicity at this announcement. Agnetha didn't elaborate any further, but she didn't appear to be too perturbed about this development.

'So, Aaron, tell us about LA. What do you do there?' Isla asked him and as Aaron began to chat, Hope felt comfortable enough to zone out and reflect on the day.

She'd found her dad and he was... Hope glanced over at him now. He was lovely. And caring. And sweet. And flawed. And, if Hope was reading him correctly, absolutely still in love with Agnetha.

Today she'd gained one father. One mother. A couple of almost-kinda-maybe stepsisters.

And she already had her mum and Maisie.

It was dysfunctional. Shocking. Completely bizarre. But if this was her family, then she was oh so happy to take it.

When she zoned back in, Skye was asking Aaron how long he planned to stay. Good question. He'd mentioned this morning that he had an open ticket, and she hadn't pressed him on when he needed to go back.

'I'm not sure, it depends on how long Hope would like me to stay for.'

'As long as you can,' Hope replied honestly.

'I can probably swing a couple of weeks,' he said, 'if that would be okay with you? I don't want you getting sick of me already.'

'Never gonna happen.' She took his hand again. 'The only thing is, I need to study and work, and my shifts are pretty long, so you'll be at a loose end with lots of free time on your hands.'

The implicit suggestion settled above the table and hung there for a few moments, as all eyes shifted to Agnetha. Hope knew what she was doing. It had been a long road to finding her father and she was determined that there would be no more wasted time for any of them.

To her surprise, it was her dad who broke the silence first. He leaned forward, as if he'd made some kind of decision and was about to act on it. 'You know... since we're all almost-kinda-maybe family here now,' he nodded to Skye when he said that and she grinned in return, 'then I'm just going to put this out there. There have been too many secrets and we've lost so much because of them. Hope, I just want to say, meeting you is now up there with the days my boys were born as the happiest of my life.'

Hope felt a rush of love for the vulnerability that was evident in the very slight quiver of his voice.

'I can't tell you how grateful I am that you found me.'

'I am too, Aaron.... I mean, Dad,' she whispered, called him that out loud for the first time. Hope was grateful to see that Maisie didn't even flinch. Calling him Dad felt right and that didn't minimise for a single second what her adoptive dad meant to her. Tim McTeer had been her father. Aaron Ward was too. They still had a lot of getting to know each other to do, but from now on, he deserved to be 'dad'.

'And, Agnetha,' he said, watching as Agnetha's head shot up and she looked at him questioningly. 'I messed up. I really did. And I want to admit that in front of the people we love because this might matter to them too. I'm so sorry. If I could take it back a million times, then I would, but I can't.'

'I know,' Agnetha said sadly, and Hope's heart broke for them.

'Pass me a napkin or I'll need to use your sleeve,' Maisie whispered, and Hope turned to see huge fat tears slipping down her sister's face as she listened to Aaron speak.

'But here's the thing. I feel like...' Her dad's voice broke, and he stopped, cleared his throat, started again. 'I feel like maybe we've been given a second chance. I've loved you since the moment I set eyes on you, and seeing you tonight, I know that I love you still. If you think our time has passed, then I'll accept that, I promise. But if you think there's any way, any way at all, that you can give us another chance, then I'm all in.'

Maisie blew her nose noisily. 'Oh my God, this guy is killing me,' she whispered, as she waited, just as they all did, for Agnetha to respond. A heartbeat. Another. Another.

'Come on, Mum, he is at a loose end,' Isla prompted gently, making her feelings on the matter clear.

When Agnetha began to shake her head, Hope's spirits crashed. Oh bollocks, her dad had put himself out there and he was about to be crushed. 'I don't know why I would do that,' Agnetha said, before falling silent and still again. Hope was pretty sure no one in the room was breathing any longer. 'But, hey, when I woke up this morning, I decided I was going to take chances, to find adventure, and happiness and love... So I guess if you're all in, then I'm willing to try.'

As the cheering started, Hope added to her earlier list.

Maybe she'd just found an almost-kinda-maybe future stepmum too.

EPILOGUE

A FEW MONTHS LATER

I remember her so clearly.

There's an image in my mind of her standing on the observation deck at the top of the Empire State Building in New York. She was about twenty-one and it was a cold day, but she didn't care that the wind made her long red hair fly and her eyes glisten as she threw her arms out wide. The sheer joy she was feeling radiated from every pore, her smile wide and irrepressible. Like it would never fade.

Another memory. Maybe a year later. Sitting on the end of a cold Scottish pier in the early hours of the morning with a man she was madly in love with. She said he was the third love of her life. Or was it the fourth? It was a standing joke with her friends that her romantic history was like a constant repetition of death defying leaps. She'd fall from a great height into the abyss, but as if on a bungee cord, she'd snap right back out again at warp speed a day, a week, a month later, leaving a few cases of whiplash along the way.

Another flashback, to the following summer. On a beach in Malibu, watching the surfers at dawn, making lines in the sand with her toes. I knew the whole holiday had been put on a brand-new credit card and the expense sent it straight to its limit, but she gave that no thought at all. All that mattered was that moment. That experience. Life is for living. Her mantra. A cliché, but, yep, life is for living, she'd say.

Along the way she met him. The one who made her forget everyone else. Dizzy with love and optimism, she said yes to the happy-ever-after dream, and prepared to waltz up the aisle with him. But they didn't make it. Life took her on another path and into the arms of someone else.

It was just a detour. A blip.

Still, she would dance, she would throw back shots and bounce the glass on the bar, she would start a party in an empty room and watch as people flocked to join the fun.

She would talk about how there were no limits to how great her life could be, and you couldn't listen to the enthusiasm and certainty in her voice and not believe her.

At twenty-three, she thought nothing could stop her, that she was indestructible, that there was absolutely nothing she couldn't do or achieve if she wanted to.

Perhaps it was the naivety of youth, but she didn't even see the perfect storm coming.

Marriage. Children. Ailing parents. A mind-blowing betrayal. A chain of events that would hijack her world, changing her until the person she was no longer existed.

Yep, life is for living, she would say.

Until she became nothing more than a battle-weary survivor, who set aside her own life just to get through the days.

I remember that young, carefree woman so clearly.

Because she was me.

And now, when I look in the mirror, older, wiser and battle scarred, I see a forty-five year old mother who is rewinding the reams of time, reclaiming that young woman's spirit and doing her dreams justice.

I see a middle-aged woman who is open to possibilities and embracing change.

The need to follow her passions have given her the courage to step back from work a little, to let her daughter take the reins of a family business that she loves and that will continue to flourish under Isla's care.

She has welcomed new friends into her life and she already adores them like family. Hope and Maisie are two of her favourite people. She even got tested in case her stem cells were a match for Hope. They weren't. And neither were Celeste's. But Aaron's were, and they all sleep better at night knowing that if he's ever needed, he'd give everything to his daughter.

It's not just new friends that are bringing her joy. She's spending more time with Val and Yvie and the others from the Wednesday Club. Will still comes, but now he brings Carol and it's lovely to see them rebuilding their marriage. It's not always a straight line, recovering from grief, but they're all taking the zigzags together.

She's growing as a person, mending fences and finding ways to forgive. Mitchell has become a regular fixture at Sunday dinners, they've found a new, very platonic closeness, and she doesn't mind at all when he occasionally brings a date. They've all been perfectly nice and shown no narcissistic tendencies, so he's clearly changed his type. He hasn't shown any signs of settling down again, but it's only been a few months. She tells him it will take time. And she should know.

Of course, none of this means she's the finished article, and there are still moments when her response lacks generosity. Yes, she did smile just for a moment when she heard that Derek Evans had gone off with a reality TV starlet and cut all ties with his event manager, Celeste.

Last anyone heard of her, she was living in a city centre flat, where she spent a month recovering from her latest facelift. Hope offered to visit her but that idea was rejected after Celeste decided that a monthly lunch with her biological daughter was as much as she was prepared to commit to. Hope was, of course, hurt, but there was a consolation prize. There was another new family out there that embraced her.

You see, that middle-aged woman is taking a chance with her heart, by giving it to a man that she loved and lost.

At the beginning, it took patience on his part as she tried to resist him, knowing that this was the greatest love and scared that losing it for a second time would be a pain too great to bear. But after a couple of months she threw caution to the wind and taking that risk has rewarded her with so much more than just a new romance. Now, as she gazes into Aaron's gorgeous grey eyes, she feels things she hasn't felt for a very long time – since she was that young girl dancing on a beach in Malibu, someone who loved, who laughed, and who grabbed the joy from every moment.

With Hope, Maisie, Isla and Skye standing beside them at sunrise on a Santa Monica beach, they finally say the vows they didn't get to share more than two decades before.

'I will love you until the end of time,' he promises.

Her smile is pure bliss. 'And I you,' she replies.

Life is for living, that young woman used to say.

And now I am.

ACKNOWLEDGEMENT

Thank you as always to my brilliant editor and publisher Caroline Ridding, for being the best damn editor and friend a writer could have. Thanks too, to Amanda, Nia and Megan, and the rest of the brilliant team at Boldwood Books, for the endless support and encouragement. I feel so lucky to have a home with you.

To Jade Craddock and Rose Fox, much gratitude for once again nudging this novel into shape.

And to every reader, blogger and reviewer who takes the time to pick up one of my books, you make it possible for me to carry on doing a job that I adore. I heart you.

Love,

Shari x

MORE FROM SHARI LOW

We hope you enjoyed reading *One Day In Summer*. If you did, please leave a review.

If you'd like to gift a copy, this book is also available as an ebook, digital audio download and audiobook CD.

Sign up to Shari Low's mailing list for news, competitions and updates on future books.

http://bit.ly/ShariLowNewsletter

My One Month Marriage, another warm and insightful novel from Shari Low, is available to buy now.

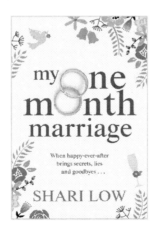

ABOUT THE AUTHOR

Shari Low is the #1 bestselling author of over 20 novels, including *My One Month Marriage* and *One Day In Winter,* and a collection of parenthood memories called *Because Mummy Said So.* She lives near Glasgow.

Visit Shari's website: www.sharilow.com

Follow Shari on social media:

f facebook.com/sharilowbooks

🐦 twitter.com/sharilow

📷 instagram.com/sharilowbooks

BB bookbub.com/authors/shari-low

ABOUT BOLDWOOD BOOKS

Boldwood Books is a fiction publishing company seeking out the best stories from around the world.

Find out more at www.boldwoodbooks.com

Sign up to the Book and Tonic newsletter for news, offers and competitions from Boldwood Books!

http://www.bit.ly/bookandtonic

We'd love to hear from you, follow us on social media:

 facebook.com/BookandTonic

 twitter.com/BoldwoodBooks

 instagram.com/BookandTonic

Made in the USA
Columbia, SC
31 March 2021